CLARE NONHEBEL

Cold Showers

GRAFTON BOOKS

A Division of the Collins Publishing Group

LONDON GLASGOW
TORONTO SYDNEY AUCKLAND

Grafton Books
A Division of the Collins Publishing Group
8 Grafton Street, London W1X 3LA

Published by Grafton Books 1986

First published in Great Britain by
Century Publishing Co. Ltd 1984

Copyright © Clare Nonhebel 1984

ISBN 0-586-06680-2

Printed and bound in Great Britain by
Collins, Glasgow

Set in Times

Clare Nonhebel worked as a freelance journalist before taking up writing full-time. *Cold Showers* was her first novel and with it, in 1984, she was joint winner of the Betty Trask Award. Since then she has written *The Partisan* and is now working on her third book. She lives in London.

1

Before you ask me out, there are three things you should know. To start with the least off-putting: I have an unusually fast metabolism.

That is a polite way of saying I eat like a horse, if not a pig. I require eight meals to the normal person's three. In self-justification, I must add that my condition has been medically proven (something to do with low blood-sugar levels) and that on anything less than eight meals a day I lose weight with unnerving speed.

I will try to spare you expense (on any date I make a point of bringing my own sandwiches) – the damage is not to the wallet but to the ego. If you ask me out to dinner, for instance, however lavish and succulent the fare, two hours later I will be in need of a refill. If you take me to the theatre, the cinema, the disco, the race-track – my doggy-bag goes too. If you take me to bed, ditto. See what I mean about the ego? Good. We'll move on to the second point.

The second point you may already have wondered about. I wear a plain gold ring on my third finger, but on the right not the left hand. I noticed you glancing at it. Then, as people often do, you glanced at the third finger of my left hand to see if it was deformed, absent, or in any other way unable to support the weight of a wedding ring. Not so. Am I divorced, you want to know? Separated, then? Married but open to possibilities? None of those. This is the part I hate. A widow. Yes, I know widows are expected to be over forty-five, prone to weepiness and addicted to Valium. They are not young (twenty-five, since you ask). They do not have red hair and freckles. Above all they do not make flippant remarks about their status, in a misguided attempt to save themselves and other people embarrassment. That is not widow-like behaviour; that is bad taste. The only trouble is, it is also the only way I can handle the situation with any dignity, without becoming prematurely middle-aged, weeping, or reaching for the Valium.

On, quickly then, to the third thing. Now for the good news, did you say? Wishful thinking. This is the pits, man; the ultimate blade of dried grass. I am temporarily, but definitely, frigid.

I say temporarily, because I feel certain that eventually lust will once more rear its familiar, inconvenient head. I say definitely, because, however strong your faith in yourself as a human aphrodisiac, I know that this will happen unaided, in its own time – and that time is not yet.

No, it is kind of you to offer, but I have had several similar offers. Should the time come, I shall know where to turn. Whichever way you like. But not now.

Admittedly, there have been times – there are times – when I have felt like rushing out into the street and grabbing the first man I see, but circumstances have deterred me. For one thing, by the time I reach that level of desperation, it would take too long. The 'Excuse me, you don't know me, but . . . ' Or the 'Listen, this may sound funny but . . . ' Or even, without the buts, 'Come here, I want to borrow your body for a few minutes.'

Then there would be the stairs, and the turning back the bedclothes – or at the very least, the closing of the front door and the removal of the spiky umbrella stand from the hall.

Then all the aftermath. The 'Sorry, I didn't quite catch your name . . . ?' The necessity, born of a decent upbringing, of offering coffee, of discoursing politely on the weather or the political situation.

I am not good, yet, at long conversations, or at unplatonic relationships, or at all the preliminary chatting-up.

My ideal date, just now, would last approximately twenty minutes. It would take place in my spare bedroom (for a change of scene); it would consist of a quick snack (to give me energy), a quick scuffle with my inhibitions, and a quick exit, on your part, before my next snack. And don't hang around for the reassuring compliments on your performance: it brings back memories and, despite my resolutions, I might cry.

You've changed your mind about asking me out then? I thought so. In your position, in search of a casual partner for tonight's roller disco, I wouldn't pick a famished, frigid widow either.

The 'famished' bit was already a problem when I met Barry. There wasn't the frigid widowhood to contend with, of course, because he hadn't even met me, let alone married me, let alone died. Not that the three were necessarily connected. (There you are, you see. Bad taste. Sorry.)

'We're all going on to another party,' he shouted, indicating the loud, cheerful group he had arrived at this one with. 'Why don't you come too?'

'I can't,' I yelled back over the decibels of the disco music and the scrunching noise of the crisps I was eating. 'I haven't got enough food.'

He thought the acoustics were deceiving him. 'You what?' he shouted.

'Food!' I screamed. 'I've only got enough to last me till midnight. I have to eat every two hours.'

He regarded me with awe. 'Every two hours?' he mouthed. Either he thought we stood a better chance of communicating by lip-reading, or he was simply struck dumb with amazement.

I nodded. He grabbed me by the hand and took me on a tour of the house, rounding up all the fragments of left-over food he could find. We did quite well, considering. There was an almost uneaten sausage roll behind one of the stereo speakers and another which only needed a bit of dusting lying abandoned in an ashtray.

'You're not fussy, are you?' he bellowed.

I tucked his hair behind his left ear and shouted into it, 'Not about food.' He liked that. At least, he liked me tickling his ear.

We unearthed quite a large fragment of cheese with some rock-hard bread still on its paper plate, under the table in the kitchen, and a scraping of Danish-blue-dip in an outsize bowl halfway up the stairs. 'We'll take the bowl,' Barry said (it was quieter out here). 'It'll come in handy for putting the other things in. Will that be enough?'

'For a couple of hours,' I said.

He bit his lip thoughtfully. 'Better get a bit more,' he said. 'Just in case.'

With the bowl of dip under one arm, he took my hand again and steered a zig-zag course up the stairs, tacking between the dozy huddles of people smoking shapeless ciggies with a spaced-out scent.

Opening and shutting doors at random yielded a fruity selection of abuse but no further edibles. The third bedroom was unoccupied. Barry looked at me. I avoided looking at him. 'Pity to waste it,' he said. His expression was that of a little boy wistfully eyeing the jars in the sweet-shop window. At least, that was my excuse.

We pushed the wardrobe against the door, just in case anyone else should wander in looking for food, and afterwards we sat up in bed and scooped soggy crumbs of bread and cheese out of the Danablu-dip.

Yes, I know I've left out the good bits. I'll get around to that later on. After all, I hardly know you.

8

Dear Blank

At 11.30 A.M. on Wednesday, 3 November, Bantam Cosmetics will be launching its stunning new range at a special press preview at the Galaxy Suite at the Baritz Hotel, Condiman Street, London W1.

No. Clumsy.

'. . . special press preview at the Baritz Hotel, London W1.'

No. Enough journalists who accept the invitation will drop out anyway, without the others getting lost en route.

Dear Blank

On Wednesday, 3 November at the Baritz Hotel, Condiman Street, Bantam Cosmetics will be launching its stunning new range of products at a special press preview.

The new range, which has been christened 'Cloud Ten' . . .

Now there's an idea.

Dear Blank

Bantam Cosmetics cordially invite you to attend the christening of its new baby, 'Cloud Ten'.

Daughter of today's trend towards . . .

No. The phone rings.

'Press office.'

'Can I speak to the press officer, please?'

'Yes, speaking.'

'Are you the press officer?'

'Yes, I am.'

'Um . . . who am I speaking to?'

What? Who is this nitwit?

'Sorry?'

'I mean, your name? I'm sorry, I don't know . . . '

'Oh. Yes. Cathy Childs. Can I help you?'

'Um . . . I was wondering . . . if it would be possible for me to come and have a look round. I mean, round the factory and . . . ' The voice tails off. She sounds very young and uncertain.

'Yes, I'm sure you can. You are a journalist, are you?'

'Oh, yes. Yes. Sally Harris. I'm a freelance.'

'Yes, I see. Is the article commissioned?'

'No.' Tremor in her voice. 'No, it isn't. Does it matter?'

'No, not at all. What would your angle be?'

Uncertainty again. 'Well, just a general piece, I thought, on how the cosmetics are made and so on.'

'Yes. The only problem I can see is that magazines are a bit wary of using that kind of article. They can lose advertising you see, from the other manufacturers, if they feature just one company. We've come across that problem ourselves in trying to place features about Bantam.'

'I hadn't thought of that.' There's a slight pause. 'So if I did a piece on several companies then, you think . . . ?'

I try to find a phrase that doesn't sound patronizing. 'Well, probably the best way is to ring round a few features editors first and see if they're interested. Then, if it's not quite what they want, you wouldn't have wasted your time . . . ' That sounds frosty, as though she's wasting my time.

'Yes. Well, I'm sorry to have bothered you.'

'Not at all. Do give me a ring back if you have any luck.'

'Okay then.' She sounds defeated already by the prospect of failure. I don't believe she will have any luck. The idea is not exactly original. She sounds very young – perhaps a school-leaver trying to get into journalism the hard way.

'Listen,' I say quickly, before she puts the phone down, 'why don't you come and have a look round anyway? It might come in useful as background or something. If you can spare the time, that is?'

'Oh yes. Yes I can.'

'When are you free?'

'I'll just have a look at my diary,' she says, regrouping shreds of dignity. 'Ah!' she exclaims. 'I can be free any time this week.'

I reach over to Alan's desk for the diary. Creative team meeting, PR department meeting, lunch with journalist, and a big scrawl across Friday afternoon which says, in Alan's handwriting, CATHY, KEEP AFTERNOON FREE FOR CHECKING HOUSE-JOURNAL PROOFS.

'I'm sorry,' I say. 'I think next week is the earliest I can make it.'

'Oh.' Desolation. 'I'm going away for a week on Saturday.'

'OK then, we'll make it this Friday afternoon, right?' It's time Alan took his turn at the tedious job of checking galley proofs, anyway. If he's otherwise engaged, I'll just have to stay on late and do it. It's unlikely to cut into my less-than-hectic social life. 'Why don't you come at about midday and we'll have some lunch first? I can tell you a bit about the company, and then we'll go round the factory.'

'Oh, lovely. Thanks a lot.'

'See you on Friday then.'

'Yes. Fine. Thanks. 'Bye then.'

''Bye.'

'Dear Blank . . . ' Phone rings.

'Cathy?'

'Marcie! How are you?'

'Fine. Are you busy, or is it OK to talk?'

11

'No, go ahead.'

'We were just wondering if you'd like to come round on Friday. Carla and Jim are coming, and possibly Vicky and Keith. I haven't rung them yet.'

'I'd love to.' Isn't there something happening on Friday? 'Oh, wait a minute, I may have to work late. What time were you thinking of?'

'It doesn't really matter, darling. Come along when you're free. Carla and Jim are arriving at about 8.30, I think; they said they could give you a lift.'

Eight thirty. Is that for drinks or to eat? In my financial situation (limited) and physical condition (permanently hungry) it is a great advantage to know beforehand whether food is on the programme.

'Eight thirty should be fine, Marcie. That'll give me time to finish work and get home for a quick meal and a bath first.'

'Oh, I'm doing food. Snack stuff, you know; not a dinner party, just quiche and things.'

Wonderful. That's just what I hoped she'd say.

'Of course,' she adds, giving her breathless laugh, 'you'll probably have to eat beforehand as well.'

'Of course,' I agree. My enforced munch-mania has ceased to seem side-splittingly funny to me, particularly since I've had to meet all my own food bills.

'Well, see you on Friday then, Cathy.'

'Thanks Marcie. I'll look forward to it.'

So there's my empty Friday evening filled; that's good. At first, after Barry died, the phone rang constantly with invitations from people who thought I shouldn't be alone; they are nice, my friends. The only trouble was that I needed, sometimes, to be alone. To think. To remember. To shut the door on the world and cry. People thought it was morbid, unhealthy.

12

'You mustn't dwell on the past,' they urged. 'You're still young: you should be getting out, having a good time.' Personally I felt I needed to cry in order to stay sane, but when I started, it was sometimes so hard to stop that I got frightened and thought maybe they were right: it was better to fight back the tears. Also, people don't want you crying all over them, and who can blame them?

Mind you, laughing could be equally unacceptable. My sense of humour refused to die until about a week after Barry did. The black depression that engulfed me only descended then; for the first few days, the crisis time, I coped okay. I saw the solicitor myself; I saw the priest, the bank manager, the relatives, even the undertaker. I did my own shopping, I made my own meals, refusing to make myself ill by not eating.

People said I was incredible. They also, I believe, secretly thought it heartless. They offered to do things for me, but I wouldn't let them. It was only when I ran out of things to do, arrangements to make, appointments to meet, that I finally cracked up.

What was I saying? Oh yes, sense of humour. It was Aunty Ida who did it. Barry's Aunty Ida, that is. She's not actually an aunty but an old friend of the family, a lovely Irish lady full of suggestions and misconceptions, and warmth and kindliness, and sayings that become classics and are quoted down the years.

We'd arrived at the church for the funeral – all in cars, nobody speaking above a hushed whisper, nobody daring to smile or to chat. Perhaps because we encounter death so rarely its taboo never has a chance to relax. I wasn't sure how I was meant to behave. I would have liked a quick ciggy, really, before going in or, better still, one of Barry's roll-your-owns that put the world into soft focus, but it was not the done thing. Brandy, yes. Tea, certainly – the time-honoured remedy for grief. But standing outside the church dragging on a Benson & Hedges, or blowing your mind on a tobaccoless wonder – no way.

So, back to Aunty Ida. It was not Aunty Ida herself who set me off but Aunty Ida's wreath. Enormous, it was, and all red, white and gold. Red roses, white blossom of some kind, and gold ribbon bows.

The card was equally enormous, black deckle-edged, and said: 'To my Darling Barry from Aunty Ida, With all my Love and Best Wishes for your Sad Demise.'

I was standing there, looking at the wreaths and the flowers, when this card somehow penetrated the numbness of my mind and suddenly it was all too much and I started to laugh hysterically. The priest came over and put his hand on my shoulder. I think he thought I was crying because he started to say something soothing, then stopped when he saw my face.

Barry's mother was horrified. I felt bad about that. She and I had never got on very well, but if she was feeling half as desperate as I felt at three in the mornings, when there was nothing for me to be efficient about, and no-one to be flippant to, then I could well imagine that she saw no cause to laugh.

But it was no use. I thought of all kinds of solemn things. I even tried to think of Barry lying on that hospital bed after the nurse had closed his eyes for him. But all I could think of was Barry alive and laughing. I could actually feel him next to me, his arm round my waist, tears of hysterical mirth running down his face. When Barry laughed, the world shook. Barry did all things in immoderation.

So we stood there and laughed together at dear old Aunty Ida and her Best Wishes for his Sad Demise, and it was good to laugh; it was like a great pressure being lifted from my body.

And then I saw all the people with their stricken, tragic faces, and I saw their shock and their bewilderment and their attempt to understand, and in that moment the laughter was gone, and Barry was gone and that was when the black period finally descended, the period that I don't want to think about because although there are lighter moments now, it is still in the background, all the time.

'Dear Blank . . . '

'Morning; I'm late. Don't tell me.'

'Hello, Alan. Another morning-after?'

He groans. 'I only hope it was worth it last night. I can't remember a thing.'

'Never mind. If you'd done anything awful you'd have been told by now.'

'Unless nobody's speaking to me any more,' he says gloomily. 'Which is a possibility, because Jerry went off to work this morning without bothering to wake me. A bad sign, don't you think?'

'Definitely,' I say encouragingly.

'Thanks.'

'Don't mention it.'

He opens his briefcase and throws a file of papers on to the floor, then carefully extracts a bottle of Paracetamol, a packet of Alka-Seltzers and a sheet of Disprin, and proceeds to swallow a selection of tablets. 'I doubt these will help,' he says bleakly, 'but I can't face the morning without something.'

'At least the stomach ulcer they give you will take your mind off the hangover,' I point out.

He regards me with loathing. 'Why don't you just . . . go and get me some coffee?' he suggests.

'Okay. That should rot whatever part of your gut the aspirin leaves behind.'

'And don't give me any of your witch-doctor crap!' he shouts, then clasps his head in agony. It is a normal morning for Alan. Alan doesn't like most mornings.

Over coffee, to divert his mind from the headache, I tell him about Sally Harris.

'You don't seriously think we'll get any publicity out of it?' he says.

'No, I don't. But it must be a bit demoralizing if magazines aren't keen on taking your stories, and if the people you're trying to write about don't take you seriously either . . . '

'So you waste an afternoon of your time showing her round – not to mention the company's time?'

'Not to mention the company's lunch,' I add contritely.

Alan raises his eyes to heaven. 'You've asked her to lunch,' he states. 'And no doubt one of the press presentation cosmetic packs will find its way into her sticky little fingers as well.'

'Well, she is press, officially.'

'Or playing at it,' says Alan dismissively. 'Well, don't expect me to waste any of my time on her, that's all. I've got better things to do.'

'Like checking the galleys for the house journal,' I suggest.

'That's your job!'

'If it's my turn, it's my job,' I point out. 'Only I've already done it for the last three issues.'

'Public Relations for Cosmetics and Toiletries is your job,' Alan argues, 'and Bantam News is mostly about cosmetics. I'm strictly Industrial and Men's Range.'

I start giggling. There is something irresistible about Alan standing there, hands on hips, head on one side, saying, 'I'm strictly Men's Range.'

'All right,' I compromise. 'I'll toss you for it.'

'You're on.' He produces a 5p and flips it in the air. 'Call.'

'Tails.'

'Heads!' he says triumphantly. 'You win the proof-read-

16

ing. You'll have to cancel Miss Smartypants and her freebie lunch.'

'I'll stay on late and do the proofs. But be an angel and give me a hand with them, Alan? I'm going out to supper and I've got to get home and eat first. Go on.'

'No way. You lost. You wouldn't have helped me if I'd lost.'

'I would.'

'Like hell. What garbage are you writing?'

'Invitation to the Cloud Ten press conference.'

He picks up a sheet. 'Dear Blank, At 11.30 on Wednesday . . .'

'That's the Mark One version. Not that Mark Four is any better.'

'Well, I'll leave you to it. What I've got to do is equally soul-destroying.'

He shovels another handful of Disprin into his mouth and retrieves the rejected file. It bursts open and discharges its contents on the floor. I find this amusing. Alan does not.

'Don't help, will you?' he snarls.

'Will you help with my proof-reading on Friday?'

He mutters darkly and clears up the mess unaided. I watch him with detached interest, unrelenting. You scratch my back and I'll scratch yours. I never quite understood that expression: is it meant to be a promise, or a threat?

When Barry used to come and visit me at my shared flat – in the shamefully short space of time between our first meeting and my moving in with him – he was having some problems with the plumbing at his flat, so he used our bath.

Clad only in my pink-flowered shower cap and a strategically-placed flannel, he would open the door and roar, Who's going to come and scrub my back, then?'

Giggling bashfully, my flat-mates refrained from poaching on my preserve, till one day I got the battalion

17

organized. Armed with loofah, soap, nailbrush, scrubbing brush, saucepan scourer, Vim and Brillo Pads we stormed the bathroom and took him at his word, while he cowered pathetically, begging for mercy, with Susie's Casa Pupo soap-dish clamped inadequately over the parts most vulnerable to wire-wool.

Funny, the things your memory retains, and those it lets go. Nights of passion gone totally unremembered. What a waste. Nor could I tell you what he had ever given me for Christmas or for birthdays. Yet I can recall, as clearly as a photograph, the way the butter would dribble into his beard when he ate corn on the cob. and the way he undressed, tearing his shirt off over his head, sending the buttons flying, and taking his socks off last, standing there absurdly naked with purple woollen feet.

I remember the sick jokes he used to make too, about his work in the research lab.

'All those nasty viruses in fragile little bottles,' he used to taunt me, 'just waiting to leap out and infect me the moment they get the chance.'

It was his usual response to my daily injunction to him to 'Have a good day at work – and be really careful, won't you?'

In the end, of course, it was not one of the little bottled viruses that got him, but cancer. Just like thousands of people working in safe plague-free offices.

It was the kind of ironic situation that would have appealed to Barry, only he didn't have a lot of time to see the funny side. And I didn't either . . .

Dear Blank
Do you fancy yourself as The Godfather? Or alternatively The Godmother? Come and exercise your megalomania at a christening with a difference.
Bantam Cosmetics' new baby, the stunning Cloud Ten range, a sleeping beauty now ready for wakening to the

18

public gaze, has all the gifts a fairy godmother could bestow: richness; fragrance; panache; smooth, smooth colours – and a few surprises . . .

Come and awaken the beauty at a special press preview on Wednesday, 3 November at 11.30.

Cloud Ten will be starring at the Galaxy Suite, Baritz Hotel, Condiman Street, W1. Drinks. Buffet lunch. Presentations.

And the new, beautiful baby.

Be there. You'll be on Cloud Ten.

RSVP to Cathy Childs, Bantam Cosmetics. Tel . . .

'Tell me what you think, Alan.'

He comes and peers over my shoulder. 'Yuck!'

'I thought you might say that.'

'Big Harry will love it,' he says. 'Probably give you a pay rise.'

'Oh yeah.'

'No, really. Send it in and see what he says. At least it's gimmicky: it'll get read. Even if they throw up afterwards.'

'Why do we waste our time writing drivel like this?' I say mournfully. 'Why aren't we expending our talents on literary epics for posterity?'

'Because posterity doesn't pay you for it till after you're dead. Send it to Big Harry. If he's got out of bed the right side and his wife hasn't burned the breakfast, you may be lucky.'

I slide the draft into an envelope, scrawl 'Harry Diggins, PR Director' on the front and toss it in the tray marked Internal Mail before I can have second thoughts. It may be rubbish but, Alan is right, it is what pays the food bills. When I'm rich, or give up eating, I'll start my Great Novel, without having to worry about not being paid till I'm dead.

That's one good thing about Alan. He doesn't shy away from all mention of death. Most people do; the word hangs unspoken in the air like Damocles' sword.

When I went back to work after Barry died, people's reactions ranged from overt sympathy to indifference. My best friends now are the ones who were kind at the time. I sympathize with the people who avoided me through embarrassment or inadequacy, but the fact remains that I don't feel as close to them as I did before.

(Before and After. It's the way I tend to date things now, like pre-war and post-war, or B.C and A.D.)

In the omelette queue at lunchtime, I study the faces of the people I know. Big Harry, ploughing his way stolidly through a plate of stew with extra dumplings. Vera from the mail room, eating crisps. Snotty Steve from Staff Expenses Clearance, who had turned out not to be snotty at all, but merely shy. 'I'm very sorry,' he stuttered when I went in for the first time After with Alan's and my expenses claim. 'I was very sorry to hear . . . if there's anything I can do . . .'

Suky was like that too. Suky is Nigerian, enormously plump, and goes round with a permanent scowl on her face. It was only After that she stopped me one day in the Ladies' and said, genuinely and unexpectedly, 'They told me about you. I feel for you in my heart.' After that, when I got to know Suky, I learned that the scowl was not unfriendliness but a defence against possible put-down because of her size and her colour. Now, when work is slack, or I feel like a heart-to-heart, I call in at the Central Filing Office where Suky works. She takes a break from her never-ending task of putting documents into pigeon-holes and we sit and drink Executive Coffee from the Cona flask in Big Harry's office, which is nicer than the vending machine slop offered to Suky's section.

Then there is Hortense from Personnel, a middle-aged lady of such muddled foreign ancestry that even she can't remember quite what her nationality is. And Patsy from

Reprographics, with all those children and a happily out-of-work husband. And Davy from Accounts. And Big Bad Bill from the van fleet, who gives us illicit lifts along with parcels, in between court hearings and probation visits and overnight detentions.

None of them enjoys working for Bantam. They are there because they are there and Bantam is there and they are too used to it, or too unsure of their chances elsewhere, to change – and anyway, as Patsy points out, who's to say that anywhere else could be better?

My own job here is an accident, not a carefully-planned step in my career. Two years ago, when I joined, I had never heard of public relations. If asked, I would probably have said a Press Officer was someone who led press-gangs. Perhaps it was just as well that, at the interview, I was not asked.

The exact nature of my job was not something that concerned me greatly when I took it. To me, fresh from a half-finished Ph.D, it was simply A Job In Business, something to provide funds for our planned move to France.

My mother was bitter about the unfinished degree. She blamed Barry for it, as she blamed him for everything from (rightly) the unexplained tyre-tracks on her precious rose-bed to (wrongly) the loss of her daughter's virginity.

'How could you give it up?' she said tearfully. (The Ph.D she was talking about, not the virginity.) 'All that studying, for nothing!' The chance of a Doctorate, she lamented, thrown away on Him. It was criminal indeed. It was the Doctor bit she minded about. 'My daughter, Doctor Childs.'

'I would never have called myself that, in any case,' I protested. 'People at parties would tell me about their gallstones.' A thesis on contemporary philosophical trends in literature is poor grounds for offering medical advice. Poor grounds for anything, in fact, which is why I gave it up.

'Who's going to pay me a salary to philosophize about Sartre?' I demanded. 'Where is the relevance of it to ordinary working life?' Not that I knew much, then, about ordinary working life.

When I found out, it was both better and worse than I had anticipated. Better in that the cut and thrust of business turned out to be quite exciting, which was an unexpected bonus. Worse in that, after four years of planning my own projects and setting my own timetable, I had to do what I was told, when I was told, to an order of priorities which often seemed nonsensical.

For better and for worse. In my job, as in marriage, the two appeared in time to merge. The worse became better: once he got used to me, Big Harry gave me quite a free hand. And the better got worse; once the novelty – or the naïveté – wore off, I began to see that much of the cutting and thrusting in what Big Harry liked to call his 'Creative Team' was actually done by one member of the team against another. Business must be the only game where the team-mates foul each other.

It didn't matter, I told myself then. None of it mattered, because it was not my permanent career.

Once we had saved enough money, sold the flat for a tidy profit and reimbursed Barry's mother for her share of the deposit, we would be off to France, shaking off the shackles of Bantam and its back-stabbing world and heading for the freedom of who-knows-what-may-happen?

In all likelihood, we stood to be disillusioned. Barry's employers – the owners of the research lab where he spent his days in the company of a thousand germs and a colony of anxious-faced rats – were French. Apart from the London project, they had labs all over Europe filled with similar viruses, similar white-robed staff and similar rodents.

The work, we knew, would be identical; the people would be much the same. Probably even the food we ate and the wine we drank would not be so different: young-married cosmopolitan quick 'n cheapies like spaghetti Bolognese, and Van Plonk in plastic bottles. *Croque monsieur* or cheese on toast, the only difference was the name.

But it would all be so much more glamorous! More exotic! More . . . well, more foreign. Even if the job I found was, from necessity, less intelligent than my present one, the banality of Bantam would be missing.

In Barry's lab, diseases would have French names. The rats would twitch their noses with Gallic charm; the lab assistant girls would wear their overalls with continental chic . . . that was the only thing that worried me, just slightly.

We were ready to go, whenever the vacancy arose. Unhampered by bourgeois materialism, we could pack our bags at a moment's notice, leaving my mother to sell the flat. Thumbing our way down the autoroutes, our few possessions resting lightly on our shoulders, would rekindle a honeymoon romance as we strolled hand in hand down the great wide highway to a new, exciting life. Something like that, anyway. The details were not important.

There were one or two little problems, apart from the major one of Barry's mother, who didn't want to lose her son to Those Foreigners as well as to That Girl (me). Our limited knowledge of French, for example.

Since language schools charged exorbitant fees, we made do with someone's not-quite-complete set of language teaching records. We had some good evenings with those records. Because Barry was at the Primary level while I was on Advanced, we took it in turn to listen to our respective discs.

As a loving couple should, we encouraged each other with mutual support. While Barry struggled manfully to repeat each phrase before the smug Parisian voice interrupted with the next one ('Hold it, you silly *vache*, I haven't finished yet!'), I lay on the floor and writhed with silent laughter.

While I attempted to enhance my scanty vocabulary, rolling my *r*s and pouting my *eu*s, Barry distracted me by pulling faces, doing gorilla impressions or, when my concentration withstood these onslaughts, performing a slow striptease. His sessions usually ended with his hurling the record across the room in frustrated fury. My sessions wound up, less frustrated, on the sitting-room rug.

Another problem came to light when, despite Barry's protestations about spontaneity, I insisted on making a list of things to take. That was the surprising (given our vaunted freedom from middle-class possession-obsession) number of things we owned.

There was Barry's guitar. 'You can carry that,' he decided. 'I'll take the rucksack. We should only need one, as long as it's big.'

'We'll need a whole rucksack just for my food,' I pointed out. Travelling light is not easy when you eat as I do.

The furniture we would sell or give away, but I was reluctant to leave behind the duvet. 'We'd have to start again with a new one,' I argued, 'and it's not the same. There are a lot of memories tied up in that duvet. Besides, they cost twice as much now as we paid for it.'

'You have to be ruthless,' Barry lectured me. 'It's the only practical way.'

He didn't say that when it came to the stereo. 'I built that stereo,' he protested. 'I bought the deck and the speakers all as bits and did it myself. You couldn't buy one like that.'

I refrained from saying we might be able to buy one with a turntable that didn't fly off at 45 rpm, and said instead that a stereo system was hardly a 'basic essential'.

He pointed out that without it the records would sound pretty quiet. I pointed out that, if we were being ruthless, they were a low priority too. Just because he couldn't bear to be parted from his George Harrison 'All Things Must Pass' . . . It was not that, Barry said with dignity; just that he wanted to continue his French course once we were there, and as we would need the stereo for the language discs it would be silly not to take a few albums as well. I would have to restrict the number of clothes I packed, that was all . . .

The argument about what was essential and what was not was cut short by the news that the move was to be delayed. The expected vacancy at the French lab was not to arise, after all, till later in the year. We were disappointed. Having secretly begun to have a few qualms about leaving our friends, our families, London, the flat and the duvet, I instantly decided that going to France was the only thing I really wanted to do. When we knew we had to stay there, London seemed dreary, our friends predictable and our families over-familiar, and Bantam Cosmetics the worst place in the world to spend one's working life.

It was a tragedy. I felt like that in those days, before I knew that worse things can happen than an upset plan.

All was not lost, however; the move was merely post-poned. Carla and Jim had a Not-Going-Away party for us, and our parents were delighted with the reprieve. We carried on with the language records, and warmed the duvet with a few more memories. Then in the end, of course, the cancer came up before the job. By the time the letter arrived from France, Barry was no longer there to answer it.

'What a good thing you hadn't already moved,' said friends to encourage me. I suppose they are really right. But at the time I couldn't see it made much difference. Cancer or *le cancer*. *La mort* or death. English or French, there was nothing romantic about it.

2

'Have a good day at the office, love?'

'Yes thanks.'

'Busy at the moment is it?'

'Not really.'

'What do you do, then? Secretary?'

'Press officer.'

'What's that when it's at home?'

'Public Relations. Publicity.'

'Public Relations, eh?' He gives me a quick, reappraising glance. 'I could do with a bit of public relations myself.'

The passengers on the bus swivel round for a disapproving stare at this bold woman who reveals her occupation to the conductor. I wish I had bought an evening paper.

'Married, are you?' he continues, unabashed by my sudden interest in the small print on my ticket.

'This is my stop,' I say, getting up.

He stretches out a hand, ringing the bell and barring my exit in one gesture.

'You married?' he pursues.

'Yes.'

'Where's your wedding ring?'

Up my . . . no, there is no need to be vulgar. Try to behave like a lady, as my mother would say – the inference being that it obviously didn't come naturally.

I wave my right hand at him, hoping he doesn't know right from left. He doesn't. That's why he's the conductor and not the driver.

'All the nice girls are married,' he says. He escorts me off the bus with exaggerated courtesy. 'See yer same time tomorrow, darling,' he bawls, as the bus draws away.

A middle-aged lady with newly-set hair sniffs disgust-edly. Not at the conductor (men will be men). At me. Making assignations with a stranger. Lusting after the uniform, no doubt. Tantalized by the promise of wild weekends on his free bus pass. Whizzing heedlessly past request stops, making unbridled love in the cubbyhole beneath the stairs, amid the weekend cases and the shop-ping-bags on wheels. Girls like that will do anything.

It is a long walk from here to my bus stop. Fool, you should have stayed on. You paid the fare, didn't you? Can't you deal with a bit of chatting-up, at your age? But how? Stony silence: ('Cat got your tongue, then? Too posh to speak to me, are we?') Devastating frankness: ('Yes, I am married, but my husband died. Eight months ago. Cancer.' Horrified silence; twenty pairs of eyes stare from twenty backs-of-heads. Then, after the silence. 'Bet you get lonely, then love? Bit cold at nights, eh?') No. No thanks. Anyway, the walk will do me good. Fresh air. Petrol fumes and rubbish bags and watch-what-you're-stepping-in. Good healthy exercise.

The supermarket near the flat sports its usual clientele of after-work shoppers buying small-size packs of frozen things and individual cardboard pies. An unofficial Singles Club, like the launderette next door where lonely youths spend Saturday nights watching their socks revolve.

I pick up a yogurt and put it down again. Cottage cheese. Economy size. One thing I don't need is small-size packs. I may be a Single but I eat like a Couple. If not a *menage-à-trois*.

'Did you want this yogurt?'

'Sorry?'

'It's the last one. I saw you pick it up. I don't want to de-prive you.'

'Oh no, that's all right.'

'Sure?' He is tall and thin, with a beard. I used to have a thing about beards. In the days when I had a thing about anything.

'Sure. It's past its freshness date,' I add, seeing him put the yogurt in his wire basket.

'Oh.' Doubt crosses his face. 'Does that matter?'

I shrug. 'Depends if you're fussy. They go runny on the top – you know, separate.'

He hesitates, torn between wanting the yogurt and not wanting to offend by ignoring my advice.

'Probably tastes all right,' I encourage him.

Sausages. No, not again. Pâté? Extravagant. Ham. Looks as though it expired a very long time ago.

The Beard reappears behind me. 'I can never decide what to get, can you?'

'No.' He is about my age, wears an army-surplus greatcoat. Ex-university. You can spot it a mile off, even without the scarf.

'I always end up with the same old things – fish fingers, sausages . . .'

Maths, I should think, or Engineering. Not Arts in spite of the beard. Not earnest enough to be Physics, nor smartass enough for Business Studies.

Do I want baked beans again? No, I don't. I lean over the freezer and flip aside a few packs of peas. The more exotic things sink to the bottom, where I can't reach.

'Can I help?'

'No, it's all right, thanks.' I dive in head first, feet just touching the floor.

'What are you looking for? Peas?'

If I wanted peas, dumbo, I could have them without getting deep-frozen ears. Peas are everywhere.

'Onions,' I gasp. 'Those little ones in white sauce.'

'Oh?' He is intrigued. 'I've never tried those.'

Well, there you are. A whole new vista opens up before

28

you. I continue to scrabble in the freezer while he hovers, uncertainly.

'Well, if you're sure I can't help . . . ' He sounds downcast. Don't be a cow, Cathy; he's only being friendly. I hit on a packet of onions.

'Here they are. Do you want them then, to try?'

'Well – is there another one for you?'

'It doesn't matter,' I say generously. 'I've had them before. Treat yourself to a new experience.'

He goes a bit pink beneath the beard. What does he think I'm offering him? I see he has rejected the yogurt; his wire basket is empty.

'Tell you what,' he says. 'Why don't we share them? Grab some beefburgers or something equally exciting and cook them at my place?'

How did I get into this? 'Oh well, thanks, but . . . ' But what? Going out? Got friends coming round? I'm not and I haven't. I'm not even washing my hair; I did that last night. Come to think of it, I'm in for a boring evening. Might just as well be bored with somebody else, suggests my inner self. My outer self disagrees. 'Thanks, but – I've got some work to do.'

'Oh yes, I see.' He concurs too quickly. It cost him to make the suggestion; he thought he might get turned down, but risked it anyway. He moves away and scans the herbs and spices. The back of his neck is forlorn.

Oh hell, that's his problem. The back of his neck is nothing to do with me. He was only trying to pick someone up; probably does it every day. Prowls round Fine Fare looking for girls to share his onions and his bachelor bed. Adds them to his shopping list as one of his weekly requirements; looking for special offers and easy conquests. Free Girl with Every Pack of Juicy Burgers. In my case, of course, he would be disappointed: Frosty Widow with Each Deep-Frozen Pea.

I don't believe it really; he isn't the type. Sociology might do that, but Engineering never. I take a tin of beans. Anyway, who cares? I care. 'What did you do with your day, Cathy?' 'Oh, nothing much. A bit of work. Bit of chat. Ruined someone's ego. Nothing much.' Nothing to be proud of.

He catches me glancing at him through the rack of salad creams above the fridge, and looks away.

Queuing at the check-out, I notice he has totted up the total and counted out his change. Perhaps he is Economics, not Engineering after all. Impressed by his efficiency, I calculate the sum of my own purchases. The cashier makes it 12p more. I pay it without question.

In the fruit shop two doors down, the Beard is there before me, buying apples. I say hello, to ease my conscience. He lingers outside, gazing intently at the pile of cauliflowers.

'Errmm . . .' he says. 'I hope I didn't . . . I mean, I hope you didn't think . . .' He is scarlet with embarrassment. 'I don't make a habit of picking people up in shops or anything.'

'Oh no,' I say. 'I'm sure you don't.' The thought never crossed my mind.

'Okay,' he says, 'I just thought . . .'

I feel sorry for him but can't think of anything to say. Perhaps on a different day, if that woman hadn't glared at me, if the conductor hadn't asked questions . . .

He turns away. He has made a fool of himself.

'It wasn't that,' I blurt out. 'It's just . . .' I am even more tongue-tied than he is. 'I don't go out much,' I say abruptly. 'My husband died,' and catch a fleeting glimpse of his startled face before I turn and flee.

You idiot, Cathy Childs. You stupid, gauche female. Whatever made you say it? Did he ask for your life history?

Is it really necessary to tell someone that, in answer to a joky invitation to share supper?

Oh well. At least he'll feel better now. He's not the only one who makes a fool of himself. The world is full of silly people, saying silly things for silly reasons. Join the club.

The Friday-morning bus is full of damp macs, steaming scarves. The awkwardness of stowing wet umbrellas makes us sociable.

'Excuse me . . . I'm so sorry. Mind your feet!'

'That's all right, love. Filthy day.'

'Yes, isn't it.'

The cosiness of small talk. (More people saying silly things.)

'The forecast promised hail later on.' 'No, did it really?' 'Well, that's all we need.' Why ever call it small talk? Because the words are meaningless, perhaps. 'D'you see that film last night on ITV? Laugh? I thought I'd die!' I notice you, she's saying. I know you exist, a fellow human being. Small talk they call it; what could be bigger than that?

Sheets of rain stream down outside the windows; inside they are misty with humid warmth and chat.The rain has dulled the morning hurry. The passengers, relieved to climb aboard, lean back in their seats, in no rush to get off. We feel like refugees, sharing a huddled safety from the rain.

An old man with haunted eyes, his hair stuck sparsely to his streaming head, raindrops like tears adhering to his cheeks, is helped on board. The bench-seat passengers move up for him. 'Sit down then, love; there's room here for one more.'

'I'm sorry; my coat is wet.'

'Don't worry love, can't get much wetter now!'

'What a day!'

'Yes, isn't it.'

Fat, motherly women. Their brood outgrown. Back to work in factories and stores. Their mother instincts reaching outside home, embracing fellow refugees, old men, strange children, cats and Pekinese. Warming the hostile city with instinctive love.

I always get philosophical on buses. If no-one seems inclined to chat, the daily ride to work is a chance to ponder on life's unending mysteries, such as Big Harry's dyspeptic temper. With Big Harry as a boss, you need philosophy.

The steamy warmth and drowsy shudder of the bus are sending me to sleep. I didn't sleep last night. I didn't cry, just lay awake, feeling the coldness of the empty bed. This morning my eyes are heavy, as if I had cried, and my mouth is dry, as though I had been drinking. I drank most of a bottle of brandy one night after Barry had died. I was sick but clear-headed, which was funny. I never drank normally. An easy lay, Barry would say. One gin and tonic and the world – and my nose – turn rosy. Two, and like Titania I'm in love with the nearest face. Three, and I wouldn't recognize my own.

Barry was never affected the same way. Time after time his glass could be refilled, and he only grew more voluble, spouting with earnest eloquence on his vision of the world, pronouncing the longest words impeccably, without a trace of a slur – till suddenly (though never before the drink ran out) he would find himself a spacious patch of floor and, stretching out full length, fall fast asleep.

It was part of his catholic scorn for moderation. Or perhaps his Catholic, with a capital C, scorn. Or was it coincidence that he and his Catholic friends made life a continual celebration? If they came to dinner, I catered for twice the number. They drank like fish and ate like starving hounds, with loud appreciation of the food; they danced like dervishes, made love (if Barry was the norm) with noisy glee; their elders bred in dozens, deeming 'a lovely family' to be eight or more. Where other religions took as their texts sobriety and sacrifice, Catholics savoured the fruits of the earth, went forth rejoicing and multiplied.

Father Delaney, who married us, was a priest in the joyous tradition. In the church he was devout, his faith serene, his sermon quite inspired. At the wedding reception, with a litre of Irish malt to swell his cassock, he lit up with an other-worldly glow. In the creeping light of dawn, amid the bodies of unconscious relatives, Father Delaney was, to be sure, an upright man. Swaying and beaming, an empty bottle in his hand, he performed the hokey-cokey solitaire.

We went to see him once or twice, and Barry went alone sometimes when I was out with a girlfriend. I never expected him home before dawn, and my expectations never were proved wrong.

When Barry died, though, Father Delaney was away on holiday; it was only on his return that he heard the news. He turned up one night, with a stricken face and a bottle of Sainsbury's brandy. 'I'll not leave you the bottle,' he said, 'for it's easy to get the habit when you're grieved. So we'll drink it all between us on the spot.' On the second glass, the stoic face I kept for visitors began to crumble. I refused a third. But Father Delaney filled our glasses and talked of Barry till the tears – his as well as mine – began to flow.

'Tell me,' he said; 'tell me how he died.'

'No. Not yet. No.'

'It would do you good to talk about it, Cathy. It's not good to keep grief bottled up inside; it goes bitter on you.'

'Please, not yet.'

So he had gone, taking the rest of the brandy and leaving me to play loud music to drown my thoughts.

'Call and see me,' he said on leaving, 'any time you want to talk.'

But I didn't want to talk; I wanted to forget, so I never went.

I am at my stop, and the bus is about to go. I grope beneath the seat for my umbrella and stumble over ankles, bags and dogs. 'Sorry! Hang on, I'm getting off.'

'Come on Missis, haven't got all day.'

It's a new conductor with a face that says his feet have corns.

'Sorry.' And out into the beating rain. Too windy for umbrellas. Head down, and dashing to the crossing, darting between bumpers of windscreen-wiping cars, then safe and dry inside the office foyer.

'Another drownded rat! Lovely day for ducks, eh?'

'Morning, Fred.'

'Wotcher, Cath. Big Harry's beat you to it.'

'Well, as long as Alan hasn't.'

'That'll be the day!' Fred snorts. 'If ever that poofed-up pansy makes it here on time . . . '

I join the lift queue. 'Morning.'

'Morning. Lovely day.' The English sense of irony. Understatement. Sorry to hear about your misfortune, Mrs Childs. Expect you feel a bit low at times. You'll be over it soon, you'll see. What a good thing you had no children. What a good thing you didn't go to France. Oh, what a good thing . . .

Third floor. 'Morning Mr Diggins.'

'Have you got a moment, Cathy?'

'Now? Of course.' Of course, Big Harry, of course I've got a moment. I stand here dripping on the carpet, undried, uncoffeed, unhugged, unwoken up. The ideal time to call an impromptu meeting.

'That invitation to the Cloud Ten launch.'

'Ah yes.' I didn't think he'd like it. On the storage cupboard floor are piles of his past letters when he had my job. He used a standard form, ready printed and varying only in

34

the details. 'Bantam Cosmetics has pleasure in inviting Blank to . . . '

'Just one point. Only a minor one, really . . . '

Oh yeah. Now where have I heard that before? It's just the style that's wrong. And of course the content, and the phrasing and the words.

'Eleven thirty you say, for the time?'

'It's the time I've fixed with the hotel conference manager.' He's not going to change the time? Not now?

'Oh, quite, It's just that I feel we should say "A.M." That's all.'

He's joking! No, he's not. 'A.M.?'

'After "eleven thirty", put "A.M." I think you should.'

'But surely . . . ' This is ridiculous. Surely they won't take it to mean at night? Imagine a group of journalists at some party: 11.00 P.M., the lights are low; the drink is too. 'Hey, girls, I've had a great idea. Why don't we breeze along to Bantam? They've got this groovy conference on a make-up range. Starts at 11.30 and they're doing lunch . . . '

'I did say there'd be lunch,' I remind Big Harry.

'That's it then,' he says, unlistening. 'Just add "A.M." and then you can send it out.' He scribbles on the draft and slides it across the desk. 'Is your typist here?'

'I haven't been into the office yet.'

He pouts. 'I do hate these temps,' he says. 'Totally unreliable.'

'Have Personnel found someone permanent yet?'

'There were a few applicants for the job. No-one who sounded suitable.'

'Oh?' Knowing Big Harry, that means no-one blonde. Or red-haired. Or even just young. Although Big Harry has his own secretary he insists on his right as head of department to choose the new secretary for Alan and me as well. We have protested with total unsuccess.

35

'I shall let you meet her first, of course,' Big Harry had conceded. 'I am simply weeding out the unsuitables.'

'There is another point,' he says now. He nods towards the chair. This is a more solemn matter, evidently, than my press conference letter, for which I could quite well stand. I ignore him. On principle, I don't respond to nods. Training staff the Woodhouse way: 'Sit! Heel, boy!' No thanks. He glares at me and nods again. 'Sit down a minute.'

'Thank you.'

Big Harry taps his engraved Perspex memo-holder with his engraved executive pen. 'I had a meeting with the MD yesterday.'

He leans back in his swivel chair, and regards me through shrewdly narrowed eyes. He needs only the Stetson, the cigar and the deck of poker cards. Big Harry of the Bantam Saloon. Don't trifle with this cookie, guys. He's a killer with the agendas.

'He is not happy,' Big Harry announces mysteriously. 'Not happy at all.'

The news does not surprise me. Managing directors do not become managing directors by being happy people: if they ever were, they lose the skill as soon as they gain the hot-seat. All that indigestible power and heavy lunches, and the ulcer-inducing necessity of being nasty to underlings. If ordinary directors feel impelled to play Sheriff of Dead-End Gulch, then the managing director has to out-John-Wayne them all, just to show who's boss.

'The MD is displeased with the quality of press attention the company has received this year,' says Big Harry ponderously.

Oh grief! Oh tragedy! Oh World, fall apart. Bantam is not this year's media favourite. The trouble with this job is that it's impossible to take it seriously. So how does Big Harry manage it? Did he start off, like the rest of us, I wonder, with a healthy disrespect for the meaningless meanderings of boardroom bores, or was he destined for public relations from his cradle: an earnest-faced baby mumbling on his dummy and drafting memos to his Action Man?

Unaware of the sentiments he is arousing in my damply-mackintoshed bosom, Big Harry is continuing. 'I assured him that Bantam's public image is, in fact, quite healthy and that the past year's coverage was satisfactory, both in terms of quantity and . . . er . . .'

'Quality,' I supply.

'. . . in terms of . . . er . . . quantity and . . . er . . .' It does not do to prompt Big Harry. 'and . . . er . . . quality. But he needs to see Concrete Evidence that This is Actually So.' When he wishes to be impressive, Big Harry talks in capitals. 'So what I want from you – by Lunchtime at the Latest – is a Compilation of press cuttings to illustrate the company's Creditable Record. Right? Oh, and draft me a brief report on the contents, summarizing the coverage given to specific achievements, and so on. You had better start straight away.'

'You don't want product cuttings, then?' I ask. 'Just articles about the company as a whole?'

'The UK company, and the international group.' He picks up the phone to indicate that he is a busy man and I have wasted enough of his time.

'All of them?' I persist.

'All of them,' he says. He begins dialling.

I forestall him. 'So that will mean including those cuttings about the vivisection protest?' I felt badly about that, at the time. A group of American animal-lovers had discovered that Bantam's central testing lab in Boston had carried out inhumane experiments on dogs, and had organized a campaign encouraging women to boycott the firm's cosmetics.

The staff at Bantam's London office had been shocked by the revelations. The cynical had professed themselves unsurprised by this latest glimpse of the ugly side of business; the idealistic had talked of giving notice.

Being one of the idealistic, 'I ought to leave,' I had said to Barry. 'I oughtn't to work for a company which does things like that.'

'All cosmetics firms experiment on animals.'

'I won't work for another cosmetics firm, then.'

'Cathy, I experiment on animals!'

'That's different. That's to find cures for diseases, not ingredients for eyeshadow.'

'Do you suppose that the rats know the difference?'

'It's not rats in this case; it's dogs.'

'Ah well, there you have it,' Barry said. 'If it was rats, no-one would give a damn. Because it's pooches, everyone's up in arms.'

I was not convinced, and he could see it.

'Look, if you really think you ought to leave, you must,' he said. 'But you'll be leaving soon anyway, to go to France. Couldn't you hang on just a couple of months? The money would be useful.'

Big Harry does not look up. 'What vivisection?' he says.

I am amazed that he can have forgotten. 'You know, that protest in America which got taken up over here, about the . . .'

'I said, "What vivisection?"' Big Harry repeats, in a louder voice.

'I'm telling you,' I say. All he has to do is listen. 'The dogs which were used to . . .'

'I don't know about any vivisection,' Big Harry interrupts. 'Or any protest. We don't have cuttings which refer to that.'

Oh, so we are playing games. Business pretend-games.

'You mean you want me to leave them out?' I say.

He does not answer. In business, it is not acceptable to call a spade a spade. I suddenly feel sick of it. 'I don't think that would be honest,' I say, feeling my face flaming. 'I mean, to report on the year's publicity but leave out the bad news . . .'

Big Harry raises his head and gives me his iciest stare. The Sheriff would be proud of him. 'Just do it, will ya?' he says. There is even a slight mid-Western drawl in his voice. 'Hello,' he says, into the phone. 'Get me John Gardner.' He swivels away in his executive chair, which has been specially designed to help harassed managers swivel out of unwanted confrontations.

I pick up my bag and umbrella – noting with satisfaction that the latter has made a damp patch on the carpet – and go, tacitly admitting defeat.

'Hullo Sharon.' The temporary secretary has arrived and is already busy at her desk, painting her nails bright orange.

'Hi.'

'Listen, can you help me dig out all last year's press cuttings on the group? Mr Diggins wants a report by lunchtime.'

Sharon purses her lips. 'They're in the file,' she says. Do your own dirty work, her tone implies.

'Yes, I know, but we need to sort out the group and company cuttings from the product ones, and they're all pasted up together on the same sheets. It'll mean taking out all the pages with company cuttings on, photocopying them, and then pasting up copies of just the relevant bits. It's going to take a while, I'm afraid.'

'Well, I don't know,' she says. 'I've still got those letters to do.'

'Which letters are those?'

'The ones you gave me,' she says. 'Yesterday morning.'

'Let's have a look. No, there's nothing that can't wait until this afternoon.'

'I'm leaving this afternoon,' she says. 'I have to go early to get paid by the agency.'

'Fine,' I say. 'Leave the letters. We'll concentrate on

this. Can you start pulling out the cuttings while I make some phone calls first?'

'Okay.' She is still painting her nails when I go out.

Sharon told Alan she didn't like working for women – Alan told me. Especially young women. Short of changing sex and aging overnight, there is not a lot I can do about that. If I was a secretary too, we'd probably get on quite well. And they say it's men who discriminate against women . . .

Dialling the factory, I hear Sharon slam the drawer of the filing cabinet. Good.

'Could I speak to Vi in Packing, please?' Now I hear Sharon typing. What is she doing? 'Vi? This is Cathy from the press office. I'm bringing a journalist round this afternoon – Sally Harris. Could you have a press pack ready for us to give her? No, not Cloud Ten; we're saving that for the launch. Yes, we'll come in Bill's van at two o'clock. Okay, fine; see you later, Vi.'

'Sharon, what are you . . . '

'This fucking machine,' she declares, 'It's smudged my nails. I'll have to start again.'

'What are you typing, Sharon?'

'Your work!' she says petulantly. My work has smudged her nails.

'But I said it could wait,' I say feebly. 'The press cuttings . . .'

'They're over there.' She points to a batch of files on the cabinet.

'Yes, but we have to sort them out . . . Probably,' I concede, 'I didn't explain very well. Look, what we need to do . . . '

Alan comes in as we are finishing. 'Morning,' he says in funereal tones. 'God alive, my head . . . '

'Make us some coffee too,' I say. 'Sharon has sugar, remember.'

'Two,' says Sharon. 'And lots of milk. I've got to

watch my figure.' She giggles.

'You don't need to,' I say.

She laughs again, and looks more friendly. After three weeks I've finally cracked the ice – and she's leaving this afternoon.

'I'll read these through,' I say, 'then give them to you to photocopy, if that's OK, while I write the report.'

'Okey-doke. I'll start your letters while I'm waiting.' Miraculous.

Alan is spooning coffee, at arm's length. His eyes are closed against the light.

'No Disprin in mine,' I say.

'Oh, very funny.'

I take the kettle from him; he doesn't look too safe. 'Jerry forgiven you yet for the other night?'

'No,' he says shortly.

'Oh. I'm sorry.'

He swallows a handful of tablets, then another. He sniffs and blows his nose.

'Hey, Alan, it's not really serious, is it?' I have never seen him cry.

'I don't know,' he says miserably. 'He didn't come home last night.'

'What, not at all?'

He shakes his head.

'Oh dear. I suppose you can't ring him up at work?'

'I'd rather die!' he says dramatically.

I remove the Disprin from his grasp. 'Have some coffee instead.' I take Sharon hers and return.

'Did you know Sharon was leaving at lunchtime?'

'Not much loss,' he says morosely.

'I suppose they'll send a new temp next week. I wish we could get someone permanent.'

'Big Harry wants a graduate,' Alan says. 'It's the latest bee in his bonnet.'

41

'A graduate in what?' I ask, perplexed.

'In anything. Pasting up press cuttings, I suppose.'

'But why a graduate?'

'How should I know? He's probably gone off blondes. This is his new fetish. Ladies with letters after their names. You'd better watch out.'

'He's gone off me as well,' I say. 'I told him he wasn't honest, this morning.'

'You didn't!'

'More or less.'

'You trying to get yourself fired or something?'

'Perhaps, in my deep subconscious.'

'There's nothing subconscious in telling your boss he's dishonest,' Alan declares. 'You'd better watch it, Cath; he'll get you thrown out.' He sits up and sips his coffee.

'Glad I could make you feel better.' I leaf through the cuttings and tick the relevant ones. Vivisection Protest. Ban Bantam, says US Animal-Lover Group. Shock Allegations: Bantam Tortures Dogs.

Blast Big Harry. Why did he bring this up? All my pangs of conscience start again. Why did I listen to Barry? 'Stay on a few months, love; what's the difference?' There was a difference: a protest has to be made, if it is to be made at all, at once. A few months later it is just convenience.

And then, of course, I didn't leave at all. The last thing I wanted to do was change my job. Bereaved and terrified, I clung to my security; the routine I had found boring became a lifeline, the straw of the drowning man.

Yet here it is again, the same old scandal. It's all blown over now. The people who protested have forgotten the boycott, I expect; when they go to buy a lipstick, they pick up the first one they see. But at least they cared at the time.

In defiance of Big Harry, I tick the protest cuttings for Sharon to include. Big Harry can leave them out if he wants to, edit all reference from the report. I'll even leave it till the end, so it's easier for him to cut. But I won't give him a censored version. It's his omission, not mine. In the long run it makes no difference. But it's a gesture.

'Hey, look at this,' Sharon remarks, when I give her the papers. 'Firm Mutilates Dogs. Is that true?'

'Apparently. It happened last year. Can you paste those up on a separate sheet?'

'Yeah. It doesn't still happen though, does it?'

'Well, they promised to change,' I say, 'but I don't suppose they did. Probably moved the dogs to another lab.'

She looks at me in disgust as well she might. 'Businessmen!' she says. 'They're all the same. Anything for money; they don't care what they do. The last place I worked for, permanent, made bombs. They never said so in the brochures, but they did. It just said "Chicago branch" but one of the managers told me that's what they did there. Anti-personnel devices, they called them.'

'They would,' I agree.

'They're all a load of shit,' she says contemptuously. 'I wouldn't play their games for anything.'

I warm to her. 'Is that why you work temp, rather than for one firm?'

She unscrews the varnish cap and touches up the corner of a nail. 'Na-ooow. The money's better.'

We are interrupted by an unknown girl, in a jacket and matching beret in vivid yellow.

'Can you tell me where to find someone called Cathy Childs?'

'That's me. Can I help?'

'I'm Sally Harris,' she announces.

'Oh! I'm sorry, I wasn't expecting you till lunchtime. Did I say morning? I must have . . .'

'Oh no, you did say lunch,' she says, 'but I thought it would be better to do the factory bit and that beforehand because I'm going away on holiday. I was going to go on

43

Saturday, but my boyfriend's got a half day off.'

'I'm sorry, but you see I'm tied up this morning.' Why couldn't the wretched girl have phoned first? 'I really don't think I can be free much before lunchtime.'

'Oh. Well, is there someone else?' she asks. 'Or else I can just wander round by myself?'

'I'm afraid they don't let visitors round the factory on their own. Look, why don't you sit down and have some coffee, and I'll see what I can arrange?'

'Oh, all right then.' She sounded so shy on the telephone, it's hard to believe it was the same girl. She sits down, depositing her bag on Sharon's desk. Sharon moves it, pointedly, and shuffles the pile of press cuttings. Sally Harris picks one up and reads it. 'Are these about the company?' she says. 'It might be useful background for me.'

'Excuse me,' says Sharon, 'but I need those. We're very busy at the moment.' And she proceeds to be, working faster than I have ever seen her before. I dive into my office before I start to laugh.

'What's going on out there?' Alan inquires.

'That girl's arrived – the journalist who isn't. She took it into her head to come now, for some reason, instead of at lunchtime. I'm just going to ring the factory to find someone to show her round.'

'I'll do it if you like,' he offers.

'Are you sure?'

'I don't feel like working,' he admits. 'What do you want me to do? I can't tell her anything about cosmetics.'

'I can talk about the products over lunch. If you could just give her a press kit, take her round . . . Vi at the factory has got some samples ready.'

'Okay. We'll get a lift with Bill on the ten thirty van.'

'That's great. Thanks Alan. I'm just making her some coffee while she's waiting.'

'I'll do that. You get on with what you've got to do.'

'Thanks.'

'Do you want some coffee?'

'I wouldn't mind.' I'm amazed at his being so nice, so early in the morning. 'You don't really think Jerry's left, do you?' You never know with Alan what is drama and what's real.

He shrugs. 'He might have. But he's probably just gone off to make me jealous by screwing somone else.'

'Ah.'

'Oh, he'll be back,' says Alan airily. 'He'll miss my cooking if nothing else. It happened once before.'

I draft the vivisection piece first, although it's to go in last. If I don't do it quickly, I might lose my nerve. Big Harry can be devastating when he's crossed.

'Although the storm has blown over,' I write, 'the vivisection issue is unresolved. Reference to Bantam is made in the press each time the vivisection topic is discussed. The Public Relations Department's work in promoting the company and its products is hindered by this flaw in the corporate image, and visiting journalists often raise the question of vivisection, even now.'

My pen keeps on writing; I'm getting carried away. This isn't the place, I know, for private theories or ethics. 'Public relations is first and foremost the job of the whole company. The company cannot act unethically, then use PR to erase the damage . . .' Big Harry will cut this instantly, but it gets it off my chest. Reading those cuttings has brought out the unvoiced protests about the firm that have festered in my head ever since I joined. And now that they're out, I find I can't ignore them. Which means I'll have to leave. Oh no; how did I get to that? I really don't want to change my job. I'm just getting back on my feet after Barry's death.

Before you drown in a tide of self-pity, Cathy Childs, remind yourself that it is eight months now, and there's no excuse for working in a firm you don't respect. No. Ridiculous scruples. I'll think about it later; now there's work to do. After the report, the arrangements for the conference; after that, the lunch with Sally Harris. She should be gone by two o'clock.

Alan puts the coffee on my desk. 'I'll go and talk to little Miss Whatshername.'

'I'll come and introduce you.'

Sally Harris is moodily kicking the desk, and looking through Sharon's *Time Out* magazine. Sharon, tight-lipped, is pasting cuttings with amazing speed. I hope Sally will stay long enough to inspire her to finish the job.

At the sight of Alan, Sally brightens.

'Alan will show you round the factory, if that's OK, then I'll meet you back here for lunch.'

'Ooh, thank you, Alan; aren't you kind?' She twinkles up at Alan, and he thaws.

'I knew a girl called Sally, when I was in kindergarten,' he volunteers.

'I knew a boy called Alan,' she returns. 'He was ever such a naughty little boy. Used to put his hand up all our skirts. Wasn't you, was it?'

'I doubt it,' says Sharon loudly. She raises her eyebrows at me behind Sally's back. I think I'll leave them to it.

When the giggling from her office becomes too loud, Sharon moves into mine. 'She's like a silly kid,' she says disgustedly. 'How am I expected to work?'

She spreads out the cuttings on Alan's desk. 'I've nearly finished the pasting,' she says. 'Then I'll run them off on the copier. You wanted the dog ones separate, didn't you?'

'Yes, that's right.'

'I'm surprised he wants those ones, that Mr Diggins.'

'He doesn't, actually. He's pretending he's forgotten they exist.'

'Gawd!' says Sharon. 'I'm glad I'm leaving here.'

'I was just thinking of leaving myself,' I confess.

'Can't say I blame you,' she says. 'Mind you, everywhere else is the same.'

'Is it?' That is what worries me. 'What about smaller firms?'

'Yeah, they're all right. The people are nicer and that. But they don't pay so good, if you're permanent staff, and they don't have canteens and things.'

'I don't mind that. I usually bring my own food.'

'You eat a lot, don't you?' she says, emboldened by her newly-offered friendship.

'Yes.'

'But you don't get fat.'

'There isn't time; I've got a fast metabolism. The food just has time for a quick wave at my stomach on its way through.'

She eyes me curiously. 'You say some funny things.'

I score a line through a paragraph and start again.

'Just going, Cathy.'

'See you later, Alan. About half-past twelve OK?'

As they go out, I hear Sally Harris say, 'Are you her boss then, Alan?'

Sharon snorts. 'She thinks men are the only ones who work. D'you know what she said to me?'

'Oh, I wouldn't take any notice,' I said sneakily. 'Some women don't like other women at work.'

She looks away guiltily, and goes back to pasting.

By half-past one, they still have not returned. I've delivered Big Harry's report, retyped (with two fingers) the press launch invitation which Sharon typed with seventeen mistakes, copied it, and signed and sent the copies off. My stomach is rumbling: I haven't eaten since eleven o'clock. That's weeks, for me.

Sally, when they return, is slightly drunk. 'Oops!' she squeals, tripping over her feet. 'I thought that was a step!' She goes into peals of laughter, which Alan shares.

47

'You've already had lunch, have you?' Hunger makes me schoolmistressy.

'Mainly liquid,' says Alan unnecessarily.

'You want to eat?'

'No thanks, we had a roll.'

Sally goes into paroxysms. 'But don't let my boyfriend know!'

'I'm going to the canteen then. You'll man the phone, will you Alan?'

'He'll man it,' Sally hiccups, 'and I'll woman it!'

Murderous feelings, I remind myself, are a symptom of low blood sugar. When I've eaten she'll seem quite tolerable. Also, she'll be gone. I wonder why I feel so strongly about her. Perhaps because I had invited her, feeling sorry for her as a struggling school-leaver, failing in her chosen career. If I was honest, I'd have to admit that I'd been looking forward to doing someone a favour. For eight months, I've been on the receiving end of other people's kindness, and I saw Sally's visit as a chance to be the giver, for a change, in however small a way.

Realizing that my motive was purely selfish makes it easier to forgive her for so obviously not needing anyone's help.

All that seems to be left in the canteen is a heap of soggy chips. 'No omelettes?'

'Too late, love; sorry. The cook's stopped cooking.'

'Salad?'

'All gone. Corned beef rissoles, that's all there is.'

'All right. Has anyone died from them yet?'

'Not yet. But the girl in the corner looks a bit pale.'

I follow her pointing finger. 'Suky!' She waves. 'Can you stay, or have you finished yours?'

'I've finished, but I'll stay!'

The cashier, a new face, hits the till with venom; she doesn't like her job. 'Tea or coffee?'

'No, that's all thanks. If the rissoles kill me, do I get a refund?'

The cashier looks grim. 'There's nothing wrong with those; I made them. I'm the cook.'

'Oh, sorry; I didn't mean it.' I spoil the apology by laughing, and she glares.

Suky, when I tell her, also laughs, her rolling belly-laugh.

'Oh, shush; she'll hear!'

'You watch it next time,' Suky warns. 'She'll put poison in your food.'

'I think she has already.' I push the plate away. 'Did you have the rissoles?'

'Yeah, I can eat anything; I don't mind.'

'I can usually, but that's too much.'

'You coming down for coffee later on?'

'I can't this afternoon, got too much work. You busy too?'

She rolls her eyes and spreads her hands expressively. 'It's just the same today as every day. Putting papers into holes and papers into holes. Sometimes more and sometimes less; don't make much difference.'

'Do you get bored, Suky?'

'I don't think about it; that's the only way.'

'Why don't you try another job?'

'I'm all right here; they don't like taking black people, other firms.'

'They have to, by law!'

'But they don't. They look at you, they say you've got the wrong qualifications, or something else. Qualifications, for a filing job!' She shakes with laughter.

'I'm thinking of leaving.'

'No, you're not!' The laughter dies. 'Not really?'

'It'll be a while. I've got to look for something else, I don't know what.'

'Don't leave, Cathy. You're the best friend I got.' Two

tears swell in the corners of her eyes. Oh no.

'You've got lots of friends here, Suky.' I pat her on the hand, and she puts her arms around me. A pinstripe-suited young executive walks past us with his tray, and looks down his nose. Mixed-Racial Lesbians Embrace in Firm's Canteen. 'It Was the Rissoles Drove Us to It,' Guilty Pair Explain.

'I know I've got other friends, but they don't make me laugh like you do.'

'I'm not having much success now, am I?' She has started me off too; we sniff and giggle sheepishly. 'I'll come back and see you, I promise.'

'How soon are you going?'

'I only decided today! Two hours ago, about. I don't even know what to look for. Probably not PR again.' The idea has taken shape; I am definitely leaving Bantam. This morning, I didn't know it. Funny how things turn out.

'I must go; there's a journalist in my office, though I hope she'll have left by now. I don't think she's really interested, but I'd better go through the motions of giving her information.'

'I'll see you Monday, then; have a nice weekend.'

'And you.'

Sally Harris is perched on the filing cabinet, giggling.

'I'm the new mascot for your office,' she says.

'Fine: we could do with some good luck.'

Alan is sitting cross-legged in his chair, drinking coffee.

'Has the kettle just boiled?'

'No coffee left,' he says. 'We finished it.'

'We needed sobering up,' says Sally. It doesn't appear to have had much effect.

'Has Alan shown you all you need to see?' I ask her. 'Or would you . . . ' Another gale of laughter. I try again. 'I mean, will you be needing any more information? About the cosmetic ranges or anything?'

'Oh no, I've got enough. The old bag at the factory gave me a box of stuff. It doesn't look my style; the colours are really old-fashioned. By the way, she sent you a sample of this glitter dust. I'll have yours as well if you feel too old for it!'

'Thanks,' I say, 'I'll wear it tonight at the pensioners' club.'

'No, really,' she says. 'Don't they make anything more up to date?'

'There's a new range out in a couple of weeks. We haven't launched it yet.'

'Oh well, perhaps I'll have some of that.'

'You ought to go to the press conference,' Alan offers. 'Free drinks and hand-outs and all that.'

'That sounds like me!' she says. 'When's it on?'

Alan looks at me. 'Cathy?'

'Fairly soon,' I say vaguely. 'I had the letter here a while ago.' I flutter papers ineffectually. I don't think Sally Harris has any intention of writing about cosmetics, or anything else.

'How did you get into journalism?' I inquire.

She giggles. 'I just thought I'd have a go. It sounded less boring than other things.'

'It's difficult to get into, isn't it?' Alan says. 'Which magazine do you write for?'

'Oh, any of them,' she says nonchalantly. 'I just decided I'd do it, and that was it. I could have done lots of things really. I thought about going to university, but I couldn't be bothered. I think it's a drain on the taxpayers, anyway.'

'So you started this straight after A levels?' Alan says.

'No, I didn't stay on for sixth form. I could have but there wasn't any point. I don't see what difference exams make, anyhow. It's only a piece of paper.'

'Careful!' Alan warns. 'Cathy spent four years collecting a piece of paper that says she has a degree.'

51

'Four!' she exclaims. 'Why four? I thought a degree took three.'

I wish Alan would keep his mouth shut. 'I started a Ph.D. Gave it up when I got married.'

'Oh yes, Alan told me . . . ' A look from him silences her – and tells me that Alan has told her about Barry.

'But I don't see why,' she starts again, 'you had to give up to get married. I think women should do what they want to do, whatever their husbands say.'

'It was what I wanted to . . . '

'If I get married, I won't let my husband dictate to me,' she declares. 'I think a woman should have her own career and not run the house and things. And as for taking her husband's name and wearing his ring and everything . . . Did you take your husband's name, Cathy?'

'I'm afraid so. And the ring. I used to wear it through my nose,' I add unnecessarily. 'My husband found it useful for tethering me to the sink.'

'I must go,' Sally decides. 'Make me some coffee first, though, Alan; be a love.'

'It's run out,' Alan says.

'Can't you get some from somewhere else? What do other people drink?'

'There's a vending machine downstairs.'

'Oh, yuck! No thanks.'

'Or . . . ' he hesitates, 'there's Big Harry's Cona flask. We pinch some of that when he's out, but he's here today.'

'He wouldn't mind, though, surely?' she cajoles. 'Who is he anyway? Big Harry! What does that refer to?' She lets out a whoop of laughter. 'Ooh, I nearly fell off this filing cabinet!'

'He's our boss,' says Alan, 'and I don't think . . . '

'So you work for him and Cathy works for you?'

I give Alan a quizzical glance, and he has the grace to blush.

'I told you, Cathy's the same job level as me . . . '

'Well, I'm off then,' she says. 'I'll see you people again sometime. Ta-ra.'

She is gone. I look across at Alan and am about to heave a conspiratorial sigh of relief when he says, 'Pretty little thing, isn't she?'

'What? Oh. Yes. Sure.'

'I think she took quite a fancy to me,' Alan says smugly. 'She's invited me to a party next week.'

'Great.'

'Perhaps I should turn straight,' he muses.

I take out my notepad and start drafting some letters.

'What d'you think?' he pursues. 'It'd be the perfect punishment for Jerry, wouldn't it – getting off with Sally?'

'Perfect for Sally, too,' I point out.

'I read about this psychologist,' says Alan loudly, 'who says everyone is bisexual.'

I pick up my pen again.

'He says anyone who thinks they're not is deluding themselves.'

'Alan! I'm trying to work.'

'You'd do well to listen,' he says severely, 'because if this guy's right then you are too.'

'I wouldn't even agree that everyone's sexual, let alone bi. If you haven't got any work, why don't you take your sex appeal for a walk and buy a jar of coffee?'

'The trouble with you,' he says, on his way out, 'is that you're repressed.'

He's telling me?

3

As if to round off the perfect working day, my mother phones, just as I am leaving the office.

'I'm glad I caught you, dear; I thought you might have left.'

'How are you, Mum?'

'What, dear?'

'I think someone's frying eggs on this line. How are you?'

'I can't hear you very well: I think it's the line. How are you dear?'

'I'm fine, and you?'

'I'm sorry I haven't rung before, Cathy. I've been so busy; you can't imagine! If it wasn't the WI it was Towns-women's Guild . . . I hope you don't think I've been ne-glecting you, dear.'

'No, of course not.' Since acquiring the status of widow-hood, I am one of my mother's 'good causes'. She even sends me food parcels – not that they are not welcome. I only hope they're not subsidized by the Rotary Club.

'But I'm ringing to say, dear, that I am now entirely at your disposal: I can come and stay for as long as you like. Now that Solly's got his chest . . .'

'His what? Do you mean bronchitis or something?'

'What, dear?'

'What about his chest? Is it bronchitis?'

'This line really is terrible; you'll have to shout.'

'I am shouting!' Big Harry will be in if I shout any louder. I give it one more try. 'Should you really leave Solly?' I yell. 'If he's got bronchitis?'

'Bronchitis? He hasn't got bronchitis.'

54

'You said his chest . . .'

'Not chest! Chess! The game, chess.' My mother's laugh, loud and clear, penetrates the crackles. 'He's joined a club in the village. Plays three times a week. Three times a week! What am I supposed to do, I asked him? I call it selfish . . .'

'Even so, you can't just leave him on his own . . .' My stepfather can't boil an egg. What am I saying? Even his tea has to be stirred for him. That's Cooking, you see. Cooking is Woman's Work. I don't know what he thinks is Men's Work. Playing Chest, maybe.

'Why can't I?' she says. 'It's about time he learned to cope on his own. It won't hurt him for a couple of weeks.'

A couple of *weeks*! 'I'm getting a lodger, Mum,' I bellow desperately. 'I'm not sure when they're moving in.'

'They? How many are there of them, Cathy?'

'Just one.' I am hoping not to have to commit myself to details of the mythical lodger.

'I hope it's a woman, Cathy?'

'Yes, probably.'

'What?'

I cross my fingers. 'Yes.'

'You won't want a man,' my mother tells me.

'No.' Mother knows best.

'How old is she? What does she do?'

I was born chicken. 'Sorry, Mum, I can't hear. The line's getting worse.'

'I said what . . .?'

'I'll call you later in the week, okay?'

''Bye darling,' she yells with such sudden force that my eardrum quivers. She puts down the receiver.

In one day I've committed myself to leaving my job and sharing my flat. Life is full of surprises.

''Night, Mr Diggins.'

'Eh? Oh, goodnight.'

'Was the report okay?' Might as well get all the bad things over in one day.

He doesn't look at me. 'Mm, fine. Have to be shortened – I'll just cut the last few paragraphs.'

'Yes. Well, goodnight; have a nice weekend.'

'Arrh.' He is hunched over his desk again, his macho black anglepoise lamp spilling a circle of light on the blank notepad. The light, in the winter dusk, softens his features; a balding, heavy-boned child. He is dreaming of lists of jobs to delegate on Monday.

Outside, the rain has stopped but there's more on the way. In the bus queue nobody speaks, conserving their warmth. The buses – all the same number and none of them mine – crush the puddles, smashing the brittle reflections of headlights, and sending a muddy spray up the edge of the kerb. The queuers accept the splashes mutely; it's no more than they expected. If they can survive, cocooned in themselves till they reach their destination, they will thaw out, once home, into human beings again. Drawing the curtains in shabby flats and bedsits, they will shut out the malice of the city night and settle to the reality of two-bar fires and tea. Till then, they suspend animation; woe betide the old man who hopes they'll make room on the bench-seat tonight.

When my bus comes, I strap-hang all the way, with someone's umbrella puncturing my knee. I am hungry again; two hours since the last cheese roll. It's an effort to elbow my way off the bus. I hurry past the supermarket, fearful of meeting The Beard. It will have to be cheese again, at home.

'Father Delaney – how nice!'

'I just called at your flat; I was with Mr and Mrs Pratt downstairs. Is it a bad time, now? Are you busy?'

'No, I'm not going out till quarter past eight. Come and have cheese on toast.'

'That sounds very nice, I've been eating your neighbour's home-made buns. But you can't take too much of that kind of thing. They're a little – what's the word?'

'Sickly?' I know Mrs Pratt's home-made buns. One centimetre of heavy sponge and two of bright pink icing.

The gas has run out and so has my change for the meter. 'I'll just go and ask Mrs Pratt; she usually keeps some change.'

'I may have some here.' He fumbles in his pocket.

'No, don't bother, please.'

'Not worrying about me being on the breadline again?' he teases. Last time, he let out – I hadn't known before – that Catholic priests receive no salary, only pocket money.

'Well, I think it's wrong,' I said defiantly. 'If the State pays Anglican vicars, why not you?'

'Sure, it's not the state religion, now it is? Your company wouldn't pay the opposition, I'm sure.'

Mrs Pratt, from the flat downstairs, obliges with a handful of change.

'Got friends in, have you?'

'Father Delaney has called.'

'Ah, yes. He was here this afternoon. I made him some of my buns.'

'Yes, he said.'

'Did he really? He always likes those; I make them specially. The secret is not to stint on the icing. So many people do.'

'Yes. Thanks for the change. I'll see you on Sunday, if not before.' We probably won't meet before. Mrs Pratt lives behind closed doors with her husband and feather duster. She hoovers and polishes every day, washes and irons twice a week and starts to prepare the tea as soon as she's 'washed up the lunch'. She hasn't much time to go out, except to compare Special Offers in Fine Fare and Safeway's.

'Will tea be all right? I've run out of drinkable booze.'

'Now even I don't drink whisky with cheese on toast.' He is sitting on the arm of the chair leafing through an old issue of *Cosmopolitan*. 'Do you read this stuff?'

'I don't buy it. Someone passed it on.' Why are women made to feel guilty about magazines? Given the chance, any man will pick one up and immerse himself in the agony column.

'Do you like tomato with your cheese on toast?'

'Don't go to any trouble now. Whatever you're having yourself.'

'I'm having tomato. They're good for you. Vitamin C.'

'Oh, well, if it's for the good of my health . . . .' He follows me into the kitchen. 'Shall I make the tea?'

'Thanks. There's a new packet on the shelf. Two spoonfuls and a bit for luck.' The sink is blocked again; a nasty smell arises from the plughole. I hope he won't think it's me.

'Are you in need of the luck, then?' he asks. 'How are things going?'

'Fine. I'm thinking of changing my job. And maybe advertising for someone to share the flat.'

'Do you need the money?'

'Not really. It would pay the rates. I could take a job I liked, even if the salary was less.'

'Why are you thinking of leaving your present job?'

Why? At Bantam, wanting to leave is a natural consequence of working there. 'Oh, I don't know. Big business is not very . . . well, I knew when I started what it was like, but I thought the job was only temporary, till we went to France. Then, when Barry died, I stayed. Perhaps I shouldn't have done.'

'So now it seems a good time to leave?'

'As good as any. I won't hand in my notice till I've found something else.'

We carry the plates to the sitting-room table: ubiquitous young-marrieds' pine. 'How's the parish?'

He sighs. 'We've just discovered dry rot in the roof. You don't expect it in a modern place – well, late Victorian I suppose it is. Not really old.'

'What will that mean? A new roof?'

'I hope not. But by the time we've raised the money to treat the rot, it may have spread, of course.'

'When I marry a millionaire, I'll give you a roof, I promise.'

'Most kind. You're not thinking of getting married again?'

'No, only joking.'

'Do you have any boyfriends now?'

'No.' His questions are uninfluenced by tact; he heads straight for the major issues and asks what he wants to know. 'I have been asked out a few times, but I don't really want anyone, to be honest. At least, not all the time. Not a proper relationship.'

'You're still grieving. Don't rush it, just because you're lonely.'

'I've got plenty of friends.'

'But it's not the same,' he finishes for me. I give him the third piece of cheese on toast. 'Are you having another yourself?' he protests.

'I'm going out to supper later. This is a snack.' He must know about loneliness too; living alone in the comfortless presbytery next to the church, with a view of the tower blocks and the vandalized playground.

'Did I tell you we'd started a meditation group?' he says.

'You mentioned it to Barry, months ago. Said you were going to. What is it – not the transcendental type?'

'It's much the same; a Christian version. Father Jessup in Lambeth started a group and I went to see. He learned about it when he was in India.'

59

'What do you have to do? Is it difficult?'

'Difficult to concentrate, at first. You get the hang of it. It's very good; spiritually refreshing. I can send you a booklet if you're interested.'

I try to imagine Father Delaney sitting cross-legged and chanting, but I can't. 'But what happens? I mean, is it meant to calm your mind or what?'

'It's meant to help you to listen to God, instead of talking at yourself all the time. To give you an awareness. Of God, first of all, and yourself as well.'

'I don't know that I'd want an awareness of myself,' I say, half joking. 'I might become aware there was nothing worth being aware of.'

He is suddenly serious, fixing me with his eyes. 'The good Lord died for you, and you say you're not worth the trouble? Isn't that a bit insulting to your creator?'

I am startled by his intensity.

'We are told to love our neighbour as ourselves,' he continues, letting his cheese on toast go cold. 'What kind of a deal will your neighbour get if you haven't first learned to value yourself? You're unique as a human being, you know, specially designed by God, with a mixture of talents and virtues that no-one else has.'

I have this horrible feeling I'm going to cry. Did I say I don't cry nowadays? Father Delaney seems to have that effect on me. 'And faults and failings,' I say lightly. 'A Special Mixture of those as well.'

'Sure, they're just the talents and virtues used the wrong way. When we shut our ears and refuse to listen to God.' He picks up his cup and drains it.

'Another cup?'

'No, I'll not keep you. You'll want to be getting on. Putting on your finery, isn't that it?'

'You don't know the half of it. Glitter dust, I've got.' It's easy to pick up the Irish intonation when you talk to Father Delaney.

'What's glitter dust when it's at home?'

'A cosmetic sample from the factory. Gold powder that you sprinkle on your skin.'

'Glory be, what will they think of next? Be sure you wear the halo to go with it!'

I see him to the door. 'It's nice of you to come. It's not as though I'm a parishioner. Or even the right religion, come to that.'

'It's the right religion if you love the Lord.' Noting my hesitation, he adds, 'He loves you, anyway. Don't you forget that now.'

'I won't.'

'I'll send you a booklet about the meditation. Don't come unless you want to, but you'll be very welcome. Monday evenings at the presbytery – seven o'clock.'

'It might be restful, anyway, after a Monday at work!'

'It's not a way of escaping from your troubles, mind. It brings you up against the root of them, if anything. But it puts things in perspective. You might find it helps.'

'You think I need to put things in perspective?' It's a genuine question. He has a way of seeing things in people.

'It could be. If you're thinking of changing your job and your home and everything else, perhaps it's yourself you're wanting to change. I'll see you soon now, Cathy. Many thanks for the tea.'

I wave at him out of the window as he unchains his bicycle in the street below.

You somehow don't resent Father Delaney talking religion at you. It's not as though he's trying to recruit you to the God Squad; it's just that he regards God as a part of everyone's life, whether they recognize it or not, and he can't help referring to him now and again any more than he can help breathing.

I remember Barry telling Father Delaney, when we were going to move, of the kind of life we planned to lead in

France. The freedom, the shrugging off of stifling traditional values.

'You take yourself with you, you know, wherever you go,' Father Delaney had said. 'What are you trying to find that you can't find here?'

Barry was angry at that. 'The only travel you care about is the journey of the soul! Travel is meant to broaden the mind, or hadn't you heard?'

Father Delaney was unmoved. 'So they say,' he agreed, holding a match to his pipe. 'And none of our minds are so broad that we couldn't do with that. I hope you will find that it deepens the spirit as well.'

It was about the time that I had suspicions that Barry was trying to leave certain problems behind, in going to France. His condemnation of 'bourgeois materialism', which had been silenced by our buying the flat, had started again now that we were to leave it.

'But we'll only exchange it for another flat in France,' I pointed out, 'and probably fill it with the same kind of possessions.'

'The point is not to get attached to the things,' said Barry fiercely. 'To keep them meaningless and valueless. We may possess things, but we won't let them possess us.'

We were attached to things, though, like the duvet, and Barry's stereo deck. They formed part of our history, a record of our past. Perhaps his real fear was of getting attached to people and he was escaping from that. Not people. Person. Janice, in fact.

I attack the blocked sink with the plunger, but with no success. It will have to wait till tomorrow. There is time to have a bath, if the water's hot. It is. I must have left the immersion on. The electricity's not coin-box metered like the gas, so I have to remember to save up to pay the bill.

Maybe a lodger isn't such a bad idea. I don't really want another person in the flat, stamping their personality on the place, erasing the memories and burning the saucepans. But it would be company, and a bit of extra cash, and someone to blame the noises on when things go bump in the night.

The bathwater cools, and I realize the time, rushing to dress before Carla and Jim arrive.

'Cathy, what have you got on your face?'

'Glitter dust. Hot from Bantam Cosmetics' production line.'

Carla bursts out laughing. 'It looks like luminous freckles. Do you glow in the dark?'

'I don't know.' We turn out all the lights to find out. 'Well?'

'No, it doesn't shine,' Jim says. 'Pity, really: could be quite erotic. Depending on where you put it, of course.'

'Shall we go?' Carla says.

I leave the light on in the bathroom, having been told by someone who was friendly with a burglar that burglars are fooled by this. I would have thought that the average burglar would conclude that the place was empty if the bathroom light stayed on for hours. Unless the burglar took four-hour baths and thought that was the norm. Come to think of it, Barry's bathtime was sometimes not far off that, once he got in there with his floating dolphin soap-dish, his Tarzan loofah-club and the bottle of Matey bubbles (or washing up liquid when money was short).

When we are in the car on our way to Marcie's I realize that for some reason, I did not kiss Jim and Carla when they arrived. I used to kiss everyone, without thinking: even the plumber once, in an absent-minded mood, when he left after fixing our burst pipe.

Since February though (it sounds better than saying 'since Barry died' all the time, doesn't it?) I have been somehow less demonstrative. It's not connected with the temporary frigidity; at least, I don't think so. It is more a reflection of my ambiguous status as a once-married female now suddenly on my own: formerly seen as a normal, affectionate person, I have now become a predator, a threat. Not to Carla, admittedly, who has known me since we were giggling schoolgirls, but even newly-acquired habits die hard.

'Have you eaten, Cathy?'

'Need you ask?'

'Oh no, of course. What I meant was, are we eating at Marcie's? Jim and I weren't sure.'

'She said she was doing quiche and things.'

'Thank God for that,' says Jim. 'Carla wouldn't let me eat, in case.'

Marcie's flat has an intercom system on the doorbell downstairs. Her voice sounds distorted. 'Hello, who is it?'

'Casanova,' says Jim.

'Come right on up, Casanova, and bring the harem with you.'

No hesitation about kissing Marcie. She flings herself at us before we reach the top stair. 'Carla, you look thinner every time I see you. Cath, the gold dust. I *love* it! Jim, darling! Isn't it lovely? Just us. I've been entertaining Sam's business friends all week, and they are so *boring*!'

Sam, from the doorway, grins sheepishly. 'Come in; what will you drink?'

As we go into the sitting room, Jim mutters in my ear, something unintelligible.

'Sorry?'

'What's his name? Marcie's boyfriend?' he hisses.

'Sam.'

'Thanks, Sam,' he says smoothly; 'I'll have a Scotch.'

'Darling, I've got wine!' Marcie wails. 'I said it was a wine evening, didn't I?'

'No,' we say in unison, and Sam adds,

'You only decided this morning, Marcie; how could they know?'

'Oh, of course. Aren't I silly?' She beams at us, confident of forgiveness. Anyone would forgive Marcie anything. The charm which eased her into a successful modelling career is combined with more than one person's quota of good looks and a total lack of malice.

'How's business going, Marcie?' At twenty-nine, Marcie has retired from modelling, and set up her own boutique.

'It's wonderful,' she declares. 'I love being self-employed. It's just so terrible having people to work for me, though. I haven't the nerve to ask the girls to sweep up and make the coffee. I do it all myself.'

'I don't know where you find the energy for all that work,' says Carla enviously. 'I'm worn to a shred just looking after Louise; I don't do half what you do, in a day.'

'Marcie's an ox,' says Sam unflatteringly. 'She may look as though she'd snap in the breeze but beneath that skinny exterior is solid steel.'

'He's right,' says Marcie unrepentantly. 'I'm as tough as old boots. Besides, Carla, children are so much more *exhausting*. All those nappies and things! Much easier to sell a few dresses. Now, don't talk! Taste the wine, and tell me what you think.'

We sip appreciatively. 'Mmm, what is it?'

'Do you know, I can't remember,' she confesses. 'Sam, have a look at the label, darling. I asked the man in the shop to choose it for me; he said it was really smooth.'

'Marcie,' says Sam reprovingly, 'if you ask the assistant's opinion, he'll invariably recommend the most expensive.'

'But it wasn't the assistant, sweetie; it was a customer. He was picking out all these bottles with incredible care; he obviously knew *all* about it so I asked his advice and really, he couldn't have been more sweet and helpful.'

Carla and I suppress a giggle at the expression on Sam's face. Later, when Sam and Marcie disappear into the kitchen to oversee the quiche, Carla whispers naughtily, 'He won't last long.'

'You women!' Jim complains. 'What's wrong with him?'

Carla shakes her head. 'Too authoritative, and too possessive. Marcie won't stand for it.'

'I think you're wrong,' says Jim. 'You girls imagine things.'

'Darlings,' says Marcie, appearing with the quiche, 'does anyone hate olives? I thought they would be lovely in a quiche, just little slices, but I couldn't remember whether you all liked them. So I made a mushroom one as well, just in case.'

When she goes out again Carla says, 'Bet you fifty p.'

'Come off it, Carla!' Jim leans forward and pours himself more wine.

'No go on. Fifty p.'

'What have you got to lose?' I encourage him. 'Male logic versus feminine intuition.'

'Feminine intuition!' he snorts derisively.

'Fifty p then? Each?'

'All right. It's your money you're throwing away.'

Marcie and Sam bring quiches, sausages, pâté, a cheese-board, salad and hot French bread.

'Marcie, I thought you said you were doing a snack!'

'Well, it's not really cooking, is it? I mean, most of it comes from the delicatessen. Not like Carla's gorgeous home-made stuff.'

'You've been cooking home-made food all week,' Sam reminds her. 'We've been having dinner parties,' he tells us. 'It's a wonder she's not worn to a shred.'

Carla nudges me surreptitiously. Jim, who notices, glares at her.

'Oh, nonsense, I love it,' says Marcie quickly. 'And

tonight is my reward, after listening so intently to all that shop-talk.'

'It was interesting shop-talk,' Sam protests. 'At least accountants talk money, which everyone can appreciate: it's not as though it was some unheard-of product.'

'But money isn't something to discuss,' claims Marcie. 'The only way to make money interesting is to spend it.'

'Then it doesn't gather interest at all!' Sam quips.

Marcie hands out plates and knives and forks and slices up the quiche. 'Just dip in and help yourselves. This one's olives and this one isn't. Jim, darling, would you like pickle? I've got some lovely mango chutney.'

'Sit down and eat, Marcie,' Jim tells her. 'No wonder you're so thin; you never stop running about.'

'I know, I know. I never stop talking either. But now I'll stop, and we can eat in peace.'

She scoops up a tiny morsel of pâté on a crumb of bread, and exclaims, 'Cathy, that glitter is lovely! It really catches the light. Did you get it at work? Could you get me some? I'll pay you for it, of course.'

'It's not being marketed yet; this was a trial sample. You can have mine if you like. I'm not likely to be wearing it every day to work.'

'Oh but, darling, you should! It makes you look so glamorous.'

'Press officers aren't supposed to look glamorous,' I tell her. 'They're supposed to look smartly efficient.'

'You always sound killingly efficient on the phone, anyway,' Carla says. 'I'm terrified to ring you at work!'

'Do I? How awful.'

'Talking of smart and glamorous,' Marcie says, 'when are you two going to come up to the boutique and get kitted out?'

'Now, wait a minute,' says Jim. 'Do I hear the chink of money going out of my pocket?'

'More like the rustle of money,' says Sam. 'Or the groaning of the American Express card. Marcie's dresses are not cheap.'

'Men have no sense of value,' Marcie declares. 'My dresses are an investment; they won't fall apart like those chainstore clothes, the first time you wash them.'

'But women don't want clothes that don't fall apart,' Jim argues, 'because then they'd have to go on wearing them. Women want their dresses to disintegrate after a couple of weeks so they can say "I've got nothing to wear", and rush out and buy another one.'

There is a storm of protest, which Marcie leads saying firmly, 'What nonsense, Jim! Good quality clothes can be worn over and over again. With different accessories, and . . .'

'Marcie, you are the last one to talk!' he exclaims. 'I've never seen you in the same thing twice. You buy more clothes . . .'

'There you are!' she cries triumphantly. 'You've proved my point. You don't recognize the same old things all the time because they look so different with accessories! If the clothes are good quality, you can make do with very few.'

Carla is laughing helplessly. Marcie's flat must be eighty per cent wardrobe.

'Now that is absolute rubbish and you know it,' says Jim. 'If you think I am going to believe that that black dress you've got on is the same as those green trousers you were wearing the other day, or that other thing you had on last week . . .'

'Ah, the green trousers!' Marcie says. 'Now there's an example of how separates can look quite different. I can wear those with at least ten different shirts and about a dozen jumpers and jackets and . . . I don't know what you're all laughing at! Help yourselves to more food and stop persecuting the hostess.'

'I will come and buy a dress from you, Marcie, as soon as I get my figure back,' Carla promises. 'It will give me something to aim for. In the meantime, you can exercise your salesmanship on Cathy.'

'Can't afford it,' I say, searching for pieces of avocado in the salad.

'Darling, I give discount to friends.'

'I doubt I could afford the discount!'

'Is it that bad, Cathy?' says Carla anxiously.

'No, not really. I suppose I'm just afraid of spending money. In case the roof caves in or something.'

'But listen, tell me, when did you last buy any clothes?' Marcie asks. 'It's very important, you know, to your whole self-image.'

'Not for a long time,' I realize. 'Not since . . . before February I suppose.'

'Then it's high time,' says Marcie firmly. 'Come up and have lunch with me one day next week, and we'll find you something ravishing. There are some lovely silk shirts in unimaginable colours.'

'I'll take a half day off and come and have lunch, anyway,' I promise. 'And drool over all your new stock, and maybe invest in a pair of tights!'

'But surely, Cathy,' says Sam, frowning, 'you can't be that hard up. If you have no mortgage to pay then it's just the rates presumably, and bills. You can't use much electricity on your own, and what's the cooker? Gas? And heating, fares . . .'

Marcie looks flustered and starts to shuffle dishes on the coffee table. She is quite strict in her own way, on what she calls the 'social code', and Sam has just breached her non-interference rule.

'Now when you say you're afraid of spending money, that's understandable in your present situation,' Sam allows, 'but in logical terms, it's ridiculous. With modern credit facilities, it doesn't make sense to save for rainy days. And I really can't see what your expenses are.'

Poor Sam. Poor Jim: I reckon he's lost his 50p. Marcie is slicing up the pâté now, with more than her customary energy.

'Oh, I eat a lot,' I say lightly. 'When I run out of food I eat bank notes.'

'But your salary must be quite reasonable,' Sam argues. 'What is it exactly?'

'You're probably right,' I agree to evade his questions. 'I do worry too much. I'll start coming into your shop every week, Marcie, and buy up all your designer clothes.'

'You do that, darling,' she says quickly. 'Do you want to open another bottle, Sam, while I change the record? Anyone have any preferences?'

Several hours and more than a few bottles later, only Marcie is still moving – refilling glasses, putting on records, fetching a cushion for Carla, who is now slumped comfortably in a corner of the sofa, her feet in Jim's lap. Sam, and Marcie between sorties, sit on one of the huge floor-cushions, while I have taken possession of most of the rug, propping myself inelegantly on one elbow. Sam has his arm around Marcie, but she doesn't lean against him.

It's all very cosy. Everyone snuggling up to somebody. Except me. To inject some discord into the harmony, I say, 'Alan's been quoting this psychologist who says everyone is basically bisexual.'

'Bisexual?' says Sam in the tone the telly-ad people use to say 'Foot odour?' 'I don't believe anyone can be. There must be a natural preference for one or the other.'

'A natural bent,' says Jim under his breath.

Marcie leans forward and, ignoring my half-hearted protests, tops up my glass. 'Fascinating, if only it could be true,' she says. 'Think of the choice it would give you!'

'You're not exactly short of choice though, are you Marcie?' Jim comments, and Sam glowers at him.

'Why did Alan bring the subject up?' Carla asks. 'Is he wanting a change from Jerry or something?'

'What do you think, Cathy?' Jim interrupts. 'Are you into this bisexual theory?'

'Don't ask me,' I say through a wine-coloured haze. 'I can't help thinking it complicates matters to have all these different labels. I have this theory . . . oh sorry, Marcie, your carpet.'

'Leave it darling, it doesn't show on brown. You have this theory . . .'

'Yes . . . now what was it?'

'I have this theory that Cathy's had too much to drink,' supplies Jim.

'Ssh, I'm thinking . . . this theory that people are quite simply sexual or non-sexual. Everyone has so many kinds of relationships – friends and lovers and husbands and wives and parents and children and so on – and if you happen to be a sexual person then all those will probably contain some physical element, and if you're not, then none of them do.'

'That's awfully good, Cathy,' Carla approves. 'I don't know what you're talking about, but I know I couldn't say it after all that wine!'

'But what does that prove about Alan?' asks Sam, perplexed.

'I don't know,' I admit. 'Maybe it proves that there's nothing to prove.'

'But I mean,' says Sam, 'the world would be terribly confusing if no-one was either homo- or hetero- but just generaly sexual, responding more or less to whoever happened to come along.'

'The world is terribly confusing,' I agree.

'Cathy is getting philosophical,' Jim says. 'Sam, you have been warned. How's the rest of your job going, Cathy? Apart from the intellectual discussions with Alan?'

'Fine. I'm thinking of leaving.'

'Well, I think you're quite right, darling,' says Marcie decisively. 'You've been there ages. I think you should find something really fascinating that pays lots of money.'

'The two don't go together,' says Jim. 'I could get you a sales rep job, Cath. The money's not bad, with commission. And you'd get a car. Not that you can drive – now there's a deficiency you'll have to remedy.'

'I don't know that I'd be much good at selling.'

'All you need,' he says confidently, 'is charm, good looks and the gift of the gab.'

'Like you?' says Carla quizzically.

'Just like me.'

'That's that one ruled out, then,' I say. 'No, Marcie really, don't give me any more wine. Can I start again on the pâté, though? Thanks.'

'What you want to go in for is computing,' says Sam. 'If you want something really well paid . . .'

'Not necessarily; as long as it's interesting.'

'But you were saying earlier that you were hard up!' he protests.

'Not hard up, no; just limited. Besides, money shouldn't be such a problem in the future: I'm getting somebody to share the flat.'

'Who?' says everyone in unison.

The temptation is irresistible. 'Oh, you don't know him,' I say evasively.

'Who is he; tell us!' Marcie shrieks.

'Well, I don't really know him either, but I'm sure it'll work out. He works in the East End somewhere, some kind of dealer. He wouldn't say what exactly, so it might not be quite on the level, but he seems to have plenty of money.'

Horror is registered on four faces.

'But Cathy,' says Carla, 'how did you meet him? I mean . . .'

'Advertised,' I say blithely. 'Lonely Hearts column in

Time Out. "Strong, uninhibited, sexy guy wanted to share flat with famished widow."' I take a generous bite of bread and pâté and watch their reactions.

'You're joking,' says Jim, relieved.

'I hope you are,' says Carla.

'Darling, you didn't really?' Marcie pleads.

'No, I didn't really.'

'I think it would be very unwise to let someone share your flat,' says Sam sententiously.

'Oh, I'm serious about that. But I haven't started looking for anyone yet.'

'Well, you mustn't do it by advertising,' says Jim firmly. 'You could get anyone!'

'I hope I'd get someone.'

'Couldn't you just advertise for a girl?' Marcie says. 'Or is that discrimination?'

'Need you really have anyone at all?' says Carla. 'I mean, I wouldn't like a stranger in my house.'

'You don't need the money,' says Jim. 'Stay in your present job till you've found something else, and keep the flat to yourself. It's the only sensible way.'

'I've already decided,' I say. It's funny how, when you're on your own, people think you incapable of making decisions. If you insist on doing so, they refuse to take you seriously. Not that I really meant it seriously, until they all started disagreeing.

'Well, in that case,' Jim continues, 'I advise you to take someone only on recommendation from a person you know and trust. And if you have to advertise, just tell any men who ring up that it's already taken.'

'Listen,' I say, 'there wouldn't be all this fuss if I was a man, would there? I mean, I can look after myself.'

'A man on his own doesn't have the same problems, obviously,' Sam points out.

'You're right,' says Jim. 'If the situation was reversed, I

can't imagine us telling Barry not to advertise for strange women!'

As usual, even after all this time, the mention of his name catches me in the solar plexus. Or perhaps it's just that the wine has gone to my head and a breadcrumb seems to be sticking in my throat.

'I think,' says Marcie, 'that if Cathy wants to share her flat with a strange man we shouldn't stand in her way. If he's nice, Cathy, can I move in too?'

'Of course,' I say through the pâté and the lump in my throat.

'I still think it's risky,' says Jim grimly.

'Actually,' I say, 'what I think I'll do is find a live-in plumber. The sink's got blocked again, and it would be awfully handy.'

'I'll come and unblock your sink for you, any time,' Jim offers.

'I've tried with the plunger but I think the U-bend needs draining,' I explain, 'and I can't get the thingy off.'

'You've got problems,' he says, winking. 'I'll come round tomorrow and sort you out.'

'On the subject of U-bends,' says Carla, struggling to her feet, 'I'm going to the loo. And then I think we really must go. The babysitter will be cursing us.'

We say goodbye to Sam, and Marcie comes downstairs to see us off. 'Don't forget lunch one day next week,' Marcie reminds me. 'Say Tuesday?'

'If I can get a half day off. I'll phone you and let you know. Is Sam coming too, or will it be just us?'

'Just the two of us.' Marcie looks over her shoulder. 'Actually,' she whispers, 'I don't think I'll be seeing Sam much longer, so you'll have to put up with me on my own for a while.'

In the car, Jim takes out 50p and hands it to me. 'I'm not

making bets with you two again,' he says. 'Carla, I'll owe you yours.'

By the time we reach my house, Carla is asleep. Jim insists on seeing me to the front door of the flat.

'Thanks for the lift,' I whisper, afraid of disturbing the Pratts.

'Anything for you,' he says. 'You know that, don't you?'

''Night then, Jim.'

For Saturday-morning shopping at her local supermarket, the modern woman wears knuckle-dusters, shin-pads and a man. The man is essential. For one thing, he can carry the potatoes and ward off old ladies with hell-bent trolleys. For another, when it comes to deciding what to buy, two hangovers are better than one.

How is that I never noticed before now how bright the lights are? The blue neon strip over the cold cabinet sears the retina like a chain saw. The noise of the tills, the loud voices ('How much is this, Mavis?'), the crashing of the trolleys ('Sorry!'), add to the cacophony of hammers inside my head. The colours of the goods on the shelves scream at my aching eyeballs. I reject tinned tomatoes (too red), decide against peas (too biliously green), and corn (a violent shade of yellow) and opt for fresh cauliflower, which comes in more restful shades.

Further down the row two ladies are fighting over the last tin of carrots. One of them is Mrs Pratt. I alter course and turn down the next aisle to avoid her.

Saturday-morning shopping is new to me, since February. Before, we never went out till lunchtime. Well, everyone else's lunchtime. Saturday mornings were lazy decadence: sleep and sex and bacon sandwiches that left crumbs in the bed. Good Saturday mornings – after good Friday evenings – would extend well into the afternoon with conversation limited to basics like, 'I made the tea last time', 'Have you finished your half of the newspaper yet?', and 'Turn over, I want to try something different.'

In between making love, and eating, and reading the paper, Barry would sleep. I might have done too, if he hadn't been curled into my back with his beard tickling my ear and one arm beneath me, denting my ribs. It would have been worth it for the warmth of his gently breathing body had he not also had the habit of edging ever closer, till I overhung the bed like a rock on a precipice. Once asleep, he was unwakable, so I would fall off the bed and run shivering round to the other side where, for five whole minutes before he turned over, I would have two-thirds of the bed luxuriously to myself.

Now I have the whole bed and can sleep undisturbed. I don't have lie-ins any more.

Even the shortest queue for the check-out reaches half-way down the aisle. The woman in front of me is wearing Aqua Manda scent. After inhaling the fumes for a couple of minutes I leave my place in the queue and join a longer one.

After eight whole months, you know, I still can't get used to sleeping on my own. It's not so much the sex that I miss, as the warmth. And that moment when you climb into bed and settle contentedly in each other's arms. And half waking up in the night and hearing the steady, reassuring breathing and flinging a drowsy arm around him and then drifting back to sleep.

The night we found out about the illness, I just cat-napped, sleeping so lightly that any change in his breathing pattern woke me.

That very first night we spent together too, I lay awake, feeling his heartbeat, as if afraid that if I slept he would somehow melt away and I'd wake up to find I had dreamed him. I was half ashamed of such soppiness till he whispered,

'Are you awake?' and I realized he hadn't been sleeping either.

The trolley behind me nudges me forward, and I move obediently with the queue.

It was unbelievable that first night. I'd thought that I knew it all. I wasn't a post-grad for nothing. Sex was sex. It was nice, of course; exciting. It was certainly better than drinking or dancing or smoking grass, or anything else you might have chosen to do. But that's all it was: an occupation, a pastime, a moment of closer contact in a life already lived shoulder-to-shoulder. Not this heart-lurching, mind-shaking, body-melting thing that threw me off balance, sending my ideas tumbling, stripping me naked of past experience. It was like diving into the sea, a confident swimmer, and finding you couldn't swim; helpless and drowning, I clung to him as he soothed and cajoled and whimpered and loved and tore me self from self and burrowed himself in between.

Scared by my own defencelessness, I opened my eyes to find the same fear in his. 'Oh, my God,' he muttered, 'don't leave me. Promise. Oh, my God.' And I was so relieved I began to laugh. 'Was I so funny?' he said.

'You were amazing,' I told him tenderly. 'It's just that, for a casual pick-up at a party, that was a bit earth-shattering.'

'Like opening a bag of crisps and finding you'd got a roast dinner,' he agreed.

That reminded me I was hungry, so that's when we tackled the bread and cheese that we'd salvaged from the party. 'By the way,' I said, 'whose party is this? I came with a girl called Vicky from university, who heard about it from someone else.'

'Some guys called Keith and Dave; I don't know them either,' he confessed. 'You are lovely in bed, did you

77

know?' he added with sudden effusion, kissing the crumbs off my cheek.

'Oh, I know,' I said smugly.

He looked anxious. 'How many others . . . . I mean, I've no right to ask, but how many other men . . .?'

I swallowed a mouthful of sausage roll and made a mental count. 'Four. Four seriously, not counting one-night stands in my far-off youth. How about you?'

'Me too. Or was it five? No, four.'

'Can't you remember?'

'Not really. They pale into insignificance,' he said, regarding me soulfully over the Danablu-dip.

'I reckon you killed them off,' I said. 'They died of exhaustion on the first night.'

'I take that as a compliment,' he said confidently, then wondered. 'No, really, was I too . . .?'

'Too nothing,' I reassured him. 'Too fantastic for words.'

'You're laughing at me again,' he accused. 'Or aren't you? Honestly, was it better than other times?'

'It felt,' I said truthfully, 'like the first time ever.'

He smiled beatifically. 'Well, here comes the second,' he said.

You shouldn't indulge in erotic fantasies in the supermarket. It is a shock to find I have reached the check-out. The couple in front of me have finished unloading their trolley; the conveyor belt is half empty.

'Go on!' prompts the woman behind me, prodding me in the back, and I hastily start unloading the goods: cauliflower, salad, chicken leg, cheese and coffee, and eggs and bread and ham. The queuers, with nothing better to do, devour my purchases with their eyes. In their place, I'd settle for the fantasies.

By the time I reach the exit I've come down to earth. So much so that when I bump into The Beard I not only recognize him instantly, but also remember in unwelcome detail the terms of our parting. He appears, however, pleased to see me. Either he has a short memory, or else he is used to lunatics. I hope the latter; it saves me the trouble of trying to appear sane.

'Hello,' he says. 'Is the sun too bright? Or was it a heavy evening?'

I take off my dark glasses, but decide immediately it's a mistake. 'Everything's too bright,' I say. 'Especially the tinned peas.'

'All those shiny wrappers,' he sympathizes. 'What you need is some coffee.'

I consider the idea. 'I think you're right.'

'Will the Wimpy do?' He has taken both of my shopping bags and is leading the way down the street.

'I can't be long,' I protest feebly. 'I said I'd call in on some friends on the way home.'

'All right,' he agrees.

The lights in the Wimpy bar are horribly bright, and everything is red, from slashed vinyl benches to tomato-shaped ketchup dispensers.

'We'll go in the corner,' he says. 'It's darker for the eyes.'

'You've done this before,' I accuse.

'Yes, I've come in here with hangovers of my own. Not this morning, though. Your Friday night was obviously better than mine.'

'I didn't drink that much,' I say defensively. 'I just haven't got the head for it.'

The waitress approaches.

'Coffee?'

'Please.'

'Two coffees.'

I don't even know his name.

'I'm Wayne, by the way,' he says.

'Cathy.'

Then the questions: the 'what do you do' and 'where do

79

you live . . .?' the chatting-up, the starting from scratch, building up a picture from scraps of information. I feel old and married and gauche, and ill-equipped for this ill-remembered game. When I lift the coffee cup, my hand shakes.

'What do you do?'

'Sorry? Oh, I'm a press officer for a cosmetics firm. Public Relations,' I elucidate, as he looks blank.

'Oh, ah.' He is none the wiser, I can tell.

'What do you do?'

'Engineering. For a consultancy in Holborn.'

I knew it! I knew it. Establish the rest of the history then. 'Where did you get your BSc.?'

He looks surprised: he didn't know it showed.

'Bristol. Er . . . did you . . .?' The hesitation. The fear that if I answer, 'Me? No, I didn't go to university,' I'll think he's patronizing. The desire that I'll say yes, me too, and forge a link between us, total strangers.

'Actually, I was at Bristol too.' I say it reluctantly. I don't want to forge that kind of link. Not yet.

'You were? Which years?' He's thrilled. We were part of the same institution, members of one club. What a small world. It doesn't make any difference, can't he see? We never knew each other; never met.

'Were you there at the same time as me?' he pursues.

I was not. I am relieved. We are the same age, or near enough, but I joined as a post-grad, when he'd already left.

'You did an MA, then?'

'A Ph.D.'

His face falls.

'I didn't finish it,' I say consolingly. 'Didn't stay a year, in fact.'

'Why not?'

I don't want to tell him that. I left to get married. Oh yes, you said your husband died . . . Or else embarrassed silence, which would be worse.

'There didn't seem much point in it,' I say finally. 'I'd planned originally to do university teaching, but I decided against it.'

'University can get claustrophobic,' he agrees. 'I enjoyed it when I was there, but I wasn't sorry to leave.'

'Was this your first job?'

'No, second. It's a big improvement on the first place.'

We drink our coffee; he offers me a cigarette. He is surprisingly easy to talk to; his very ordinariness makes him seem familiar. I find myself telling him of my plans to change my job and he doesn't question the reasons.

'It's useless if you have no respect for the firm you're working for,' he says. He tells me about the people he works with, the house where he has a bedsit, one among seven.

When he offers more coffee, I suddenly realize the time. 'I must go; I told Vicky I'd be there at eleven! Thanks for the coffee, anyway.'

'Can I see you again?' he says. 'Would you like to come out to dinner one night?'

I hesitate. Coffee is just coffee; dinner is Going Out. 'Oh, I don't know . . .'

'No strings,' he says persuasively. 'Just a meal. Not beefburgers!'

When I still hesitate, he says, 'You don't want to, do you?' He is rebuffed; he thinks I don't like him. I decide to be honest with him. 'It's just the idea of going out, I suppose. I mean, I haven't been out much really, since . . .' The plastic spoon I have been twisting in my fingers suddenly snaps in two.

'Of course,' he says immediately. 'Well . . . how about something a bit more casual – would that make any difference? I could cook us a meal at my place. The other people are quite nice.'

It would be churlish to refuse again. 'Okay. Don't go

to any trouble, though; beefburgers will be fine!'

'Tonight?'

No, not tonight. Not yet. Oh, don't be such a coward, Cathy.

'Yes, all right. Tonight.'

'About seven thirty? I'll call round for you if you tell me where you live.'

'No, don't bother please. I know where your road is. I must go now.'

'See you tonight then, OK?'

Vicky opens the door with a mug in her hand. 'I'd given you up for lost!'

'Sorry I'm late.' I take off the dark glasses.

'You look like I feel,' she says. 'Did you have a good time at Marcie's last night? She invited us too, but we'd been asked to this party. We didn't get home till quarter to four this morning.'

'Congratulations on being up so early, then! Is Keith still in bed?'

'Well, floating six inches above it, to be exact.' She pushes open the bedroom door and Keith waves dopily through a cloud of scented smoke. 'Hi, Marcie.'

'It's Cathy.'

'Hi, Cathy.'

Vicky raises her eyes to heaven and closes the door on him. 'I don't know how he can face it, this time of the morning. Coffee?'

'Yes please.'

'Toast?'

'Lovely.'

'Doesn't even a hangover spoil your appetite?'

'It takes the edge off it. I'll skip the egg and bacon.'

'Ugh, don't!' she says feelingly.

'Whose party was it? Anyone I know?'

'Remember Dave, the one Keith used to share a house with? It was at one of their parties that I first met Keith, come to think of it. Heaven help me.'

'I was there,' I reminded her. 'It was when I met Barry too; actually I was just thinking about it this morning.'

'Oh yes.' She spoons the coffee into the mugs. 'But you left early, didn't you? You weren't there when that guy fell down the stairs?'

'No, I missed that.' We had wondered what the commotion was but didn't go out to see.

'That was a funny party,' she muses. 'Do you know, the next morning they couldn't open one of the bedroom doors, and when they shouted there was no answer, so Dave climbed up to the window on a ladder, and d'you know what?'

'What?'

'The window was open, the wardrobe had been pushed against the door, and there was no sign of anyone there at all.'

'No, really?'

'So someone must have barricaded themselves in and then climbed out of the window.'

'How strange; perhaps they were drunk.' We had clambered out of the window at three in the morning, I remember, when my stomach said it was breakfast-time and commonsense said that if we emerged now it could be awkward. We had tried to shift the wardrobe, but it made such a noise that we left it, in the end, let ourselves down on to the flat kitchen roof and stole off into the dawn, in search of an all-night café.

'There are some funny people about,' Vicky concludes.

When I leave, two hours later, I call in on Keith to say goodbye, but he has fallen asleep, slumped sideways on the pillow, mouth open and tongue hanging out.

'He's always asleep or smashed these days,' says Vicky

bitterly. 'He'll wake up this evening and then go out and get drunk. He doesn't talk to me any more and he doesn't hear when I talk to him. The other day when he was asleep I pinned a notice over the bed saying "Artist's Impression of a Man".'

'What did he say when he saw it?'

'He didn't understand it. I'm not surprised. He must have killed off most of his brain cells by now.'

'Why don't you leave, if it's getting you down? I know you've been together a long time . . .'

'But it's not as if we were married,' she concludes. 'Thank God for small mercies. But he won't go; he says he was the one who found the flat so he's got first right to it.'

'Why don't you go, then?'

'Why should I let him have the flat?' she demands. 'I've been paying more rent than him because I earn more; I don't see why he should have it!'

'Well, if you decide you want to leave, there's a room free at my flat. I'm looking for someone to share it anyway.'

'That's sweet of you Cath, but I'll hang on here. I'll get this place in the end, if I have to change the locks while he's out.'

It's sad to see a relationship going sour. Keith and Vicky used to be lovely together; we often went out, the four of us, and they would be joking all evening, teasing each other – bickering even then but in a friendly way. There is nothing friendly about it now.

It began to go sour when Barry and I got married, which gave Vicky ideas that Keith didn't like.

'Not me,' he said. 'I'm not signing any registers. What does it prove anyway?'

'It proves that people want to stay together,' she told him.

'But they don't,' he argued. 'It's hypocrisy. No-one stays

happily married to one person for a lifetime. They're just deceiving themselves.'

'Do you think he's right?' I asked Barry anxiously, when we were back in our own little flat.

'No, I don't,' he said firmly.

'You think that a couple can stay in love all their lives?'

'Not every minute of every day,' he conceded. 'But everyone has their moments. You just have to keep going, from one to the next.'

I leaned against him on the sofa. 'You think we'll still have our moments when we're old and grey?'

He kissed the top of my head. 'I'll be the randiest grandad in history,' he promised me.

4

Saturday evening at Wayne's goes surprisingly well. The meal is almost ready when I arrive; lamb chops, potatoes and peas – and onions in white sauce. It turns out he's addicted to them now. One of his house-mates from the bedsit across the landing is in the kitchen too and he's just bought some new records so we take the meal into his room and listen to them.

And then we just chat, and one or two other people drop in, and it's very relaxed and easy and not at all the ordeal I was expecting. In fact it's easier being with strangers who see me as myself and not as Barry's widow.

Wayne walks me home, and I don't invite him in for coffee but he doesn't seem to mind; he just says he'll see me on Tuesday night, as we arranged, and then says goodnight. He wanted to make it Monday but I said Tuesday would be better. Playing it cool comes naturally when you're frigid – though in this case there's no need as he's moving to Sheffield anyway, next week.

The hall light works on a time-switch, and normally I run up the stairs and round the corner to my own front door before the light runs out. This time I linger in the doorway to give Wayne a wave and then go slowly upstairs humming the tune from one of the album tracks we've been listening to and feeling in my pocket for the key.

Two things happen at once. The light goes out, and a figure rises from the top step. I want to scream, but my breath stops and my throat has gone dry. I cling to the stair rail and manage a useless croak.

'Cathy,' says a voice.

'Who . . .?'

'It's me. Jim.'

'Jim, for God's sake!' I am laughing with relief and shock. 'You frightened the life . . . Push the light switch. I thought you were . . . The light switch. By the door.'

'I've come to see you,' he says. 'To mend your sink.'

'You what? Jim, turn the light on, will you?' Panic begins to rise again. His speech is slurred. I want the light on. I reach past him and push the switch.

'You gave me a real fright,' I scold, but reassured now by the familiar sight of him.

'You can't be frightened of me!' he chides. His breath smells of Scotch.

'I didn't know it was you, did I?' I locate the key and open the door. 'What are you doing here?'

'Came to see you,' he repeats.

Another fear dawns. 'Is something wrong? Carla? The baby?'

'No, 'course not.'

'Where is Carla?'

'Home. Let me out for a drink. Don't I deserve it after working hard all week?'

'You can't have been working hard enough to deserve all that,' I tease, hoping to get a laugh out of him. I don't like him serious, with those glazed eyes. This is ridiculous; I've known Jim for years. I'm getting neurotic.

'I've fixed the sink, anyway,' I tell him. 'I did it this afternoon. So thanks for the offer but . . . It's really late, Jim. Do you know what time it is?'

'Any time's a good time,' he mutters, taking a step towards me.

I switch on the inside light. He continues moving towards me. I retreat, putting on the kitchen light on my way past the door, then the sitting-room light and both the lamps. He blinks at the sudden brilliance.

'Carla will be worried about you,' I say. 'You'd better go home.' We are circling each other like strange dogs.

'Aren't you even going to make me some coffee?' he says, aggrieved. Half-joking, he sounds more like his normal self. There is nothing to fear from Jim, even drunk. If you can't trust your oldest friends, what kind of suspicious creep are you?

'All right,' I concede. 'A quick cup of coffee. Black. You're not driving, are you?' I ask, on my way to the kitchen.

He is suddenly behind me, arms round my waist. 'I'm not driving anywhere,' he says. 'Not tonight.'

'What . . .? Jim, I really think you'd better go. Carla will think you've had a crash or something.' I turn to remonstrate with him and am pulled against his chest, his face, his mouth. 'No . . . listen, Jim.' I am twisting my head away from him. His arms are like a vice. God, what do I do? If it was a stranger I'd make a fuss, but you can't start screaming at a friend who's just got a bit pissed on a Saturday night, can you?

I escape by suddenly ducking out of his grip. 'Jim . . .' He advances. I back away from him. 'Listen, this is silly. You're pissed. Tomorrow you're going to feel a right idiot.'

'Tonight,' he says blurrily, 'I'm going to feel . . .' One hand slides round the back of my neck; the other is inside my sweater. If this was anyone else I'd have kneed him in the groin by now. But a friend who . . .

'Don't be so bloody stupid.' It's intended to be a shout, but my breath has run out on me again. 'What d'you think Carla would . . .?' I keep invoking her name, like a talisman, hoping it will bring him to his senses. Soon. It'll have to work soon. Oh God, what do I do?

'Go home,' I say desperately, as he corners me by the cupboard, one hand on the wall each side of my head, his feet caging mine between them. His pelvis crushes my back

against the sharp handle of the drawer; it's this final dis-
comfort that makes me lose my temper.

'Get out of here!' I scream, pushing him in his flushed,
perspiring face, and my sudden anger unsettles him. I push
him roughly in the chest, aiming a kick at his shins to clear
my way out. 'Get out! How dare you come round here, pretending to be a friend . . .'

He is stunned by the outburst. 'I am a friend,' he says
stupidly. 'Don't be silly.'

'Silly?' I yell. 'You come here at gone midnight, lurking
there in the dark and scaring the bloody wits out of
me . . .!'

'I'm sorry,' he says. 'Sorry. I only wanted to . . . look,
Cath, I know you're lonely. It's not easy being on your
own, all this time.' His voice is still slurred. He hangs his
head sentimentally. 'A girl like you, all alone at nights.
Must feel, sometimes . . .'

'That's my problem,' I snap, but the anger dies. I can
cope with him in this mood. Just agree with him and ease
him out of the door and then into the street . . . It's not my
fault if he drives home drunk. Carla can't blame me if he
has a crash. Oh God, I wish I was on the phone.

I manage to lead him as far as the door, then he stops.
'I'm staying,' he says firmly. 'I know you'll tell me to go but
you don't want me to, do you? Be honest. All alone, every
night . . . S'not right, is it? His breath, strong and sour,
on my face again.

'You're a good friend,' I say briskly. (Like some bloody
almighty Scout-mistress or something. Why is he making
me behave like this? I hate myself.) 'And a friend is exactly
what I want. So go home to Carla, now, okay?'

'A friend,' he agrees, his hand up the back of my sweater
again. 'And who better than a friend . . . ? See, I haven't
forgotten what you said last night.'

'What?' I am caught off balance.

'About relating sexually to people – friends.'

'I didn't mean it like that; you know I didn't!' Anger rises again. I fight it down. One more try at keeping it light. Carla is one of my oldest friends. I sat next to her at school, for heaven's sake. 'In any case,' I say into his face, forcing myself to smile, 'I don't qualify as sexual right now. I'm on sabbatical. Frigid. Dead. Okay?'

His sense of humour is on sabbatical too. 'That's nonsense and you know it.' His body flattens mine against the wall with familiar, forgotten pressure. I don't want to remember how it was – not now, not like this. Oh God, not with him! My body softens. It has a mind of its own. I'm too tired to fight . . . His hands are persuasive.

'Come on,' he says. 'Come on.'

The sound of his voice, the voice of my best friend's husband, gives me a shock of energy.

'No.' Then more strongly. 'No! Go home, Jim. Please. Please go home.' My voice is shaking. This is a nightmare. Make him go. Please God, make him go and I'll start believing in you.

Jim holds me at arm's length, not roughly. 'Stop fighting it, Cath, eh? You've got to rejoin the human race some time. If you leave it too long you're going to find you can't.'

He sounds so normal. Perhaps he isn't that drunk. Perhaps he's right. Eight months. Is something wrong with me?

'No!' I shout.

He watches me, sensing my doubts. 'And you're not cut out to be a nun, are you Cath? You can't tell me you're frigid . . .'

'You don't know! Mind your own bloody business!' If I cry now, I'm lost. Anger's the only way. He's wrong. I'm right. Stay angry. 'And don't be so bloody patronizing!' I shriek. 'Treating me like the poor little widow! You think

I'm so desperate I'd want you?' Bugger the friendship; he's gone too far. I can't take it.

His face hardens. 'Yes, I think you are desperate,' he says with no trace of a slur. 'Hanging on to a shadow. Staying faithful to a ghost. Fucking hell, Cathy, the guy didn't deserve that even when he was alive . . .'

'Shut up! Shut up!' I am screaming now. I'll wake the Pratts. They must be awake anyway. So why don't they bloody well come and rescue me?

'. . . turning Barry into some little saint. He wasn't exactly the perfect husband, was he . . .?'

Blinded with fear and fury, my hand has seized the umbrella standing by the door, but he immediately wrenches it from my grip.

'All right,' he says breathlessly. 'I'm going. I just hope you sort yourself out soon, Cathy, for your sake.'

'Get out,' I say brokenly. 'Get out. Get out.' I continue saying it while he goes down the stairs, like an incantation. '. . . out. Get out . . .' till I hear the front door slam and the car start up in the street.

Even then I don't move: I am shaking so much that I can't shut the door but stand there leaning against the frame. I don't cry. I've trained myself not to cry. You can't tell where it will end. A heart of steel. No-one. Need no-one. That's the way. Not even friends. Oh God, if friends can treat you like that, then what is there left? Don't think about it. It's shock, that's all, just shock. What's the treatment for shock?

Close the door. The sitting-room cupboard. A glassful of nasty sherry. A thimbleful of Cinzano, gone stale in a loose-capped bottle. And a full new bottle of Scotch bought by someone a few months ago. I don't like Scotch.

The cap is sealed on but I finally wrench it off. My hand won't stay steady; I spill some over the edge of the glass, so

I leave the glass and drink it straight from the bottle. After the first few mouthfuls it doesn't taste so bad.

I switch on the gas fire and gas hisses out. No coins in the meter? Oh no – got to light it first. Fancy forgetting that, silly cow. I leave the gas hissing and go to fetch the matches. Striking one, it snaps. And the next one. I'm all thumbs. I start to giggle feebly. Now I've turned the gas tap off. What d'you do that for, then? Oh. That's right. Match. Okay. Bang. What a bang! Nearly burnt my hair off, bloody stupid fire. It's all bloody bangs this evening, isn't it? I laugh and some of the tears fall on the whisky bottle.

Another drink. No problem. He got a bit drunk, that's all. He won't remember anything tomorrow, and I won't either in a little while. More whisky. Good for you. Warms the bones. I need that just now; I'm so cold. Cold and dirty. Bloody Jim! Dirty hands, dirty eyes, dirty breath. I need a bath or something. In a minute.

I felt so good, before Jim, in the house with Wayne and the rest. 'This is Cathy. Stewart, meet Cathy.' 'Cathy, nice to see you.' Normal, see. Accepted. They didn't know. But other people know. Another drink. Where the hell are you, God? This is a crisis. Hiding, huh? In the bottom of the bottle. But I pass out before I get there so it seems he's eluded me once more.

I don't know what time it is. It could be any time. The light is on, but the fire has gone out. My feet are like lumps of frozen lead. When my head hit the floor all the thoughts spilled out of my brain and I don't know where they are. But I find the door of the bedroom, and the bed, and the duvet wraps itself round me – warm outside, frozen in the middle, like Arctic Roll. Somebody come and eat me so I won't have to wake up, ever again.

Funny, I didn't know you could throw up in your sleep. Did you know that? When I wake in the morning I've been sick all over the bed. I never knew you could do that.

Up, out, no thinking allowed. Clothes on. They are on already – still – from last night. And my shoes. Better change, then, hadn't you? Keep going. Get moving. Cold. Move.

I bend down to take off my shoes, which detonates a bomb inside my head. Clever, that. Just by bending down. Yes: does it again when you stand up. Some sadist invented that one. When he had a hangover probably.

What a mess. What a terrible, sordid mess. Get out. Fresh air. Too tired, too sick and tired. Out – did you hear me?

Machine-gun fire as the cold air penetrates my ears to my exploding brain. Meant to be good for you. Like the whisky. A whole bottle, Cathy! Or near enough. Well, and what of it? It helped at the time. It's even helping now. At least I'm saved from thinking; I'm too busy making sure my head won't fall off.

Plenty of people about for a Sunday, neatly dressed, chattering. Of course, they're going to church. I am swept along with the purposeful tide. It must be either nine o'clock or half-past eleven.

I used to go with Barry to that church. They never knew I didn't belong. I did belong, when I went with him. Not now, though; I couldn't go in now, singing 'Soul of My Saviour' and watching the priest hold the chalice aloft as a symbol of redemption. If Christ has redeemed me, where's the difference, I'd like to know? Never there when I need him, to redeem me from getting groped or getting drunk.

The people turn in through the gates, and I turn away. I haven't the stamina for the spiritual journey; I just want to have arrived. So, home.

My watch has stopped but the clock on the cooker says half-past twelve when Mrs Pratt knocks on the door. She looks surprised when I open it. 'Oh – d'you want to come and have lunch with us then, dear?'

I don't want food, but I'm overwhelmed with gratitude. 'Thank you. Oh yes, thank you.'

'Give us ten minutes, then,' she says, 'while the carrots boil.'

They greet me heartily, seat me at the table, new two years ago and still in its plastic wraps. Mrs Pratt hands me a Pyrex plate with a slab of dry beef, tinned carrots, a greasy potato and one round Yorkshire pincushion.

'All right for you, dear – not too much?'

'Yes. No. That's fine. Thanks very much.'

'For what we are about to receive . . .' intones Mr Pratt. 'We heard some shouting last night. Did you hear it?'

I choke on the sawdusty beef. So that's why they've invited me in; they want the full story – now, the day after, when it's all safely over and they can't be expected to help. I could have been murdered up there, for all they knew. Not much use coming up the next day to see if I'm still alive, is it? For all they care.

But I'm sitting here eating their food, so I can't say what I think. That's the trouble with being brought up ladylike. You don't bite the hand that feeds you, don't kick the balls of the friend who tries to screw you; it's not the done thing now, is it dear?

They are watching me, waiting for my reply. I keep my gaze fixed on my knife and fork as they grind their way through the beef. 'I didn't hear a thing,' I lie.

There is a pause. 'Must have been somebody in the street,' mumbles Mr Pratt.

This potato is cold. I feel sick. 'It could have been,' I agree. 'Some poor girl got raped in this area a while ago – did you read about it? She screamed and shouted and people heard her but no-one came to help.'

Mrs Pratt relieves me of my plate. 'Ready for your dessert?'

Tinned pears topped with shaving foam. The clink of spoons in the dearth of conversation.

'Not enough milk in this whip, dear,' Mr Pratt comments.

'I didn't make it with milk,' she says indignantly. 'Had enough then, dear?'

'Plenty, thanks. No, no tea, thanks all the same. I must be going; got some work to do. Thanks so much for the meal.'

The spectre of Jim rises from the top stair as I round the corner, and follows me into the flat. He is behind me everywhere I turn – in the kitchen when I fill a glass of water, lurking in the empty sitting room, close on my heels when I run to the bathroom and vomit him down the sink. The sour taste of friendship. Friendship makes me sick.

Was it my fault in some way? I may not have been flirty or even demonstrative in recent months but have I – even subconsciously – been signalling availability? Acting pathetic, sending out mute communications of loneliness? People have been following me recently – in the subway, in the street, on the tube. Homing in on me with unerring instinct as if I was walking naked through the well-dressed streets. Without Barry, I feel naked. Have I let that show?

By two o'clock I have been sick twice and feel better. I am getting him out of my system. How could it be my fault? Even if I was lonely and it showed, is vulnerability a sin?

My mind and the ashtray are full of burnt-out endings. I am smoking too much. I go out to the off-licence and buy another packet. Once out of the flat I can't face going back so I wander on down to the park where couples stroll with pushchairs, and kids race by on bikes. It's easy being a child. That reminds me: I ought to phone my mother. There's a phone box just outside the park gates.

The prospect of having her to stay for several weeks no

longer seems overwhelming. If the blackness continues, I will be glad of the company. Not to mention proper meals. I haven't outgrown my selfishness towards my mother. I contact her when I need mothering, not when I think that she may need daughtering.

'Hello, Solly? It's Cathy. How's the chess?'

When he goes to fetch my mother, there is a gap, during which I have to feed in more coins.

'Sorry to keep you waiting, dear. I was in the garden. I've been spreading compost round the roses; you wouldn't believe the difference it made to last year's. It's the first time I've had a breathing space for weeks, and now there's so much to catch up on . . . And how are you?'

'Oh, fine. All right.'

'What have you been doing?'

'I've just been to lunch with the Pratts. Saw Marcie on Friday, and Carla and Jim.' (And went out last night with someone I picked up in a supermarket. And fought off advances from my best friend's husband. Nothing to phone home about.)

'Well, you have been having a busy social life!'

My mother sounds relieved: one less burden to worry about. Now she's free to concentrate on her roses and the WI. And the problem of Solly's chess.

'I'm so glad you rang, darling, because after I spoke to you on Friday, you'll never guess what happened. Guess.'

'What happened?'

'Mrs Bassett from the WI came round (you remember Mrs Bassett with the terribly ugly daughter?) and *insisted* that I come on the committee. Mrs Pargeter is in hospital, as you know, and now she's been told she must have absolute rest when she comes home, so of course she'll have to give up the WI.'

Of course. The local WI is no place for an invalid. It makes women's wrestling look like a soft-shoe shuffle; it's survival of the fittest down there among the Crimplene and the weekly shampoo-and-sets.

'And so the rest of the committee unanimously decided that I was the one to step into the breach. Well, you know how much I hate any kind of prominence, but in the circumstances what could I say?'

'You said yes.'

'And of course I'm being completely thrown in at the deep end, because the Yuletide Fayre's only four weeks away and hardly a thing has been done. They're all terribly well-meaning, I'm not saying they're not, but when it comes to organization they haven't a clue!'

Pip-pip-pip.

'I've put some more money in, Mum, but that's the last.'

'Oh, have we still got a few minutes then? So – what was I going to say? Oh yes . . . so darling, I really won't be able to spend as much time with you as I'd hoped. I'll have to at least get a few of them sorted out, and then I'll have to get back in good time for the actual "do" of course, and then I suppose Christmas is nearly upon us. It's amazing, when you think, isn't it?'

'Amazing.'

'I suppose you'll be coming home for Christmas, won't you? How much time will you get off work?'

'I don't know. I haven't thought about it yet.'

'Well, you must come home, darling, unless you've got something arranged. Christmas is no time to be alone.'

'No.'

'You're not letting things get you down, are you, Cathy? You sound a bit down.'

'Well . . .'

'Just remember you should be over the worst soon, darling. They say it takes nine months.'

'You're thinking of pregnancy, Mother.'

97

'What dear? I know it took me that long to get over your father.'

'But he didn't die.'

'No, it was worse for me, of course. The shame.'

Pip-pip-pip.

'I'll let you know when I'm coming,' she says. 'It'll be sometime . . .' Brrrrrrr . . .

'Bye mother. How unreasonable of me to feel betrayed. I lost my mother to the WI. The shame. Like poor old Mum losing greedy old Dad to his secretary who wasn't even glamorous and only had a hairdo once a fortnight. It took Mum nine months to get over losing him – not bad going, when you consider it took her twenty years to get over marrying him.

Then, nine months after the break-up, almost to the day, along came Solly, sent by Providence and matchmaking friends from the Rotary Club.

Back to the flat, then. You can't call in on people on Sunday afternoons. It's cosy-couples time; putting their feet up in front of the telly, digging things up in the garden or raving it up in bed. Jim is probably stretched out in front of the fire while Carla tries to keep the baby quiet because poor Daddy has a hangover from his night with the boys. I feel sick and hungry at the same time. I've only had one meal today, and that didn't stay down long. By the time I reach home I could be fading away. Fading away. What a tempting thought. For God's sake pull yourself together, Cathy Childs, or I shall disown you. I shall. Oh yeah? You and who else? Oh shut up, for heaven's sake.

I knock on Mrs Pratt's door for more change for the meter. Aren't you wet, dear! Is it raining out? Yes, it is actually. I should go in and get dry if I were you, dear. Yes, I will. Thanks for the change. And thanks for the lunch. Did you enjoy it, dear? Oh yes, it was lovely. I'm so glad, you must come again. Oh no, you must come to me next time. No, no, we wouldn't dream of it; we don't expect it, you know, with you all on your own.

'All on your own.' 'Christmas is no time to be alone.' Last Christmas – our second – it was our turn to go to Barry's mother's. We'd tried to put it off till lunchtime, but she wasn't having any. 'I shall expect you by eleven o'clock,' she said in a tone that brooked no discussion. So we opened our presents after midnight Mass, in bed with a bottle of Cointreau and the mince pies and nuts we had promised to take as our contribution to the feast. ('She won't miss just one or two.') And we giggled silently, so as not to disturb the Pratts, over Barry's present to me of a Beryl Bainbridge novel and a red suspender belt (nothing expensive or heavy, since we were soon off to France) and mine to him of a one-pound box of Black Magic with a written promise that I wouldn't eat them, and a *Mayfair* magazine.

He took the *Mayfair* with him to his mother's and disappeared, halfway through charades, to the garden shed.

'Barry! Everyone's looking for you. You're meant to be doing *Look Back in Anger*.'

'Just listen to this one, Cath. "My girlfriend and I have recently discovered an inventive new way . . ." . . . Oh dear!'

'Don't laugh so much; I can't hear. Let me read it. Oh rubbish! That's impossible.'

'No, no it isn't. Not necessarily. If you put one leg . . .'

'You still couldn't do it. No-one could. You'd have to be a contortionist.'

'No, listen to me, Cath. Look, if I lay like this, then you came round this side . . .'

'Barry, everyone is waiting for you!'

'This won't take a minute, Cathy. I just want to show you . . .'

'Not with that lawnmower there. It's got a sharp edge.'

'I'll go next to the lawnmower. Now stop complaining and come here.'

'It's *Woman's Weekly* for you next year, I'm warning you . . .'

It's *Woman's Weekly* for me this year instead. And helping Aunty with her knitting and making Solly cups of tea. And walks with Mum around the estate to criticize the neighbour's shrubs. The only trip to the garden shed will be to inspect the hyacinth bulbs. 'And mind the blades of that lawnmower, Cathy; they can be very sharp.'

Perhaps I'll get used to it in time. Four Christmases hence, I could be counting stitches and talking manure and saying, 'I think I fancy a cup of tea: who's going to make it?' Or I could be here alone in my flat, feeling glad that there's no-one to stop me from watching my own choice of films on TV. And making the tea in my own special cup, and washing the spoon as soon as I've used it, and setting out one little plate and a knife on a tray. And conning myself that there's no need to worry about other people: that my comfortable life is all that matters. 'I've earned it, haven't I?' Oh God help me; there must be more to life than that.

At seven o'clock I don't want to eat, but I'm feeling faint. I delay the meal three-quarters of an hour by putting a potato and an apple in the oven. Cheese on the potato, top of the milk on the apple. Oh Lord, for someone to squabble with over the top of the milk. 'Don't be a pig, Barry, you always have it.' 'Oh, come on, Cath; I'll let you have the yogurt.'

In the end I don't eat more than one mouthful anyway; I'm too tired. Before I can go to bed I have to wash the sick off the duvet cover and put on a clean one. Then I can't get to sleep. I wish I had something to knock me out. Nothing gentle like pills or dope. A mallet would do. Or maybe a drunken friend. How long can you stop yourself from thinking about things?

Tomorrow I will wake up cheerful and go to work full of good resolutions.

I wake up late, having dreamed that I'm in Vicky's flat.

'Just look at him!' she tells me, pushing open the door of the bedroom and there on the bed with a half-smoked reefer burning between his fingers is a skeletal Barry with a beard but no flesh. 'Stop it!' I scream at him, over and over again. 'Stop it, stop it; you're killing yourself!'

I wake up sweating, to find that it's gone half-past eight. The rush to the bathroom, the shock of the cold water (I forgot to switch the immersion heater on), banish the image along with the sleep. Merciful Monday mornings, with their spartan demand for five days of unthinking work before the empty vista of another weekend.

I am late for work. Big Harry will be pleased. 'Women executives!' he will say triumphantly. 'I knew it would never work' – ignoring the fact that Alan rarely arrives before twenty to ten. Only today I'm even later than him.

I won't bore you with details of my morning. You know what the average Monday morning is like. Well, this one is much like that except that the phone rings twice as often, Alan is in a bad mood and throws files about, the new temp typist can't type and doesn't know that c.c. stands for 'carbon copy' and asks me to call the mechanic because the electric typewriter comes to a halt at the end of the line. Also, the advertising agency has missed our deadline for artwork for the conference, the photographer sends the wrong prints, and Big Harry comes in to ask why (in a very cross voice) I've requested a day off tomorrow. You know the kind of Monday morning. Oh yes, and I'm sick again. Got the picture? Fine.

Monday afternoon is OK, as fortnights go. Five o'clock is another week away. I feel terrible. I'll never get drunk again, just as long as I never need to as much as I did on

101

Saturday. Two days ago, nearly, and I still feel like this. Dreary and edgy and stomach-achingly hungry. Light-headed. No concentration. A total disaster area. I wonder if I'm ill and that's what's making me depressed – or whether I'm depressed and that's making me ill. I went to the doctor shortly after Barry died, dragged along by my mother, who thinks there is no malaise that cannot be cured by the NHS, not even bereavement.

The doctor, who obviously shared her belief, gave me Valium 'for depression'. I pointed out that the depression had a cause and the cause would not be removed by the Valium, but he insisted. So I took the tablets, under my mother's eagle eye, and felt decidedly worse. To the de-pression was added a sense of unreality, a feeling of floating in a void.

'If you want me to get high, I'd rather have cannabis,' I told the doctor at my follow-up appointment. He glared at me with resentment and increased the dose. When I got dizzy and woolly-headed and started making silly mistakes at work, I flushed the Valium down the loo, which apparently found the wonder-tablets as hard to swallow as I had done.

'I do get low blood sugar, you know,' I told the doctor. 'Could that be the trouble now?'

'Lot of nonsense,' he snorted. 'It's very rare.'

'I had a test for it and . . .'

'I've seen the results. The levels aren't low enough for hypoglycaemia.'

'But surely the tolerance varies from person to person? I get the symptoms, after all.'

'You take these tablets my dear, and I think you'll soon notice a difference.'

'What are they?'

'Tranquillizers.'

I gave up. That was several months ago. I didn't see much point in going back.

It's not that I'm doing nothing, you understand, sitting here with my head on my arms on my nice cool metal desk. I'm working, mentally planning next week's press conference. The highlight will be Big Harry delivering himself of an 'informal personal message'. 'Journalists get sick and tired of official speeches,' he is fond of telling Alan and me. 'What is needed is a simple, direct, spontaneous little chat – just talking one to one in a friendly natural way, about the products.'

He nearly said 'man to man', but beauty editors and their staff tend to be mainly female. Big Harry is out of his element in the beauty world. He feels more at home at Alan's press conferences, talking one to one to half a dozen trade journal staff on the joys of surgical soaps and Bantam's Gunjo cleanser which banishes sump oil from honest hands. He finds it more virile than eau-de-toilette and eau-de-nil and Oh-de-bore-of-finding-something-new-to-say-about-yet-another-eyeshadow.

And yet he has to be there to do his Public Relations Director bit – publicly relating to hurried beauty writers by shaking them painfully by the hand and telling them ponderous anecdotes about research into new ingredients for surgical scrub. And delivering his spontaneous friendly chat, which he has asked me to prepare for him. 'A few rough notes,' he told me last time, so I gave him a little list of points to make, and received a heavy reprimand for skimpy work. What Big Harry means by a few rough notes for an off-the-cuff little talk is a typewritten speech to take home in his briefcase a week before the launch, which he can memorize ready to deliver, carefully unrehearsed, on the big day.

'You look as though you're working hard,' says Alan, returning unusually early from his business lunch.

'You're right; I am. How did your meeting go?'

'Oh, not bad,' he says. 'The guy's preparing an article on

industrial packaging. I think he'll give our stuff a reason-able report.'

'Congratulations. You can tell Big Harry that all your bullying was worth it, to make him change the packaging last year. You've got the most design-conscious gunge-remover on the market.'

'Yeah, the packaging's OK,' says Alan wryly. 'All they need is to fill it with something that works. What are you doing?'

'Not a lot. Pondering on Big Harry's speech for the press launch between bouts of throwing up. I'm not sure which is the most worthwhile of the two.'

'Throwing up?' says Alan. 'You must be pregnant.'

'And you must be joking.'

Phone call from Big Harry all the way from the other side of the partition wall. 'I rang your secretary but she wasn't there. Can you find me the telephone number of Jarvis Chemical Supplies?' I can. 'And by the way, Cathy, you haven't forgotten those few notes for next week's product launch?' I haven't. 'On my desk first thing tomorrow morn-ing, if you will.' I will. By tonight. I have the day off tomor-row, thank God.

Phone call, via Alan, from a Mr Slindon. 'He rang while you were on the other line. I didn't catch the name of the firm. Here's the number anyway. I said you'd call him back.'

'What's it about?'

'Don't know; he didn't say.'

'Could I speak to Mr Slindon please? Hello – Mr Slin-don? This is Cathy Childs from Bantam Cosmetics. I had a message to call you back.'

'You don't know who this is, do you?' says a low, amused voice.

'No, I don't.' The voice does sound familiar, though. 'Oh – Wayne?'

'Well done!'

'Is that your name – Slindon? I didn't know. How are you?'

'Fine. Listen – about tomorrow night . . .'

'Yes. Has something come up?' It might be just as well, the way I'm feeling. We arranged to go to a roller disco. My stomach is skating all by itself already.

'No, no. I was just wondering if there was any chance . . . you wouldn't like to come out tonight as well, would you?'

Oh.

'Don't feel you have to say yes; it was just a thought,' he adds.

'I would, but I've had a bit of a rough day, actually. I keep being sick. I was just beginning to wonder, in fact, about tomorrow . . .'

'I'm sorry to hear that.' He sounds it. 'What is it – something you've eaten?'

'More like something I haven't eaten. I have low blood sugar –at least, my present GP doesn't believe it, but that's what the last one said – and I don't think I ate enough yesterday.' Also I got drunk, but I don't think I'll tell him that.

'Low blood sugar? I've got a friend who has that. Are you on a special diet?'

'I have to eat every couple of hours.' There, that's out. Bad news item number two. He already knows about Barry, so that leaves just the frigidity he hasn't been warned about, and if he's only around till the end of the week, with any luck the subject won't arise.

'Yes, so does Steve. But don't you have to avoid certain foods – sugar and starch and so on?'

'*Avoid* sugar? Surely not, if it's low . . .'

'I'm sure that's what Steve was told, because I can remember thinking it sounded illogical. He went to a homeopathic doctor, I think. I could ring and ask him if you like.'

'Oh no, don't bother, please. I'll probably be fine by

tomorrow. I hope so, anyway; I've got the day off to meet a friend up in town.'

'Well, is there anything I can do? I mean, do you need to eat a big meal or anything?'

'Ugh, no! I mean, yes, probably, but the thought of eating at the moment . . .'

'Yes, I see. Well, look, if there's any way I can help, just let me know. I can't phone you tomorrow, can I, if you're not at work?'

'No. Shall I say I'll phone you if I can't make it tomorrow evening? Otherwise assume it's all right.'

'Okay then. And if you're not better in the morning, give me a call and I'll come and take you to the doctor's.'

'No, really. I'll be fine by then, I'm sure. It's nice of you to offer . . .'

'I'll see you tomorrow then. Take care.'

It's kind of him to sound so concerned, though when he puts the phone down he'll probably curse me for a nuisance. I'll have to try to get there tomorrow evening; it's not fair to mess up his last week in London. The phone call has cheered me up; I'll tackle Big Harry's 'few rough notes' for him now.

The phone rings. 'Press office.'

'Cathy? It's Wayne again. I've got the phone number of that doctor that Steve sees if you want it. He says he's very good.'

'Thanks. I'll write it down. I might call him if it doesn't get better soon. Thanks.'

'What was that?' says Alan curiously, 'Business or social?'

'Business.'

The typist leaves early because she has to take her jacket to the dry-cleaner's, so I seat myself at the typewriter to do the speech, first removing the temp's half-finished sheet which says: 'Dear Sor, I have just recieved yior latter about . . .'

Big Harry comes in, with his usual perfect timing, as I am being sick again, into the wastepaper basket. He retreats. 'You all right?' he says, from the safety of the doorway.

It is obvious that I am not.

'I should go home if I were you,' he says, from the corridor.

'Mr Diggins, could you possibly call me a minicab?'

'Yes. Yes. Got the number?'

'No, I'm afraid not.'

'I'll look it up. I'll get Hazel to look it up.'

He returns in a few seconds. 'Hazel is up on the fourth floor in Expenses. Will you wait till she gets back?'

'No. Don't worry; I'll do it.'

'Sure? All right. Take the morning off tomorrow if you're still not right; you needn't come in till eleven.'

'I've got the day off tomorrow.'

'Have you? Ah, yes. Did you finish those notes?'

'In your in-tray.'

'Typed up?'

'Typed up.'

'Fine.'

I find the number of the minicab firm and dial it. Engaged. I find another one. Engaged. I'll get the bus.

Actually, it isn't that early. By the time I walk out of the foyer it's nearly ten to five. It seems even later because of the dark and the rain and the fact that this afternoon seems to have gone on longer than any normal afternoon. Mind you, considering . . .

'Cathy!' Someone is hooting a car horn. 'Cathy! Over here.'

A long, low sports car that I don't recognize.

'Oh, Jerry! Hello.'

'Hop in,' he says.

'You're an answer to a prayer,' I say gratefully. 'I was just . . .'

'I've got to talk to you Cathy, all right? Alan and I – well the situation has got quite ludicrous. We simply can't go on like this.'

'No, I see, but . . .'

'Something has to be sorted out one way or the other. I mean, I can't phone him and he won't phone me and I thought . . .'

'Yes, I see. The thing is, Jerry . . .'

'So be a love and come and have a drink with me and you can tell me what you think.'

'Why don't you come back to the flat, Jerry, and you can . . .'

'Sweet of you to offer, but I should really be at the theatre, even if it's only sitting with you in the dressing room having a heart to heart.'

'Yes, but it wouldn't take very long, would it, and to be honest I'd love a lift home because . . .'

'No can do, lovey, really. Not that I'm shooting my mouth off about being the great indispensable director and all that, but really I should be somewhere around. God!' he says. 'This situation is really eating me up. My emotions are churning like a tumble-dryer.'

He drives emotionally, slamming the gears and stamping on the brake.

'I know what you mean,' I say. My stomach is tumble-drying in sympathy.

The theatre is fifteen minutes' drive away, but the rush hour has started so it takes half an hour.

'What play are you doing at the moment?'

'They're just finishing *The Maids*, but I'm not involved in that. I'm rehearsing a new play by a guy called Nicholas Wasser.'

'Haven't heard of him; sorry.'

'Oh, he's very contemporary. Lot of new actors in the cast as well, so I've really got my work cut out. And then to

108

have all this hassle just at the worst possible time . . .'

'What's the play called? Is it good?'

'It's quite – well, you know. Commercial.' He grimaces, and brakes violently as the car in front slows down.

'Is that bad?'

'Well, it makes money, which can't be bad in these times, but it isn't – what shall I say?'

'Art?'

He looks at me quickly to see if I am mocking him, but I am not smiling. My smile has ceased to function by now.

'Art, I suppose you could say.'

'What's the play called?' I know he wants to talk about Alan, or about himself in relation to Alan, but I am putting it off.

'It's called *L'Aimande*. That's French for magnet and it's also a pun on "*Le monde*", you see – the world.'

'*L'aimant*,' I say.

'What?'

'French for magnet. *L'aimant*, not *l'aimande*.'

'Oh my God!' he groans. 'Are you sure?'

'Sure.'

'Oh, Christ Almighty, this just isn't true!'

'Go.'

'Huh?'

'The lights are green. Go.'

'Oh, shit in hell!' he declaims. 'That stupid little . . . That ruins the whole pun, doesn't it? The whole meaning of the whole fucking play. So what does *l'aimande* mean, then?'

'Never heard of *l'aimande*. *L'amande* means almond,' I say helpfully.

'That's no bloody use to me, is it?' he says furiously.

'No, I suppose not.'

Jerry strikes his brow with his fist. 'Let me think.' He thinks. '*L'aimant*, did you say? There wouldn't be a pun we could use with that, would there?'

109

'Well, *aimant* on its own means loving. Or there's *l'amant* which means lover.'

'Yeah!' he says, inspired. 'Yeah, I believe we could do it. It could be very relevant, in fact. It might even be an improvement. Thanks, Cathy.'

'Don't mention it.' The only edible thing I have with me is the cheese roll I brought for lunch, and I don't fancy cheese again. I suppose I could eat the roll. I burrow in my bag.

'The thing about me and Alan . . .' Jerry says.

I can't find it. What did I do with it?

'. . . is that we're both creative people. I mean, in our own way. I can't appreciate what he does, probably; he's always saying I don't, but quite frankly, I tell him I couldn't do his job and he couldn't do mine . . .'

Oh no. I left it in the drawer of my desk. I haven't got anything else to eat. I am starving. I feel faint. I feel sick. I wonder if Jerry would stop off at a sandwich bar.

'. . . so why argue about which job is more *artistic*? I mean, we're both in it basically for the money – well, everyone is, aren't they?'

'Jerry, do you think you could . . .'

'Not just for the money, of course, but really if you look at it that way, there's no *merit* in doing a creative job, is there? I mean, if you're a creative person then that's what you do, just as if you're a practical person then you become a bricklayer or something; I mean, it's only a way to make a living, isn't it?'

'Yes. Jerry . . .'

'But the whole trouble comes, you see, when you have two creative people living together. You get problems that simply wouldn't arise with other people. I mean people who aren't creative, such as . . . well . . .'

'Bricklayers?'

'Exactly; bricklayers. Now the thing with Alan and me

is that physically we're great together, but . . .'

'I feel sick –'

'Oh God, Cathy, don't tell me after all this time you are so narrow-minded . . .'

'I am going to be sick!'

'Oh shit in hell!' He swerves the car violently, mounting the kerb with a bilious lurch. I fling the door open and throw up on the pavement. Furious drivers sound their horns and fastidious pedestrians stare with acute distaste.

'Have you finished?'

'Yes.'

Jerry restarts the engine and pulls out into the traffic, indicating that he has started moving. More hooting and a spate of vocal abuse.

'Jerry, could I just go home?'

'Look, we're nearly at the theatre now. Come in and have a drink or something and then I'll run you home straight afterwards. I promise. Okay?'

'Okay. But I'll have to get something to eat, else I'll keep on being sick.'

'Don't worry; we'll get you something to eat.' He sounds like a weary parent placating a child who wants sweets. 'I'll drop you off here at the stage door,' he says. 'Save you walking from the car park.'

'Thanks. Where do I go?'

'My office. Ask anyone the way; everyone knows me.' He drives off in a cloud of dust, screeching the Pirellis at the corner.

'Excuse me, can you tell me where Jerry Canver's office is?'

'Yeah. Find the door that says Broom Cupboard . . . No: up the stairs, first left, through the fire doors, down a narrow corridor then, let me see, second or third on the right? Can't remember.'

'I'll ask again when I get there. Thanks.' It must be like

111

working in a rabbit warren here. 'Excuse me, can you . . .'

'It's Barry's wife, isn't it? Cathy?'

'Yes.'

'Adrian. Adrian Soper. Remember me?'

'Yes, of course. You used to play squash with Barry, didn't you?'

'That's right. I came to supper at your place afterwards once. Fantastic lasagne; I can still taste it!'

'I must have put too much garlic in it.'

'No, I'm just greedy.' He laughs. 'I haven't seen you since . . . I was sorry about Barry; he was a good guy.'

'Yes.'

'Well, what are you doing here? I'd like to think you'd come for the pleasure of seeing me rehearse, but that isn't the reason, is it?'

'I'm here to see Jerry Canver; he's a friend of a friend. I hadn't realized you worked here.'

'It's only recent; I used to be with Pavement Theatre, remember?'

'Oh yes.' I don't remember really. I only met Adrian once or twice, because on Barry's squash nights I usually went out with Carla or Marcie or Vicky or Elsa or sometimes all four.

'Are you going to be here for a while? We're still in rehearsal, but if you're free later we could go for a drink.'

'I'm not staying, actually. It's a nice idea, but . . .'

'Tell you what! I'll look into Jerry's office when we finish and if you're still there I'll drag you off down to the pub. Probably be about an hour's time.'

'Fine.' Easier to agree than to go into details about the state of my stomach. In an hour's time I'll be gone for certain.

5

'So what happened then?' Marcie asks.

We are sitting in what she calls 'the little kitchenette' (which is both larger and smarter than my kitchen at home) at the back of Marcie's boutique, waiting for the kettle to boil. The kettle, being red and streamlined and space-age, matches the kitchen. Someone got paid a lot of money to design that kettle.

The cakes are equally beautiful, though in a quieter colour scheme. Each one a sculptured edifice in glistening sugar, they look architect-designed.

'I was going to take you to the little bistro down the road,' Marcie lamented when I arrived. 'But a customer phoned and said she'd be coming in at one o'clock. She's quite a special customer, so I thought if you didn't mind just staying here to eat . . .'

'Of course I don't,' I assured her. 'Do you want me to go out and get some sandwiches?'

'I have a better idea. What would you say to some really figure-threatening cakes? There's this wonderful patisserie which makes the most beautiful little gateaux.' Her eyes were sparkling with enthusiasm. When Marcie sparkles, it's hard to refuse, especially on the unpoetic grounds of a still-queasy stomach.

'It's a crime to eat those cakes,' I say now. 'They're works of art. Except that Picassos were never so fattening.'

'Who cares?' says Marcie blithely. 'Tomorrow I'll go on hot water and lemon juice.'

'With willpower like that you deserve a figure like that. Tomorrow I'll probably go on egg and chips and carry on

113

degenerating into a happy slob.'

'As long as you're happy,' says Marcie generously. 'Start eating while I make the coffee. And tell me what happened with Jerry.'

'Not a lot. I told him I thought he ought to swallow his pride and go to see Alan, and he went off to do just that.'

'He didn't just leave you at the theatre?'

'He did. He leapt up, gave me a big kiss, and rushed out of the room. When I followed him, he said, "This is wonderful advice, Cathy; I must go home straight away. You do understand, don't you? I'd give you a lift any other time but I have to be alone right now to think this one out." And off he went. Marcie, how do you eat these cakes without getting cream up your nose?'

'Oh, I'm sorry. I'll get you a knife.'

'No, don't, that would be cheating. I really like having cream up my nose. You try it.'

'I'll have one of the white ones,' Marcie decides. 'White has to have less calories than pink, don't you think?'

'Definitely.'

There is a squelchy silence.

'Tell me about Sam,' I say finally. 'Has he been relegated, then?'

'Darling, what an awful way to put it.' Marcie fetches two sheets of kitchen paper and hands me one, wiping her fingers delicately on the other. 'Milk in your coffee?'

'I'll get it.' But Marcie has already got up again.

'Sam was very sweet,' she says, dismissing him into the past tense. 'We had a good time together.'

'But . . .?'

'But I met Desmond,' she confesses.

'Marcie, how on earth do you meet all these men? I think you must have a regular order with the factory – a new one every Monday morning.'

114

'It's not quite that often!' she says, looking pleased. 'And if you must know I met Desmond when I was shopping.'

'Not the man in the off-licence?' I accuse. 'The one who you said was terribly helpful when you were buying the wine?'

'That's right. Now tell me off for getting picked up in a shop.'

'I'm sure it was a very high-class shop,' I console her. 'I got picked up in the supermarket the other day. Smoulder-ing glances over the deep-freeze cabinet.'

'Really? What was he like?'

'Quite nice actually. Ordinary, but nice.'

'You should have taken him up on it, then,' Marcie admonishes. 'What does it matter where you meet people as long as you meet them?'

'You mean men, not "people".'

'Well, who else do you want to meet? Women?' Marcie demands. 'No, seriously darling, you shouldn't discourage people, just because it's a supermarket.'

'I didn't. I'm seeing him tonight.'

'Darling, that's wonderful!' Marcie exclaims. 'I am so glad.'

'I'm only going skating; don't get excited. And he's mov-ing up north on Saturday anyway.'

'Oh, what a shame,' Marcie sympathizes. 'You know, Cathy, I don't like to give advice but I really do think what you need is a new man.'

'Trouble is,' I say, 'I liked the old one.'

'Yes, darling, I know.' There is the slightest hint of impatience in her voice. (It's a common enough reaction to reminders of grieving: 'Hasn't she made up her mind to forget him *yet*?') 'But if you could meet someone nice it would make all the difference, you know.'

'I don't think it would,' I say honestly. 'I already know

115

lots of nice people and it does help, a lot, to have such good friends, but I don't see them as a replacement.'

'But lovers are different from friends,' Marcie says, and I have to remind myself, quickly, not to mention Jim. It would be a relief to tell her about it, but not really fair, as she knows him. Besides, I realize with a slight sense of shock that I don't know what Marcie's reaction would be. No, that's silly. She wouldn't of course, recommend that I use a friend's husband as an anti-grieving therapy. Surely. Would she?

'To have a lover,' I tell her, 'you have to be able to love. Which I can't, at the moment.'

'How do you know till you try?' she says, then adds, 'Honestly, darling, I don't mean to sound hard but you don't want to leave it too long, you know.'

There it is again. They're all worried about me, thinking there's something wrong. It's unnatural, unhealthy, for somebody young to miss her dead husband so much that she doesn't want anyone else.

'It isn't that I don't want to,' I tell her. 'If I found some- one I could love, then it would be great. I don't like being alone. I didn't choose it.'

'Does it have to be love?' she asks.

'I don't know. It has to be something; affection, liking, whatever. I've got too spoilt by marriage for one-night stands. Not that they really suited me when I was single; I used to get my emotions in a twist.'

'But you're older now,' Marcie points out. 'More mature. You could handle casual relationships now, I'm sure: just a bit of fun with no ties?'

'I don't know that I could,' I say slowly. 'I think it's a question of temperament more than age. In a way it's easier when you're younger, but even then I found biology got in the way. The pair-bonding instinct or whatever it's meant to be called. At university I used to sleep with people I

116

didn't know very well and didn't have any particular feelings for and however good it was, all next day I'd feel – I don't know – restless, dissatisfied. It gave me a sense of loss. Don't you ever feel like that?'

'Sometimes. You get used to it.'

'I don't want to get used to it. When I had sex with Barry, I used to feel marvellous. Relaxed and sexy and peaceful and warm and contented.'

'Cathy,' says Marcie gently. 'Sometimes you just have to take second best.'

'Second best is being on my own,' I say stubbornly. 'At least I wake up in one piece.'

'Fine,' says Marcie. 'I admire your standards. I couldn't live with them, but I admire you for having them.'

'I don't know how long I can live with them either,' I admit. 'But anyway, tell me about this Desmond. What does he do?'

'I'm not too sure. I know he's a director of a smallish firm but whether it's his own business and what the business is, I don't know yet. I'm only going out with him for the first time tonight. He's taking me to Patchelli's, so he can't be poor.'

'Trust you to get picked up by a millionaire! He's probably a full-time tycoon whose only leisure pursuit is popping into the off-licence every night for a magnum of champagne. He'll take you back to his mansion tonight in his chauffeur-driven Rolls, and call the butler to turn back the monogrammed sheets.'

She laughs. 'As long as he doesn't call his wife to turn back the sheets.'

'Is he married?'

'I didn't ask. Probably. He doesn't look divorced.'

'What does divorced look like?' I inquire.

'Like me,' Marcie says. 'Haggard and antiquated.'

'Oh yeah.'

'Have another cake.'

'No, really.'

'But Cathy, you must! I couldn't possibly eat my second one without some moral support, and I'm really pining to; you wouldn't deprive me?'

'No wonder you became a saleswoman! Oh, all right, then.' My stomach is feeling better anyway, along with the rest of me. One thing about sickly food is that it gives you a great lift. It's as good as a double Cognac.

Talking of sales, one of Marcie's assistants appears to tell her the customer has arrived. 'She's wearing the mink,' Shirley whispers, 'and she's told the chauffeur to go and park, so she must be planning to try on the whole shop.'

'I'll be there in a second.' Marcie whisks the crumbs from her mouth with the kitchen paper, rinses her hands and replenishes her make-up carefully before entering the shop, like an actress getting psyched up for her cue. 'Come in when you've finished your cake,' she invites, 'and get the girls to show you some things. I want you to try on one of those silk shirts. Do I look OK?'

She doesn't wait for an answer: she knows she looks OK; it was part of her training as a model. You can call in on Marcie any time – early morning, late at night, weekends – and she always looks fantastic, in coordinated clothes and with never an eyelash out of place.

Barry used to say there was something inhuman about a woman who always looked beautiful. I told you that Barry used to go out with Marcie, didn't I? I didn't? Probably because it made me slightly jealous. Or slightly insecure. How could he, after Marcie, settle for a slob like me, with an indeterminate waistline and spots on bad days of the month? 'I married you for your cooking,' Barry said. 'Marcie cooks such healthy food, it made me feel quite ill.'

Their relationship was brief, and already history by the time he met me; it was some while before she was married;

and her divorce was quite a few years ago now. But still, it made me jealous when I first knew Marcie.

'What was she like with you?' I asked Barry once. I was feeling neurotic, probably before a period, and he had been taunting me, enjoyably, about getting fat. When I started thinking that he meant it, he retracted, taking refuge instead in backhanded compliments.

'It makes you cuddly,' he said. 'You're the cuddliest woman in the world.'

'Makes me sound like a teddy bear,' I grumbled. 'What about the sexiest woman in the world?'

'What about her?' he said innocently. 'Oh, I see what you mean. Do you know, I can't decide which of my many women was the sexiest. I think it was Raquel who said to me – but then it may have been Brigitte – "Barry," she said, "darling, I have met many men in my time but never one so superbly equipped as you . . ." Don't throw that coffee-pot, Cathy; it was a wedding present.'

'So who *was* the sexiest woman you've ever known?' I demanded . 'Was it Marcie?'

'Mind your own business, can't you? My torrid past is a secret.'

'Then why do you keep on talking about it? Go on Barry, tell me, what was Marcie like?'

'If you mean in bed, you can mind your own business.'

'No, I can't; you know me better than that.'

'That's true. Well, and you know Marcie. She was the same in bed as she is out of it, basically. People don't change character as soon as they slip between the sheets. She never kept her mind on one thing for more than two seconds at a time. Most frustrating. Worse than you, getting up to eat; at least you wait till I've finished.'

I was fascinated. 'What did she do?'

'Really, Cathy, I think you should curb these unhealthy voyeuristic tendencies . . . all right, all right. Well, she

119

didn't do anything really. It's just that it's off-putting to have someone saying, "Are you sure, darling, you don't want more coffee?" in the middle of being screwed.'

'You exaggerate!' I accuse.

'Perhaps, but only slightly.'

'But she is a lot more beautiful than me,' I said enviously.

'I'll grant you that,' said Barry serenely, 'but she's basically cold.'

'Cold? Marcie? She's the most demonstrative . . .'

'Outwardly, yes,' he agreed. 'But her head rules her heart. She'd never get carried away; her feet are firmly on the ground.'

If Barry was right, then that could be what makes Marcie such a good businesswoman. Through the open door, I can hear her in the boutique.

'You could try the blue, with one of the lace blouses – bring the wide-collared one, Shirley – and a very narrow belt. Then a silk scarf tied – so – and a pouch-bag and very plain classic shoes.'

Then the customer's voice, vintage Roedean . . .

'Not too formal, you think?'

'Not at all,' Marcie assures her. 'The same suit could look absolutely casual with a little cotton T-shirt top or – no, Karen, the striped one. There, you see, and leave the jacket open . . .'

To be appreciated, this has to be seen. I leave the rest of my cake (I'm feeling sick again and the 'lift' has descended abruptly) and go into the shop.

The customer is straight out of *Vogue*; off-the-peg aristocratic nose, hand-made eyelashes and anorexic eyebrows, teamed with a mouth too well-bred to use for laughing, a porcelain complexion which wouldn't know a spot if it met one, and a hairstyle so immaculate that no wind would dare to ruffle it. Even the fingernails are of uniform lengths, perfectly filed to a perfect shape (not so sharp as to be vulgar nor so rounded as to suggest a working hand), and perfectly painted. The clothes on the mannequin figure, which she has just dismissed as 'These awful old rags' look as if they have never before been worn.

'How do people manage to look like that?' I whisper to Karen, the younger assistant. 'On a weekday, too!'

'Money!' she whispers back, but there is more to it than that. Behind the aristocratic perfection lies a history of breeding to rival any racehorse. The pedigree has been charted, over century-spanning generations, to outlaw undesirable traits. No hybrid blood, no taint of work, no penchant for cream cakes to ease that marble figure out of its sculpted lines, no troubling thoughts to bring wrinkles to the smooth brow or giggles to cause unsightly laughter lines. No grief to drag at the corners of that shapely mouth or love to soften its cool outline; no emotions beyond an attractively pouting petulance; no sticky-fingered children allowed within range of the crease-resistant heart. No, it's too great a price to pay. I'd rather be a slob. Except when, as now, I am looking in a mirror with an expensive silk shirt held incongruously against my unaristocratic jersey-clad bosom.

'Not the cream, Cathy,' Marcie calls, seeing me with the extra pair of eyes she keeps at the back of her head. 'Give her the emerald, Karen.' Without any apparent interruption, she is pinning the the skirt of the Roedean customer's suit. 'See the difference just those few centimetres make? The whole outfit seems to hang better.'

'Emerald?' I say doubtfully, as Karen obediently brings it. 'I don't normally wear green.'

'Try it on,' she encourages. 'Marcie's usually right.'

She is. The customer is toeing the line, I notice. She makes a point of trying other accessories with the blue suit, but ends up with exactly the ones Marcie recommended. Marcie, without apparently speaking, through her mouthful of pins, has sent Shirley scurrying for fresh supplies of blouses and skirts and woollen masterpieces that could never be insulted with the name of sweater.

The emerald-green shirt, I have to admit, is amazing. In the cream one, I look like a girl wearing an expensive shirt; in the green one I look expensive. The only thing is, when would I have an occasion to look expensive?

'I'd never wear something as good as this,' I explain to Karen.

'If I were you,' she says, 'I'd wear it all the time.' She has a point. Can I bear to relinquish this new image to return to my ancient jersey and skirt? I can't. I look at the price tag. I can. I have to.

'It's not really expensive,' Karen consoles. 'Think of it as an investment.'

'You've been listening to Marcie,' I accuse, and she has the grace to laugh.

'Karen!'

'Excuse me a minute.'

She returns. 'Marcie says,' she whispers, 'that you're not to pay for it.'

'Oh no, I couldn't . . .'

'But there is one condition.'

'What's that?'

'You have to buy this brooch to wear with it.' She opens her hand to reveal a pin with a translucent plastic-winged butterfly. It looks cheap and nasty. Because my stomach is churning uncomfortably, I am rude enough to say so.

'Well, it isn't cheap,' says Karen frankly. 'But it costs a lot less than the shirt. I should have it if I were you.'

I take it from her. 'Do most of Marcie's customers do as they're told?'

'All of them,' she says cheerfully. 'Shall I pin this on for you?'

'If you must.'

The plastic butterfly picks up the colour of the shirt and is transformed into an emerald wonder with glinting silken wings.

'Actually,' I say slowly, 'it's not bad,' and Karen grins.

'You see?' she says complacently. I see.

'But I must pay for the shirt,' I say firmly.

'What nonsense,' says Marcie, whisking past with an armful of coloured scarves. 'I give discount for bulk.'

'Are you talking about my figure?'

'No darling, of course not. I'm talking about those French-cut jeans you're going to buy to go with it.'

'Oh no.'

'Karen. Try the ones with the little pleated pockets.' She is gone again.

The important customer is saying, 'No really, I do think the pink would be too strong . . .' Marcie drapes the pink scarf over her shoulder.

'Well . . .' she demurs. 'Perhaps you're right . . .' and Marcie tosses the scarf on top of the growing pile of purchases on the counter.

A tailored lady has just come in with a sullenly pretty teenage daughter. 'It's far too expensive,' she says, 'but we'll just have a look.'

'This is an old people's shop,' the daughter complains. 'There aren't any young clothes here.'

Shirley, dispatched by Marcie's left eyebrow, goes to serve them and has a quick conversation with the mother. 'Something for a party?' she repeats. 'And it has to be black?'

'Not a dress,' says the daughter quickly. 'Something I can wear with jeans,' and her mother sighs.

'Oh, EMMA!'

Shirley steers them towards the silk shirts but Marcie, without turning round, says, 'What about the black blouson T-shirt? With a bead collar-necklace perhaps,' and Shirley changes direction.

'Too old,' says the daughter at once.

'At least it's *decent*,' her mother says.

'Who wants to be decent at a party?'

Karen has brought the French trousers. I look at the price tag first, this time.

'Oh no,' I say. 'I wouldn't pay that even for a winter coat!'

'You'd wear these much more than a winter coat,' Karen coaxes. 'They make everyone look a size eight.'

'They're a whole week's salary!' I exclaim.

'More than one week's, for me,' she says sadly, 'even with the discount. I'm saving up for them myself.'

'Well, don't sell them to me then.'

She laughs. 'It's all right. Marcie's put a pair aside for me. I already borrow them on Saturday nights.'

The trousers (they're far too elegant to qualify as 'jeans') make me look, if not a size eight, then considerably more streamlined than my usual shape. But the price! I couldn't spend that amount on myself. Could I? I could go out with anyone, anywhere, in this outfit, lack of confidence forgotten. I feel like a million dollars. Not surprisingly. They cost almost that much. No, I can't. People are starving; living on bowls of rice. But then, that's in India. In England people are wearing designer underwear and paving their bathroom floors with hand-made ceramic tiles, and it's really not so extravagant, in the circumstances, to buy a pair of French trousers. Even if they cost the equivalent of a month's supply of rice.

'No, I can't,' I tell Karen.

'Perhaps,' she suggests, 'you could pay for them in instalments or something?'

'Have you still got much to pay off on yours?'

'A quarter. It's still quite a lot.'

'I'll just take the shirt and the brooch, Karen. But tell Marcie I'll pay for them both.'

'I'll tell her, but she won't let you.'

Marcie's customer is writing out a cheque while Shirley and the other assistant are tissue-paper-folding a pile of garments into innumerable chic little carrier-bags. The tweedy lady is trying on a hand-woven jacket while her daughter is in the changing room.

'Look at me in this!' The sullen expression is gone, as is the teenager. In her place is a sophisticated young woman in a deceptively demure get-up that shows curves where before there was puppy-fat.

'Not too old?' says Shirley teasingly.

'Far too old!' says the tweedy lady. 'No, really, Emma – you look about twenty in that.'

'I know,' Emma breathes, 'great, isn't it?'

'So lovely to see you,' Marcie enthuses to the porcelain beauty. 'Come again soon now! Yes, that's very good,' she says, turning instantly to Emma. 'Now, I think there's a black bracelet that goes with that collar-necklace. And what are you going to do with your hair, for the party? Just as it is? In that case, what about twisting a string of beads through a few strands down one side . . . let me show you what I mean . . .'

I have to go. My stomach is not going to last much longer, and I would hate to spoil a sale. I wave my cheque book at Karen, and Marcie says, without looking up, 'We'll take for the brooch, Karen, and the shirt will go on account.'

'I haven't got an account,' I say weakly.

Marcie sidles round Emma, inspecting the back view. 'A little present,' she murmurs. 'So use it wisely, darling – like tonight. Now, that's perfect, Emma. What kind of shoes did you have in mind . . .'

I can't be sick in Marcie's beautiful kitchen; they'd hear me in the shop. Perhaps, though, if I sat down for a minute. I steal a look at the emerald shirt in its black and silver carrier-bag to help the recovery process. There is just one more thing, before I leave. I scribble a second cheque and fold it in a sheet of paper, torn from my diary. 'Marcie – for the final half-leg of Karen's trousers. And thanks for the present. C.' It's a kind of insurance, to make it too embarrassing for me to return later to buy those jeans. I'll call in to Etam's in the High Street when I get home and buy an ordinary pair. They won't make me look thin and leggy but they won't represent quite so many bowls of rice either.

It's all hypocrisy of course. If I had the courage of my convictions, I should be sending the balance to Oxfam, not giving it to Karen who by Third World standards is quite as wealthy as me. But I haven't. I mean, I haven't any real principles on these things, no moral code or anything like that. It's just an impulse thing, the same kind of gut feeling I had about Bantam's experiments on dogs. In general, I have no ambitions to change the world; it would take too much effort and moral integrity. I'll close my eyes to most things, along with the rest of the apathy brigade. But some things just stick in my throat.

Like those cream cakes. I make a dash for the door, but once outside in the cold November air the urge to be sick recedes. Instead I am left feeling light-headed and the pavement beneath my feet bounces like a waterbed. I feel as though I am high – but you can't get high on sugar. Could this be the secret success of Marcie's little patisserie? Illicit dope in the cream slices? Cunning move, eh? Meringue with marijuana. Dope doughnuts. The bakery doors are besieged every morning by glassy-eyed Chelsea ladies clamouring for Speed Cake for their elevenses.

Seriously though, I do feel strange. I fumble in my pocket for my return tube ticket and my hands are nerveless, with hardly the strength to hold it. An American asks me which way for the Piccadilly Line and my voice is slurred when I answer him. I can hardly get down the steps to the platform. My face feels funny, as thought it's being dragged down by some extra-gravity force. My heart is thumping, my mouth is dry, my palms clammy and my feet frozen. What the hell is happening to me? I can't focus. This is silly. Concentrate on something. A torn-edged poster for a film: 'The ultimate experience in . . .' and then the tear. The ultimate in what, we'll never know. The white-lined edge of the platform. Feet in boots, clogs, shoes, sandals. Sandals in November? Rubbish – cans and crisp packets – lying between the gleaming rails. The train. At last, the train.

Sinking into the seat, eyes closed. The noise and vibration and swaying – and the train hasn't started to move yet. The noise is inside my head. What is happening to me? Maybe it's flu. It doesn't feel like flu. I don't feel feverish; I feel . . . oh, God, I feel like I'm dying. Is this how people die? Those cakes. My stomach. You can't faint on the tube; everyone would ignore you. They'd sweep you up in the depot and throw you away with the cigarette packets and Coke cans. Another one died, Fred. Okay, George, chuck her in the mincer. We'll sell her to British Rail for the hamburgers.

Don't panic. Things get worse if you panic. What is wrong with me? Things get worse . . . Which station is this? Is that all? I'll never get home at this rate. That long walk from the station to the flat. Never any taxis. I'll never make it.

If I went to Carla's . . . That's three stops earlier. They don't live far from the station. I don't want to see Jim. Jim won't be there. At work now. Only Carla and the baby. Carla might be out. Then I'd be worse off. Worse . . . Couldn't be worse. Their house has a porch. Could lie in the cold tiled porch till somebody came. Someone would come. 'Mavis, there's somebody dead in that porch!' 'Don't look, dear. It's bad for your blood pressure to get upset.' 'She's only young. It must be drugs.' 'Come away dear. Let the police deal with it; it's their job.'

I'll risk it anyway. Carla will have to come home eventually. Poor Carla. First Barry, now this. It was Carla and Jim who came to take me home when Barry died. Two o'clock in the morning. Both white-faced and bleary-eyed with shock. Carla heavily pregnant. 'Carla, you shouldn't have come.' 'Of course I came.' Sitting awake at five A.M. in their sitting room with the dawn breaking through the closed curtains. Carla, upstairs, sobbing her heart out, shutting herself away for fear of upsetting me with her grief. Jim, haggard, drinking whisky mechanically. 'She'll lose the baby if she goes on like this.' Me, frozen and speechless, numb with lack of grief and lack of all emotion.

Read the adverts. Anything. Don't think. I haven't let myself think about that night. At first I couldn't. My mind shied away from it, repelling the thoughts as a magnet repels another. When this natural resistance began to subside, the repulsion became a deliberate effort of will. Don't dwell on it, people said. Don't let yourself become morbid. Bury the emotions along with the coffin, that's right. Forget it. Don't think about it. That's the way. You'll soon get over it.

Eight months ago. And I haven't let myself think. For eight months I haven't dwelt on the thought of that night. It's been hard. Almost impossible sometimes. Like now. When you're sick or you're tired, your resistance is low. But you have to resist it. Fight it, people said. Till what you are fighting takes on the proportions of a monster. No longer grief that you are resisting, but insanity.

What station is this? One more stop. No thought until then, just hanging on, staying awake, staying alive. Consciousness receding, images coming and going like a bad dream. The sound of voices now muffled, heard through cotton wool, and now amplified – booming, vibrating. Noise without individual sounds. Concentrate. Keep awake. Only one more stop. Sliding, falling, into a dark weightless void. Keep holding on. Stay awake.

The doors sliding back with a crash like the trump of doom. The platform, very far down, moving with breathtaking speed beneath my heavy feet. Steps and more steps. The station is empty. All the people have gone. Rushing ahead with the effortlessness of the fully alive, moving without conscious movement. I never thought of walking as a skill. Now it's an ordeal, a superhuman effort, like wading through treacle.

Out on the street. The air, dry and dusty, now damp, now hot, now cold. Loud chattering people, droning like aeroplanes. Waves of sound. Drowning through the ears. Jostling groups of people, buffeting me with electric waves of shock. Searing brightness of cold light. Lasers of pain through the nerve-ends. Dwindling reality returning in roaring rushes through the thickening haze. Is this sickness or madness? Or are they the same? Nightmare world of noises and images half understood. Sickness and darkness and fear.

What number is Carla's house? I can't remember the street. I hardly know where I am. Now I can only see my feet, still moving mechanically along the whizzing ground.

When I find myself in front of the door I can't understand how I got here. I thought I had died, there on the station, eliminated by dusty winds blowing straight from eternity. When I lift my hand to the doorbell it seems a disembodied thing, far away and belonging to somebody else. Soon be over now. Must tell her. Must find words to explain when the door opens.

Opening the door a looming, sinister figure. Mother and baby depicted by a surrealist; swollen to huge proportions and ugly voices. 'Cathy . . . what's the matter?'

'Sick . . . going to be sick . . .' Clashing and roaring in my ears, like cisterns and water-pipes and cymbals orchestrated by maniacs. Then darkness and falling, at long last, into the void.

Waves of sickness inside the machine which is pumping me alive. Let me be. Let me die. It's too much effort to come alive again. It hurts too much in my head. Let me fade away into blackness again.

More waves and roaring around the room. The walls closing in, ceiling tilting, voices rising and falling. 'Cathy. Wake up, Cathy. Are you all right?' The sound of a telephone being dialled and a voice again, farther away. 'Hello, could I speak to Dr Kennedy? Yes, it's an emergency.' Emergency. What can a doctor do? A doctor inhabits the normal world, not this callous flesh-and-blood machine which is pumping my chest and churning my stomach and filling my head with noise and pouring cold sweat down my funny, sagging face.

'The doctor's coming, Cathy. He's on his way. Can I get you anything? Can you open your eyes?'

A warm hand in my cold one. I can feel its warmth. There is someone there on the furthest edge of the void, anchoring my sightless, drifting body with the weight of its normality.

Out of the blackness, another voice, 'Not my patient . . . wouldn't like to say . . . history of diabetes?'

Carla's voice. 'Low blood sugar . . . something . . . I believe.'

Sugar, yes. Give me sugar. Somebody. Please. Please think of it. I've forgotten the words; can't seem to speak.

Then being lifted and a voice saying, 'Drink,' and a sweetish liquid poured into my mouth. 'Swallow.' My throat won't work. 'Swallow.' All right for him; it's hard work. 'And again. Another sip. That's right. And another.' Sweet-tasting water. Not sweet enough. More. 'That's better. She's coming round now.'

Mists clearing. Carla and a man I don't know, holding me up. 'Just drink the last of this.' I am so cold. I have never been so cold.

'Are you all right, Cathy?'

I don't know. Am I? I seem to be alive again, anyway. Was it like this for Barry? When I left him in the hospital when the nurse had closed his eyelids, was he really adrift in a black nightmare, crying silently, 'Don't leave me!' with a mind that couldn't frame the words?

Can you speak to me now?' The man. Must be the doctor.

'Yes.' But what use is it? Depression, heavy as a fall of snow, blanketing my thoughts.

'You're not a diabetic are you? As far as you know?'

'No.'

'What about the low blood sugar, Cathy?' Carla says. 'I couldn't remember exactly.'

'Oh, yes.'

'You have hypoglycaemia?' the doctor prompts.

What?

'Low blood sugar,' he translates. 'Have you been tested for it in hospital?'

'Yes, long time ago.'

'Were the tests positive?'

'Some of the doctors said yes and one said no.'

'I see. Look, I think we'd better get you into hospital again.'

Oh no. 'No.'

'You ought to, to be on the safe side,' Carla coaxes.

'No.' Not hospital, no. All those tests and then no conclusive results. White-coated doctors arguing over normal and subnormal while I sat and retched. 'I'll go to the doctor,' I offer. 'My own doctor. He's got all my notes.' If he ever bothers to read them. Pessimism, like a shroud. 'Can I have some more sugar?'

'Yes. Did you eat breakfast today?'

'Yes.'

'What did you have?'

'I . . .' What did I have? 'I can't remember.'

'And lunch?'

I shake my head. It must be after lunchtime, then.

'I still think you'd be better in hospital,' he says, but as I shake my head again: 'You'll see your own doctor, then, at the earliest opportunity? I'll give you a note for him.'

'Here you are. Eat this and I'll make a pot of tea.'

The cheese on toast smells lovely, but it is so far away. Such an effort to reach my hand to the plate, to my mouth. Is this how disabled people feel? All that effort of will for one slow and clumsy movement? How humiliating. Is this what happens to old people? Clever people, ex-heads of industry. Talented people, painters and athletes; capable mothers of families who depend on them – all reduced in the end to this pathetic ritual, weakly lifting shaky hands to trembling mouths, spending their dwindling energies on staying alive.

As I eat I feel better. The doom-cloud lifts. Perhaps I won't die after all. Maybe I'll leave it till tomorrow. I get up and go into the sitting room where Louise is sitting in a pool of toys. Carla comes in with tea.

'Feeling better?'

'Yes, thanks. I'm sorry you had to play nursemaid; I didn't think I could make it home.'

'You only just made it here, by the look of it. Sit down. You still look putty-coloured.'

'Thanks for the compliment.' My fingers and my feet have gone dead; I can't stop shivering.

Carla turns the gas fire up. 'When you were lying there and I felt how cold your hands were, I panicked,' she confesses. 'I thought you were dead.'

'I thought so too.'

'Do you want some sugar in your tea? Does it make you feel better?'

'No, I won't have any more, thanks. I'm sure it was something to do with those sticky cakes I had at lunchtime. Wayne said a friend of his who had low blood sugar wasn't allowed to eat sweet things at all.'

'Who's Wayne?'

'Oh Lord, that reminds me; I'm meant to be going out tonight. Can I use your phone to ring him at work? I've got the number in my bag.' I get up and walk straight into the door.

'Are you sure you're not just drunk?' Carla says. 'Sit down, for heaven's sake, and I'll phone him for you.'

'Sure you don't mind?' Carla hates talking to people she doesn't know. She once confided that her idea of hell would be a never-ending party where everyone knew everyone else, except her. 'You can forget the weeping and gnashing of teeth,' she said. 'My hell will be playing wallflower for all eternity in a roomful of happy drunks.'

'Of course I don't mind,' she says airily. 'What's his name?'

'Wayne. Wayne Slindon. Here's the number.'

'I'll ring him first and interrogate you afterwards,' she promises. 'What have you been keeping from me?'

'Not a lot.'

When she goes out of the room, Louise screams.

'Come here, Loulou. Look at Teddy!' Teddy does not pacify her, so I stoop down and pick her up. The room stoops with me and stands up more suddenly than I do. 'Oops-a-daisy. Now what's all the fuss about, baby?'

I hear Carla on the phone to Wayne, going into unnecessary detail about my precipitate arrival. Knowing Wayne even as little as I do, if she makes it sound too dramatic he'll be here on the doorstep if she's not careful. She puts the phone down.

'He's coming round,' she says.

'Oh no!'

'Why "Oh no"?'

'Well, haven't you had enough bother for one afternoon?'

'Not at all,' she says cheerfully. 'It's the most exciting thing that's happened in weeks. Apart from the washing machine breaking down when it was full of nappies. Besides, he sounded quite nice. What's he like?'

'Quite nice. Look, I can just get a minicab home . . .'

'Don't you dare. I want to meet this Wayne what's-his-name. How long have you known him?'

'Five minutes. He's nobody special and he's leaving on Saturday to go and live in Sheffield – okay?'

'You are boring!'

'I know. Is there any more tea in the pot?'

'Yes, plenty. Here. What are you doing off work today, anyway? Were you ill this morning?'

'No, I had the day off and went up to town to have lunch with Marcie.' My memory is coming back, all by itself. Amazing what cheese on toast can do for the brain.

'Is that what the fancy carrier-bag is, in the hall?'

'What carrier-bag? Oh yes; I bought a shirt. Have a look. Try it on.'

Carla returns wearing the shirt. 'I can't do the buttons up. Don't ever have babies, Cathy; it has a dire effect on your boobs. This shirt isn't me, is it?'

'There was an apricot-coloured one there that would have looked good on you. Marcie talked me into getting the green, but she was right, as it turned out. She's the most amazing saleswoman; have you ever seen her in action?'

'No, but I can imagine. She persuaded Jim to buy me an antique silver bracelet once for my birthday. He was going to get me a frying pan. Cathy, I think he might be having an affair.'

'What?' It's too much of a switch from frying pans, all of a sudden.

'I know it sounds silly. And I know you'll say he couldn't

134

be – not Jim. I mean, he's the last person you would think of being deceitful, isn't he?'

'Oh, yes.' Please don't let this be anything to do with Saturday night.

'But he came home terribly late on Saturday; he's never done that before. I mean, he often goes out for a drink with his friends from work; sometimes I go too, but I'd been up all Friday night with Louise and I was too tired to go. But he's never stayed out so late, it was ages after the pubs shut and he wouldn't say where he'd been and he was in a terrible mood . . .'

'Oh Carla, he was round at my flat!'

'At your flat?'

'I'm sorry. I should have told you, but I thought he'd be embarrassed. He came round to fix my sink – you remember he offered, at Marcie's on the Friday? He'd called round earlier apparently, but I was out so he came again on his way home – some chivalrous impulse prompted by the booze!'

Carla let her breath out slowly. 'Is that all? But why wouldn't he tell me where'd he been?'

'As I say, he was probably embarrassed; he was far too pissed to start unblocking sinks! And I'd done it anyway, by that time. So he stayed for a chat and a cup of coffee and went home. It was obviously later than I thought. I should have realized you would be worried. So you see, it was my fault.'

If Wayne arrives soon, I can leave in time to phone Jim before he leaves work.

'God, Cathy. What a relief! You must think I'm stupid, getting in such a state!'

'No, of course not.' Of course I don't. When it was Barry and Janice, I was frantic.

'No, Louise! The fireguard is not a climbing frame, darling. Will that be Wayne coming up the path, Cathy?'

135

'I left work straight away,' Wayne says. 'I reckoned they wouldn't sack me as I'm leaving anyway. Are you all right?'

'I'm fine,' I assure him. 'Just thinking about going home. Come in while I get my coat on.'

'You're not going anywhere yet,' Carla says. 'She isn't fine at all.'

'Wayne, this is Carla. Wayne.'

'Hello, Wayne. Do you want to come in and have a cup of tea?'

'Thanks, I'd love one.'

'Jim will be back soon,' Carla says. 'He said he'd be home early tonight.'

Oh no. No I can't see Jim, not yet, and especially not while my brain is only half working. On the other hand, if I can't catch him before he leaves work, to tell him what I've told Carla . . . Perhaps I should stay, to try to have a quick word in his ear as soon as he gets in, and then get lost . . .

Carla, who is usually shy with strangers, warms to Wayne immediately. He carries the tea-tray for her and rescues the baby from the wastepaper basket.

'Why don't you both stay to supper?' Carla suggests. 'It'll only be beans or something, but you're very welcome.'

'That would be great,' Wayne accepts. 'As long as you're feeling all right to stay, Cathy?'

I am going off him rapidly. I do not want to spend a whole evening with Jim. I know I will have to eventually, but not yet, and not today. In ten years' time maybe.

'Well, actually I am still feeling slightly . . .'

'You haven't eaten enough,' says Carla solicitously. 'You need a proper meal. She only had a cream cake for lunch,' she informs Wayne. I feel they are ganging up on me.

He is properly scandalized. 'That's the worst thing you could do,' he accuses, 'according to Steve's doctor. I thought you were going to see him today? Did you ring him?'

'Well, no, as a matter of fact . . . .'

'I'll ring him now,' says Wayne firmly. 'Can I use your phone, Carla? Thanks. And then I'll go out and buy some steak. Do you and Jim like steak?'

'We love it!' Carla enthuses. 'We don't live on beans from choice.' When he goes out of the room, she whispers, 'Isn't he NICE!'

'Yeah, lovely.'

'Don't be like that, Cathy. You must like him, to go out with him.'

'I'm not going out with him.'

'He's got a very sweet face. Nice eyes. And he seems really kind.'

'Sounds just like a spaniel,' I say ungratefully.

'What's he like in bed?'

'Like a spaniel, for all I know. Shut up, will you, Carla? I've told you I'm not going out with him. Come to Aunty Cathy, Louise; Mummy's talking baby-talk again.' Louise leans her head against my shoulder and grizzles.

'She's getting grumpy,' Carla says, 'just like her Aunty Cath. It's nearly her bedtime. Stay here and watch the news for me Cathy, while I go and give her a bath.'

'He'll see you tomorrow,' Wayne announces. 'At 11.45.'

'I'll be at work!'

'No you won't. Because I've also rung your mate Alan and told him you won't be in tomorrow.'

'Listen, what makes you think . . .?'

'Of course you can't go to work tomorrow,' says Carla in the voice she uses when Louise goes too near the electric sockets. 'Don't be silly!'

I give up. I'll do what I'm told. I sit and watch the news while Wayne goes out to buy steak, and Jim comes in while Carla is still bathing the baby. I feel sick again suddenly.

'Oh Cathy. Hi.' He looks as thrilled to see me as I am to see him. 'Where's Carla?'

'Bathing Louise. Just a second, before you go. I told Carla you'd been round to my flat on Saturday.'

'You did what!'

'Will you listen? She said she was worried about you coming home so late, so I said you'd called in on your way back from the pub to fix my sink, but as you were a bit pissed and I'd already fixed it anyway you stayed for a cup of coffee and then went home.' I say it all in one breath to get it over with.

'Oh, I see.'

'And if you ever let on that I told you she was worried . . .'

'I won't. I'm not likely to, am I? What do you take me for?'

'You don't want me to answer that, do you?' I hope he can take being teased; it would ease the situation. He glares at me for an instant and then relaxes and we both laugh.

'Maybe not. I'll just go and say hello to Carla; have a drink if you want one.'

Wayne turns up with four huge steaks.

'Looks like you bought a whole ox!'

'I thought you'd need feeding up,' he says. 'I bought you some bacon too, and half a dozen eggs so you can have a proper breakfast tomorrow morning.'

Maybe Carla is right and he does have something. 'That's very sweet of you.'

He smiles at me, very sweetly. Have you noticed how men don't normally smile much? Laugh, yes; look amused, yes; but they don't seem to go in much for normal, friendly smiling; it's not considered macho or something.

He sits down beside me on the sofa and doesn't watch the television. Instead, he asks me about my lunch with Marcie, and tells me about his successor at work, who has started early for a hand-over period.

'He doesn't seem to be getting the hang of it,' Wayne worries. 'He's got all the right qualifications and a glowing reference from his last job so he must be all right, but he seems a bit unsure of some of the basics.'

'Should you have left him on his own then, this afternoon?'

'He'll have to start on his own soon enough. He might get on better alone. Could be it makes him nervous with me standing over him.'

'He probably finds you terrifying,' I agree.

'Yeah. It's the Rasputin beard.' He strokes it thoughtfully. 'I've been thinking of shaving it off. What d'you think?'

'It's up to you.' I might not like him without the beard. Barry had a beard. He didn't look anything like Wayne apart from that; Wayne is thinner, more serious-looking.

Carla and Wayne cook the meal. Jim and I sit in front of the television. I wouldn't describe the atmosphere as relaxed.

'Carla says you were ill?'

'Yes. I'm OK now.'

'Good.'

'Have a good day at work?'

'Not bad. Busy.'

'Ah.'

Formalities over, we breathe a sigh of relief and settle back to watch a man who breeds crocodiles in his Surbiton semi.

During the meal, Jim and Wayne wash down the steak with whisky and talk about sport.

I am so tired I can hardly keep my eyes open. Wayne keeps looking sideways at me, suspiciously. I wish he wouldn't because then Carla and Jim look at me too. I would rather be left to vegetate in peace.

'You feeling ill again?' Carla says.

'I'm fine.'

'You don't look fine.'

'I'll take you home,' Wayne says, 'as soon as we've washed up.'

'We'll wash up,' Jim and Carla say simultaneously. Carla wants Wayne to take me home and convince me that there is life after Barry. Jim just wants me to go home. Wayne wants – I don't know what Wayne wants, but I'll go home anyway. Carla insists that Jim drives us home. Wayne insists on sitting in the back with his arm round me, which probably makes Jim feel like a minicab driver.

'Thanks for the lift, Jim. See you.'

'Take care.'

'I'll look after her,' Wayne assures him. I hope he isn't going to get proprietorial. Not that it matters. Nice though he is, the nicest thing about him is that after Friday he will simply evaporate. Does that sound nasty? Yes, it does. But from a selfish point of view it is ideal to have just the first week of a relationship without all the follow-up. Perhaps I can tackle my rehabilitation in easy stages. What I need now is to meet someone who is going to Sheffield in two weeks' time, then someone who is emigrating in three weeks . . . By the time I'm about eighty maybe I'll be ready to commit myself to a lifetime with somebody. Then I'll probably die on my wedding night; the shock will kill me.

'You go straight to bed,' Wayne says, taking the key from me and opening the door, 'and I'll bring you in some coffee.'

'How kind of you,' I say unkindly, 'to invite me in for coffee.'

He looks sideways at me. 'It's a pleasure. Milk?'

'Please.'

'Toast?'

'Please. The bread-bin is in the cupboard by the cooker.'

'I'll find it. You get into bed; you look knackered.'

'Thanks; how flattering.'

Looking at myself in the bedroom mirror, I have to admit he is right. I look about eighty. I feel about eighty. Only this isn't going to be my wedding night. I obviously can't sit up in bed drinking coffee in what I normally wear in bed, which is nothing, so I rummage in the drawer for the nightie my mother bought me when I went to university. It is seven years old and brand new; quite pretty really if you like that kind of thing. Except that now I remember I lent it to Carla when she went into hospital to have Louise and told her not to bother to give it back.

I can hear Wayne clattering about in the kitchen. What am I going to wear? My dressing gown is one of those wrap-over kimono things that parts like the Red Sea every time you lean forward.

Finally, I find a pyjama jacket of Barry's. I bought him two pairs of pyjamas when he was taken into hospital and he never got the chance to wear the second pair. I hated seeing him in that hospital bed, wearing pyjamas. When I first went in to see him and found him propped against the stacked pillows in striped pyjamas and with his face a shade of grey, he looked no different from all the old men who were coughing their guts up in the adjoining beds. I knew I'd lost him then. That's why when he was fighting for life I told him, 'Don't fight it, Barry. You'll be all right, darling: just let yourself go,' and it was as if I'd given him permission to die: he relaxed against me and half an hour later when the sister came she said that he was dead.

Even when I start crying I can stop as soon as I have to – like now, when I hear Wayne knocking at the door. One of these days it will all catch up with me and I'll find myself in a padded cell, tearing my hair out and screaming and weeping such oceans of tears that the whole asylum will float away, and all the poor crazy people who see life too clearly and can't bear the reality of it will drown in a sea of grief, as they always knew that they would.

'You've made enough toast for an army!'

'I'm having some too,' he says, 'if that's okay. There seemed to be plenty of bread there.'

'I reckon I can spare you the odd crust, after all that steak you bought tonight. You must let me pay for it.'

'Of course not.'

'No, really, I wouldn't want . . .'

'Eat,' he says firmly. 'And don't worry about it. I did tell you I was a millionaire, didn't I?'

'Me too. Or I will be when the rich lodger arrives.'

'Are you taking a lodger?'

'I'm going to advertise for someone to share the flat, yes.'

'Are you finding it hard to manage financially?'

'Not really. The mortgage was endowed. It's just sheer greed. So that I can afford a pair of jeans from Marcie's boutique.'

'Where you went today?'

'Yes. I bought a brooch and she gave me a blouse which will make all my jeans look like floor-rags. I could have bought these beautiful French-cut jeans to match but I got pangs of conscience about the price.'

'Why conscience?'

'Oh well. You know. They would have kept an Indian village in rice for the next ten years.'

He puts his head on one side and considers the problem. 'Why don't you save up twice the amount, buy the jeans and send the rest of the money to Oxfam?'

I laugh. 'I hadn't thought of that one.'

'It's what my sister used to do. She went to school at a convent and got very religious at one time. She was all set to become a nun when she was thirteen; my mother was quite worried. Then at fourteen she discovered boys and we never heard any more about it.'

'Are your family Catholics then?'

'No. My parents sent Debbie there because they thought convent girls grew up to be nice young ladies. But she turned out quite normal after all.'

'It didn't work with Barry's sister either; she ran away from school at sixteen and went to Katmandu with a guy who lived in a horse-box. She's respectably married now with four kids who all go to convent school.'

He settles himself more comfortably on the end of the bed. 'But you're not a Catholic, are you?'

'No. Barry was. I'm a nothing-in-particular.'

'I wondered. Only, being nosy, I saw that pamphlet in the kitchen.'

'The meditation one? Father Delaney – the priest who married us – sent it. I haven't had a chance to read it yet.'

'I had a girlfriend once who did transcendental meditation. She went to classes. She said it was really difficult at first and then she got hooked; said it changed her life.'

'I could do with that,' I say wryly, then to forestall any questions add quickly, 'Did you try it?'

'No; I was going to but then we broke up so I never did. But Lesley was really enthusiastic.'

'That's what puts me off,' I admit. 'People seem to get hooked on religion and things. There are no half measures; you can't carry on as you were before except that now you believe in God or Krishna or whoever. You have to go round looking radiant, in last year's ethnic clothes.'

He laughs. 'I suppose fashion must seem a bit irrelevant if you've just discovered the secret of the universe.'

'Yes, but if no-one else has discovered it and they're all wearing this year's fashions you're going to be out of step with the rest of the world, aren't you?'

'Maybe that's why we're all so scared of it,' Wayne suggests. 'If you go with the crowd you feel safe. You can kid yourself that you're not alone, facing God.'

I look at him curiously. 'That sounds vaguely religious in itself.'

He shrugs. 'Religion is one of the things I've always postponed thinking about. Like you, I suppose, I'm afraid if I give it an inch, it'll take a whole lifetime. I'm as chicken as the next guy; I want to be one of the crowd.'

I feel like crying again. So everyone is alone and everyone is afraid – of grief or of God or of something. Even Big Harry must wake in the night sometimes with a chill midnight knowledge of his own nothingness.

'Are you feeling all right, Cathy?'

'Yes, I'm all right. Just tired.'

'I'll leave you to get some sleep.' He takes the coffee mug from me. 'And I'll come round tomorrow at elevenish to take you to the doctor; I'll get a minicab.'

'I don't expect you to do that! You have to be at work . . .'

'You really must stop arguing,' he says. 'It's very bad for the blood sugar.'

Once he's gone, I can go to the loo in the too-short pyjama jacket and wonder, drowsily, without using too much brain-power, why I don't resent him bossing me about. But the question requires too much intellectual effort, so I leave it unanswered and go back to bed and sleep.

6

At twenty past seven – A.M. – my mother arrives.

'Darling!' she exclaims, charging in on a blast of Ma Griffe, 'I phoned you yesterday to tell you I was coming but you weren't there.' She kisses the air beside my left ear. 'Let me look at you. You look peaky. Why were you on sick leave yesterday?'

'I wasn't. Come in. I had the day off. What time is it?'

'Seven thirty. I thought I'd have to catch you early to make sure you didn't go to work. So you're not ill after all, then?'

'Well . . .'

'If you knew what time I got up this morning!' she accuses. 'I really don't know how I did it; I feel quite exhausted. But after I spoke to that young man in your office I thought, "I must go to my daughter; she'll be needing me." That's what I thought. But you're not ill, you say?'

'What time did you ring the office yesterday, Mum?'

'About five. I was going to phone you before but then Mrs Grantley called and she *wouldn't* stop talking. But that young man definitely told me you were ill.'

'Yes. Yes I was. If you rang at five o'clock.'

'But you said . . .' Her face becomes pink with exasperation, like her hat which is full of pink petals nodding irritably.

'I didn't get sick leave; I had the day off,' I explain. 'But then I got ill.'

'Ah!' she exclaims. 'So I'll have a chance to see you after all. You won't be going to work.'

'This afternoon I will. This morning I'm going to the

doctor's. Tea or coffee, Mum?'

'Going to the doctor's? What's wrong with you? I saw you looked peaky – I said so, didn't I? It's a good job I came, Cathy. I can take you to the surgery.'

'It's all right, thanks; a friend's taking me.'

'Nonsense, darling; that's what mothers are for. The surgery's only down the road anyway; you can walk that far, for heaven's sake! What's wrong with you? I must sit down, Cathy; my feet are killing me.'

'Yes, come in and sit down. I'll put the kettle on. I'm not going to that surgery, Mum; I'm seeing a homeopathic doctor.'

'A what doctor? Nothing wrong with your hormones, is there? You look all right to me.'

'Not hormones, Mother. Homeopathy. They're into natural remedies and diet and stuff. It sounds a better idea, for things like low blood sugar.'

'You haven't got low blood sugar. The GP said so last time. Aren't you going to offer me a cup of tea, Cathy? My feet are killing me.'

'I'll put the kettle on. I know he did, but I think he didn't know much about it. I want another opinion. Come into the kitchen if you want to talk to me.'

She stays in the sitting room and shouts.

'Did I tell you about . . .? D'you know what that Mrs Grantley said to me about Mrs Pargeter . . .? I told you about Solly's chess, did I? Well, d'you know what he's done now . . .?'

I shout back yes and no and quite and no really and how amazing, and in between shouting I spill boiling water over the bread and drop the packet of tea and knock the teapot lid on to the floor. What a wreck. I feel wobbly still. There goes my lie-in this morning as well.

'Would you like some toast, Mum?'

'Oh, tea. I thought I was having coffee.'

'I'm sorry. I did ask you and you said tea.'

'Did I? I wasn't thinking. I have tea first thing in the morning but for breakfast I prefer coffee.'

'I'll make you some coffee.'

'Don't go to any trouble. I can make it myself if you like. That train was so noisy and dirty; it's given me a headache. Trains never used to be like that.'

'Would you like some toast, Mother?'

'I used to travel by train all the time when your father and I were first courting . . .'

'Do you want TOAST!' I yell with sudden impatience.

She looks at me, shocked. 'Don't you speak to me like that, Cathy. After I've come all this way . . .'

'I'm sorry. Sorry. I didn't mean it. Would you like some toast?'

'I think you must be ill, dear; it's not like you to be irritable. When you were a little girl you were irritable when you were ill. I remember when you had measles . . .'

She follows me into the kitchen. 'You woke up one morning covered in a rash and do you know what you said?'

'Excuse me, Mum. Can I just get to the cupboard?'

' "Mummy," you said – just like that; you had a funny little voice. "Mummy," you said . . .'

'Could you just pass me the coffee jar, Mum? Second shelf on the left.'

'. . . "my chest is blushing." That's what you said. It was so sweet. "Mummy," you said, "my chest is . . ." What's the matter, dear?'

'Could I just get to the cupboard? Thanks.'

She corners me by the cupboard, back to the wall, just like Jim. I want to scream and hit her. My blood sugar is low. I must remember that. That's why I feel murderous; it always has that effect. Lack of sugar to the brain; the hospital doctor explained it to me that time. Aggression is just a symptom; I don't really feel aggressive.

147

'Here's your coffee, Mum.'

'Thank you, dear. There's no milk in it.'

'The milk's in the fridge. Behind you. You go ahead and sit down and I'll make the toast.'

'I don't want toast, thank you, dear. I don't have toast in the morning nowadays. I read somewhere that it's bad for the small intestine.'

'Can I just squeeze past you, Mum? Thanks. Can I just open this drawer?'

'Am I in your way, dear? Just tell me if I am. Blocks the bowel, it said. Something to do with refining the starch or whatever.'

''Scuse me, Mum. I'll just light the grill.'

'I'm not having toast – I said.'

'No, but I am. Do go and sit down; you must be tired. I'll be with you in a minute.'

She steps into the hall and continues to talk. 'Mrs Pargeter's daughter – you know, the ugly one, with the terrible acne? She had a blocked bowel. You know what they do . . .? That toast is burning, Cathy. You won't eat burnt toast. As a child you would never eat burnt toast. "I don't like the black bits," you used to say. So funny. "The black bits." Aren't you having butter?'

'I've run out.'

'You want me to go and get you some?'

'No, it doesn't matter.'

'No, I don't mind. I'll go.'

'The shops won't be open yet, Mum.'

'What about the milkman? Does he do butter? Or shall I go and ask your neighbours downstairs?'

'It doesn't matter. I'll have it without.'

'You can't eat toast without butter. You always loved butter, even as . . .'

'For God's sake, Mother!'

She is silent, pursing her lips.

'I'm sorry. I didn't mean to shout. Sorry. Come and sit down.'

'You're not well,' she tells me. 'I can tell. It's making you bad-tempered. I know you don't mean it.'

'No. That's right.'

'You aren't well, are you? Be truthful, now.'

'No.'

'There you are, then. Now come and sit down and let's have no more arguing; I'm taking you to the doctor's. You ring that friend and tell her I'll take you. We can get the bus if it's too far to walk.'

I give in. As a token bid for freedom, on my way back from phoning Wayne I call in at the newsagent's and sit down on the wall outside for a full ten minutes before going home. There are a couple of jobs in the Sits Vac pages that sound all right; public relations again but what else am I qualified for? Not a lot.

When I get back my mother has done all the washing up. Three days' worth.

'Thanks very much. Like some more coffee?'

'I wouldn't mind something to eat, now you mention it. I don't often eat at this time of day but travelling makes you hungry, doesn't it?'

'Do you want some toast?'

She looks reproachful. 'No, darling, I told you, it blocks the bowel. What I fancy, really, is a nice boiled egg. With a little bit of crispbread, if you have any.'

'Crispbread is just the same as toast!'

'No it isn't, dear.'

'Yes, it is!' After five minutes with my mother I appal myself by reverting to my teens. 'Sorry. I don't think I have any. How about egg and bacon?'

'I can't eat bacon, dear; it's too greasy. The doctor told me to stay off grease. "It's not good for you," he said. Crispbread is good, you see, because it's easy to digest.

It doesn't upset the intestine.'

'Well, I would go and get you some, Mum, but the shops won't be open yet and to be honest I'm feeling a bit kind of faint . . .'

'Fainting is a nervous thing. I read it somewhere. You can stop yourself from fainting by just not letting yourself think about it. It's like these hypochondriacs – they think about themselves too much. Don't boil that egg too long, Cathy; I don't like them hard. Three minutes after the water boils or three and a half if it's a large one.'

'How long are you able to stay, Mum?'

'Four o'clock, dear. I have to be back for Solly's supper. I've left him bread and cheese for lunch. "I can't help it, Solly," I said, "I'll have to go to my daughter if she's ill."'

'You've come up just for the day?'

'Four o'clock the train goes, but I like to be there a bit early just to be sure.'

'That's fine. I'll have to go to work this afternoon, Mum. We've got this press conference coming up . . .'

'But you'll come and see me off at the station?'

'I don't think I can. You see, I didn't go in yesterday and there'll be . . . I'm sorry.'

'No, it's all right. I quite understand. I got here on my own, didn't I? Got a taxi and everything . . .'

'That reminds me: I'd better go and phone for a minicab to take us to the doctor's.'

'Don't bother, dear. We'll go by bus. There is a bus, isn't there? No, I'm perfectly all right. I don't mind. They're such a waste of money, these minicabs, and I don't believe they're any quicker in the long run . . .'

The surgery – when we finally arrive – is part of a terraced house, with the bedrooms turned into a surgery and waiting room. The waiting room has four chairs and a coffee table on which a joss-stick is burning.

('Terrible smell!' exclaims my mother, in a piercing whisper. 'They burn those to cover up the smell of drugs, you know.'

'Homeopathic doctors don't use drugs, Mum!'

'No, but you know – dangerous drugs. These students. Mary-wana. It's true; I read it somewhere.')

'Cathy Childs?'

'Yes, that's me.'

'Would you like to come in?'

'Yes. No, don't come in with me, Mother. Yes, I know you don't mind, but I'd rather . . . No really, please . . .'

'I won't keep your daughter long,' says the doctor in his authority voice. 'Please make yourself comfortable here. Shall I turn the fire up for you?' Mother subsides, mollified, and I follow the doctor into the surgery alone.

'I shall have to ask you a few questions,' he says. The guy is a master of understatement. My medical history from the day of birth, my relatives' medical histories, my preference for heat or cold, my temperament . . . It goes on and on. Mind you, a couple of questions are really on the nail, like whether I ever get cravings for sweet things and if I feel ill at particular times of the day.

'Have you been under any stress?' he says finally, half-way through examining me, hitting my knees with a hammer while I cower on the couch with all my defences down.

But I'm not having that one. 'I don't think this illness is due to stress,' I say firmly. 'I think it's physical. And it's something to do with food – I know.'

He raises his eyebrows at me. 'If I am right – and I'll want you to have tests to confirm this – you are suffering from reactive hypoglycaemia. Blood-sugar imbalance. It can be triggered off by a number of things – and one of them is stress.'

'Oh, I see,' I apologize.

'So have you been under any stress?'

'No, not really. Not specially.'

He gives a patient sigh. 'Okay. Just tell me what circumstances in your life have undergone a change in the last twelve months. Right, I've finished. You can get dressed.'

'Well, I'm just about to change my job,' I say, struggling into my tights. 'And get a flat-mate, but I haven't done either of those yet. And my mother remarried a few months ago – does that count as a change of circumstance? And my husband died in February.'

He looks at me over his glasses. 'So,' he says dryly, 'you haven't been under any stress?'

'I've had this illness before,' I say defensively. 'You can't put it down to my husband dying. It's just that recently it's been getting worse . . .'

'You had the imbalance before,' he tells me. 'Over-production of both insulin and adrenalin. It's a form of diabetes; the blood sugar somtimes gets too high and sometimes too low. You were probably born with it, but it's worse at certain times – like puberty or when you're under stress or when you're overstimulating the system with artificially refined foods. So try to cope with the stress, OK? Talk to a friend when you feel upset, or take up yoga or a relaxing hobby. And what about your sex-life?'

'What about it?' I say, hostile. Why is everybody so interested in my sex-life?

'Does it exist?'

'No it doesn't, since you ask.'

He nods. Apparently he doesn't think it necessary to let me know the reason for his question because he goes straight on: 'And I want you to watch your diet. No refined carbohydrates or stimulants.'

'What does that mean? Cut down on the booze and dope?'

152

He looks at me sternly. 'I hope you are joking.'

'Yes, of course,' I say meekly.

'No alcohol or coffee,' he says breezily. 'No refined starches – sugar, sweeteners, white flour. Nothing containing preservatives. And keep off the high-sugar fruit – bananas and grapes. Oh,' he adds, 'and eat every two hours. Carry a snack with you always. All right? I'll give you a diet sheet with all this written down so you won't forget.'

'I won't forget,' I tell him. 'Don't eat anything worth eating but eat it every two hours – is that right?'

He pats me on the shoulder to cheer me up. 'Don't worry,' he says. 'You'll lose your taste for sweet things once the condition is stabilized. And it'll be worth it when you see how much better you'll feel.'

'It had better be,' I say hollowly. I write out a cheque for his services, though why I should pay the man to ruin what's left of my life, I can't think. If I've given up sex and dope, what the hell will I do without booze or coffee or food?

'I do think,' the doctor says, as I reach the door, with the diet sheet clasped ferociously in my hand, 'that you ought to open up a bit about your husband's death. It's not at all good to keep things pent up inside.'

'I've got over the worst of it,' I assure him. 'Really,' as he looks disbelieving; 'I coped with it okay.'

'I'll see you in three weeks' time,' he says, not committing himself.

'Well?' says my mother. 'How did you get on?'

'I've got to give up food,' I tell her gloomily, 'and take up nutrition instead.'

'Oh really, Cathy!' my mother exclaims, her temper popping like the gas fire in the overheated room. 'Why can't you give a straight answer to a straight question, for once?'

But then she relents and takes me out to lunch, which can't be bad – even if I do have to order cottage cheese salad without the pineapple chunks. It is nice of her to buy me lunch.

'This doctor seemed to think,' I tell her in a rush of confidence, 'that I ought to talk about Barry more.'

'I think he's right,' she says surprisingly. 'You'd feel better if you did. You've hardly mentioned him to me, since it happened.'

'You didn't like him very much,' I say sadly.

She looks uncomfortable. 'Oh, I don't know.'

I am surprised. 'Did you?'

'I didn't think he was good enough for you,' she admits. 'But what mother thinks anyone is?'

I shrug. 'I saw Jim the other night,' I say carefully.

'You told me. Jim and Carla. You said you'd seen them.'

'No. Yes. Anyway. Jim said he didn't think Barry had been much of a husband.'

My mother sniffs. 'He would.'

'What?'

'Sour grapes,' she says firmly. 'He always had an eye for you, that Jim. And he never liked Carla being so fond of Barry.'

'Really?' My mother amazes me sometimes.

'You may think your mother's a fool,' she says astringently, 'but I do notice things sometimes.'

'More than I do,' I agree. How humiliating. 'So you thought Barry was a success as a husband?' I pursue masochistically.

'What man is a success as a husband?' my mother asks rhetorically. 'I suppose he was, if he made you happy. He did make you happy, didn't he?'

'Oh,' I say, 'yes.' The knife slides off my plate and clatters on to the floor. Unaccountably, tears come into my eyes. 'Shall we go back?' I suggest. 'And have coffee before I go to work?'

It seems a long walk home.

154

'I'll make the coffee,' my mother offers. 'You sit down.'

It's good to sit down. For some reason I feel tired.

'Oh God!' I say, waking up with a start. 'What time is it?'

My mother is sitting by the window, holding a magazine up to the fading light. She peers at her watch. 'Quarter to four. I didn't wake you; I thought you needed to sleep.'

'You'll have missed your train!' I realize.

'I'll get a later one; I can phone Solly. Shall I make you that cup of coffee now?'

She's not bad really, my mother. 'Thanks.'

Halfway through drinking it I remember that coffee is one of the things on the banned list. Oh well. I'll start tomorrow.

I walk with her to the phone box, and while she's in there I go in the newsagent's and write out a card for the window, advertising the room in my flat.

'I'll go now,' my mother says, coming into the shop. 'Solly says I should get the next train if I'm lucky, and he'll meet me at the other end.'

'You go then. Thanks for coming up, and for the lunch and everything.'

'You'll be all right now? You're not going into the office really, are you?'

'No, it's too late now; I'll just phone. See you, Mum.'

When she is gone, I queue up for the phone box and call Alan. 'I'll be in tomorrow. Any messages?'

There is just one, from Diane Crosswell, who is beauty editor of one of the women's weeklies, to say that she's leaving the magazine to set up her own business and so can't attend the press lunch. I count out a pile of coins and call her back.

'I'll be taking a week off and then coming back to the office to tie up the loose ends,' she tells me. 'I would have liked to do a piece on your new range but the press conference is the week I'm away. I'll try to send someone along, but it's bound to be a busy time.'

'Mm. That's a pity. There are a few good things in the range.'

'Are there? Anything really new?'

'A couple of ideas that might be good for a story: a lot of glitter dusts in different colours, stick-on teardrops and hearts and things, toenail transfers – that kind of thing. But all in very subtle colours, coordinating pastel shades. A sophisticated version of teenage gimmicks, trying to tempt the older, up-market buyers to be a bit more adventurous.' When I get a new job, it will be nothing like this, I promise myself.

'That sounds interesting. We're a bit short of copy just now. My successor can't take over till later than she'd planned and I can't stay on, so I'm having to stockpile a few features to see us through. It's a shame your press do is just that date.'

'Well listen – what about having a preview? The story would have to be embargoed till after the press conference date, but I don't suppose that would cause you any problems, would it?'

'Could you do that?'

'As long as you've got the time before you go away. If you can manage a lunchtime we could make it a farewell lunch too.'

'That's sweet of you, but I don't think I can. Would it be too much to ask you to make it after work? Latish-early evening, Friday, say?'

Friday. That's Wayne's last evening.

'Could you make it Monday instead?'

'I really can't; I'm sorry. My partner and I will be working every evening from next week, to set up the business.'

'Okay then. Friday will be fine. If I book a table at Escargot and Friends for seven – would that suit you?'

Not that it makes much difference, really, if I say goodbye to Wayne on Thursday evening or on Friday. It's not important. It's just that I thought if he did want to go out on Friday it would be unfair to refuse, seeing as he's been quite kind and everything. But it really doesn't matter to me.

It's only when I've rung off that I realize that I didn't ask Diane what the new business was. Pity I didn't know before about her leaving; I could have applied for her job. Not that I would have got it, probably, without magazine experience.

Marcie comes round in the evening; she's been on the grapevine to Carla and knows all about me getting ill yesterday.

'And anyway I was going to come and thank you for leaving that money for Karen – she was thrilled. But why didn't you take those jeans for yourself? I was sure they'd look perfect on you, with the shirt.'

'I've had second thoughts,' I admit. 'Next time I come up, if they're still there I'll buy them.'

'Funny you should say that, darling,' Marcie says, 'because I brought them with me, just in case!'

So I write out a cheque to Marcie's boutique, and another one to Oxfam, as Wayne suggested. It will hardly redress the world balance of wealth but it means I can wear the jeans without feeling like an oppressor. And they do make me look nice and thin.

'If you have them dry-cleaned they'll last for ever,' Marcie claims. 'So don't go fainting on dusty pavements or anything! What happened to you yesterday, anyway? Have you seen a doctor?'

'This morning – though I wish I hadn't. I'll show you the diet sheet – God knows what I'm going to eat. But whatever it is, it has to be every two hours.'

'You already do that.'

'Not quite that often! I won't have time to work!'

'What does he think is wrong with you then?'

'Low blood sugar. Big surprise.'

Marcie pours herself more coffee. 'What causes it then?'

'Don't know. All kinds of things can, apparently. In my case he thinks it's been made worse by stress, but I don't know that I agree.'

'What stress?' Marcie says.

'That's what I said. I told him I wasn't under any stress but he didn't seem to believe me. So now I've got little white pills and a diet sheet and he's recommended yoga or something to calm my shattered nerves.'

'Now that's awfully good!' Marcie says. 'I used to go to yoga classes for years – did you know? It was when I was modelling. I used to go straight from a hard day's work with throbbing feet and a face that ached from smiling at the camera, feeling like nothing on earth, and afterwards I would feel so relaxed and full of energy, I would go home and clean the whole flat. You ought to do it.'

'I'm going to start meditation; it must be roughly the same.'

'Cathy, how fascinating! All that chanting. Someone was doing it on the tube the other morning: I couldn't take my eyes off him.'

'No, this is a silent form; you do have a mantra word but you say it to yourself. I have given it a try but it's really hard to concentrate. I kept thinking of things I should be doing at work.'

'You should go to a group. It's much easier,' Marcie advises.

'I'm going to, but you're meant to do it at home as well every day. There's a group on Monday evenings. Father Delaney runs it.'

'Father Delaney?'

'You remember, Barry's friend. The priest who married us.'

'But you're not going to him? A Catholic priest!'

158

'You don't have to be Catholic to go. A lot of the people aren't, apparently.'

'But Cathy, that's not what I meant! I mean, you don't want to get mixed up with that kind of thing. They'll try to convert you or something.'

'I don't think he's into conversions. I remember him and Barry talking about it once and he said you couldn't talk anyone into believing anything; the wish had to come from the person himself, like wanting to give up smoking. I can't see him trying the foot-in-the-door approach.'

'That's just where the danger lies!' Marcie declares. 'It's when you don't suspect it that you're most at risk.'

'Risk of what? You make it sound like a disease, Marcie! I've no intention of being converted to anything I don't want to be. If anyone tried to I'd just leave. They don't go in for brainwashing, you know!'

'Not directly, maybe,' concedes Marcie. 'But that kind of thing is awfully insidious. They can be peculiar, these religious people.'

'Well, Barry was one and he wasn't peculiar, was he?'

'No. No, not in general.'

'What do you mean, not in general?'

'Well . . . I mean, don't take offence, darling, will you, because it was all such a long time ago, but he did have some funny ideas, I used to think. About sex and so on.'

'In what way?' Barry may have been overenthusiastic about sex, but at least he was fairly normal. Or so I thought.

'He told you, didn't he, that ages and ages before he met you we had a brief . . . um . . . you know, darling . . . nothing serious. You know how it is. We'd known each other a long time and one night there was a party and we'd had too much to drink and Barry was a bit high and – well, there we were in bed together the next morning. You know how it is.'

'Yes.' I know how it used to be.

'So I didn't think anything of it. You can't let that kind of thing spoil a friendship, can you?'

'No-o.' I think of Jim. 'But what was so funny about Barry's ideas on sex?'

'Well, that was just it. He seemed a bit upset by it all. Thought it shouldn't just happen like that; there should be some sort of relationship. I did sleep with him a few more times, but it was obviously not going to work, so I pointed out to him that we were the best of friends and should really stay just that, because in bed we weren't too terrific together. I mean, we'd never been each other's type. If it hadn't been a boring party it would never have happened at all. But as I say, he was upset.'

'Maybe he wanted to think you fancied him not just because of the boring party.'

'Oh no, it wasn't that. He was quite honest about that. It was more that he seemed to think that as it had happened he had some kind of obligation – to me or to himself, I don't know – to make something of it. He thought that sex ought to mean something.'

'Well, maybe it should.'

'There you are, you see, Cathy! You have been influenced without even knowing it. It's terribly easy to pick up these points of view.'

'Perhaps it's my own point of view!'

'No, it's not. You used not to be like that. Not when I first met you, when you'd just met Barry. You were as casual and uninhibited as anybody. More so, if anything.'

'It's age that's done it, Marcie. Age and marriage and probably lack of stamina!'

'And living for two years with a Catholic.'

'Oh nonsense! Living two years with anyone would have the same effect. You just get used to a relationship and it spoils you for one-night stands. Barry compared it once to roast dinners and bags of crisps: once you get used to dinners you're reluctant to make do with snacks.'

'That's a typically Catholic viewpoint,' says Marcie seriously. 'You want to be careful, Cathy, honestly. I wouldn't go in for this meditation thing; I don't like the sound of it.'

'For heaven's sake, Marcie! I'll make some more coffee and we'll talk about something else. We're going round in circles. Did I tell you I put in an advert today for a flatmate? And I wrote off for a couple of jobs as well. Both public relations ones. I wanted to do something else really but when it came to the point I didn't know what else I could do. It's difficult without qualifications or experience and I'm too old to be considered for beginners' jobs in anything.'

'Darling, you've got hundreds of qualifications!' Marcie exclaims. 'I remember I was quite terrified when I first met you.'

'But they're not the kind that qualify you for anything. Were you? Why?'

'Your reputation went before you, darling. We heard that Barry had this terribly brainy new girlfriend; I was convinced you'd think me as thick as two planks and we wouldn't get on at all.'

'And to think I was terrified of you!' I return. 'I thought you'd be far too glamorous and successful to have anything in common with me.'

Marcie lets out a most unglamorous yelp of laughter. 'So when did you change your mind?'

'I think it was when you confided to me that the nurse at the family planning clinic scared you stiff.'

'She did! Awful woman! The first time I went there she came at me with this freezing cold metal implement and when I yowled – quite understandably I thought – you know what she said to me? "Ooh, we are a baby!" she said. "It's no different from having intercourse, after all." Well, I told her. I said, "I'm afraid I can't see the resemblance.

The men in my life actually aren't made of solid steel with a little clamp on the end." '

'Marcie, you didn't!'

'I did. Well really, of all the ridiculous things to say!'

We giggle into the coffee.

'Didn't you ever get the same nurse?' Marcie inquires. 'Nurse Broadbent she was called. She probably was, too.'

'More likely frustrated than bent,' I suggest. 'If she couldn't tell the difference between sex and smear tests, her love life must have been lacking in something. No, I never went there; you put me off. I used to go to the GP instead.'

Marcie sips her coffee and says, 'Are you still on the pill? Tell me if I'm being nosy.'

'You're being nosy. Yes, I am. I stopped taking it for a couple of months but I went back on it because I got period pain.'

'Ah yes.'

I can tell she doesn't believe me. She thinks I waited a couple of months then took a conscious decision to become available again.

'Is that someone at your front door, Cathy?'

'I'll go and see. The bell's just packed up; I must get it fixed.'

It's Carla. 'I've left Jim babysitting,' she says, 'so I can't stay or they'll murder each other or something. I came to see if you're all right.'

'That's nice. I'm fine, thanks. Did you drive over?'

'Yes, in that horrible car Jim's got while his normal company one's being serviced. I can't get the hang of the gears. Hello, Marcie!'

'Hi. I'm just going; don't take it personally, darling, but I have to cook supper.'

'I'm sorry – I never asked you if you'd eaten,' I realize. 'Why not stay and have something here?'

162

'Thanks darling, but no. You did offer me something actually, when I arrived, but I've got a friend coming round.'

'Desmond?'

'Mm-hm.'

'Who's Desmond?' says Carla suspiciously. 'You don't exactly waste time, Marcie, do you?'

'All this criticism!' Marcie complains. 'Anyone would think I was a man-eater or something.'

'Can't be,' says Carla promptly. 'You're too thin. OK Marcie, see you.'

'See you darlings.'

As she is going out, Elsa is coming up the stairs. 'This is becoming a party!' Marcie declares. 'And I have to be just leaving and missing it all!'

'Come back later then and bring Desmond.'

'I might just do that.'

She won't, of course. Who would, with the option of an attentive Desmond and a candlelit sofa for two?

Marcie, as she always does, continues talking all the way down the stairs, so I have to lean over the banister to finish the conversation.

'I'll phone up and ask you over for supper one evening, darling,' she calls from the hall.

'You must come here next time; I'm looking forward to meeting Desmond. I should have a proper party instead of an impromptu one really, shouldn't I?'

'Great idea, darling; we'll keep you to it. 'Bye now!'

Carla and Elsa have found themselves the Liebfraumilch in the fridge and the corkscrew and are having a discussion about flat-sharing.

'Cathy should stick to men; they're much easier,' Elsa declares. 'I was just saying, Cathy, that you should get men.'

'Have a harem, you mean? I could send them all out to

163

work and stay at home all day drinking Liebfraumilch. Provided you left me any. Those tankards are meant for beer, Carla!'

'Couldn't find any other glasses,' she says. 'Listen, did you buy this wine for anything special? Because if you did I'll nip down to the off-licence and get some more.'

'I bought it to drink; go ahead.'

'You're not expecting anyone, are you?' she says suspiciously.

'No, no. Well, Wayne is coming round later.'

'There you are!' declares Carla triumphantly. 'What did I tell you, Elsa? No-one wears a silk blouse on a freezing cold day in November without a reason.'

'Oh shut up, Carla. Pour me a tankard of wine. Oh no – better make it a thimbleful; I'm meant to be on the wagon. This is going to be a real drag.'

'You should drink Perrier water,' Carla advises. 'With ice and a slice of lemon, so it'll look like gin and tonic.'

'Well, it wouldn't taste like gin and tonic so that's not much consolation,' I say ungratefully. 'What were you saying, Elsa, about sharing a flat?'

'You should share with a man,' she repeats. 'They're easier to live with. Look at me; three of us in a flat, two men and one girl and we never have any problems. If one of the guys gets sore at the other he tells them to fuck off and it clears the air immediately.'

'I bet it does. It probably clears the flat immediately.'

'I don't see what's so good about that,' Carla says. 'It just proves that men are uncivilized.'

'Rubbish!' Elsa declares. 'It's far more healthy; look at those awful girls Cathy used to share with in Maida Vale.'

'What was wrong with them?' I say indignantly.

'Oh come on, Cathy, you remember. They were always going round not speaking to each other for borrowing each other's tights or something stupid.'

'That wasn't all of them, that was Moira, once, that time when she'd split up with her boyfriend. The rest of the time we got on really well. And at least they never left smelly socks in a heap in the bathroom, like your flat-mates do.'

'I'd rather put up with smelly socks than deep silences every time someone hurt someone else's feelings,' Elsa says.

'I wouldn't,' says Carla. 'Though I'd rather have smelly socks than smelly nappies. My only advice to you, Cath, is to share your flat with either a man or a woman but don't share it with a baby.'

'I won't. Babies aren't good at paying rent.'

'So, have you advertised yet?' Elsa asks.

'It goes in on Saturday. Local paper and the newsagent's window.'

'That answers what I came round to ask you, then,' Elsa says, 'which was what were you going to be doing over the weekend. I thought we could go to the wine bar or something.'

'I suppose I'll have to stay in, won't I? It's awkward not having a phone at home; I won't know when people are coming – if anyone comes.'

'They'll come all right,' Elsa says. 'They'll keep arriving till you barricade the door.'

'In that case I'll take the first person who turns up and stick a notice on the door to say the room's taken.'

'You must be careful, Cathy,' says Carla anxiously. 'You could get some really weird people.'

'I won't take anyone weird. What do you think then, Elsa? Do you want to go out?'

'Better not – really. You'll be up to your ears in people, I'm telling you. We'll go another time. How about Monday evening, or Tuesday?'

'Not Tuesday – it's the night before the press conference so I'll be working late. Monday would be fine.'

Somebody knocks at the door again. It must be my lucky night.

'By the way,' says Carla, 'your doorbell isn't working. That's going to be a nuisance if you've got people calling round.'

'I know. I'll have to fix it.'

It's Wayne, with a bottle of wine.

'I'm glad you bought that,' I say. 'We've almost finished the one I got to have with the meal.'

'It's for me,' he says, smugly. 'You're not allowed alcohol, remember? I might let you have one glass.'

'Very generous of you. You know Carla don't you, Wayne? And this is Elsa. Elsa, Wayne.'

'Hi. Goodness, is that the time? I must go.' Elsa drains her glass in one gulp and stands up.

'Me too,' says Carla. 'If I leave him too long, Jim will never offer to babysit again.'

'Don't rush off! Stay and start on the new bottle. I'm only cooking spaghetti; there'll be plenty to go round.'

'No really – must go.'

If it had been a girlfriend arriving, they'd have stayed the whole evening. Their haste to depart and leave me alone with Wayne is embarrassingly obvious.

'Frankenstein's monster must have felt like this,' he says ruefully. 'One glance at his face and people ran away screaming.'

'Elsa and Carla thought they were being tactful,' I apologize.

'I know. I don't mind really. I can put up with your undiluted company. Shall I open the wine?'

'Yes, do. Let it breathe or whatever it's meant to do. And while it's breathing we can drink some of it. I haven't started cooking yet. Are you starving?'

'Peckish,' he admits. 'I didn't have time for lunch.'

'Tell you what. How about having the pudding and cheese and biscuits first? Then we can have the spaghetti as a second supper afterwards.'

'You made a pudding? Great.'

'It's only cheesecake out of a packet. I did it while Marcie was here. Hell – and I can't eat any, can I? I'll have to sit and watch you.'

'We'll start with the cheese and biscuits then,' he says consolingly, 'and you can carry on eating them while I start on the cheesecake.'

So we have the meal in two stages, solemnly drinking coffee after the cheesecake before starting cooking the Bolognese sauce, for which Wayne chops the onions.

'As a farewell meal this isn't very impressive,' I acknowledge, 'but I've got out of the habit of doing organized cooking.'

'What's with the "farewell meal"?' he says, aggrieved. 'I'm not going until Saturday. It's only Wednesday.'

'I've got to see this beauty editor on Friday evening. It's the only day she can manage.'

'What time will that go on till?'

'Hard to say really. I don't want to rush her. But she's in the middle of setting up a new business so maybe she won't have much time.'

'And you're doing something tomorrow night?'

'Not as far as I know.'

'Well then – how about having a farewell meal tomorrow? We'll go out somewhere.'

'Okay, that sounds nice.'

Do you think I should tell him I'm frigid or let him find out? Or maybe he isn't like that. His manner is not what I'd describe as platonic, but you never can tell. Perhaps he likes my company, but doesn't fancy me. I wonder, idly, what he'd be like in bed. Warm and friendly, I should imagine, and not very exciting.

'You're miles away,' says Wayne. 'What are you thinking about?'

'I was just thinking,' I say glibly, 'that the sauce looks almost ready to eat.'

7

On Thursday, Alan and I stage a mutiny and demand a new
secretary. Or rather, I do the mutinying while Alan stands
behind me providing moral support. That's what he calls it
anyway.

'We must have a temp, at least,' I say firmly. 'A proper
one from an agency, who can type fast. I've got all the press
kits to do and the ring-round for the conference on Wednesday.'

Big Harry wears his most forbidding frown. 'I'll get Personnel to organize someone for Monday.'

'We need someone today,' I say, standing my ground.
'Monday would only give us two days to prepare the whole
thing, and Alan's got loads of work to be done as well.' I
feel Alan could back me up a bit more at this stage: he is
halfway out of Big Harry's office, his hand apologetically
caressing the door handle.

'Not possible,' says Big Harry with finality. 'Not the
same day.'

'No,' agrees Alan, cravenly. 'Not the same day.'

'It's been done before,' I point out. 'It's worth a try. Shall
I have a word with Hortense in Personnel and see what she
thinks?'

Big Harry shrugs. 'If you want to. I think it's a fool's
errand, personally.'

'Then I'll send the fool to try it,' I say evenly, and exit
from the office, sped on my way by the force of Big Harry's
glare.

'What the hell got into you?' Alan says when we're
safely behind our own desks. 'You were a bit over the top.'

'Desperation,' I say, 'at the idea of having to do all that work myself. I've used up the weekend and all my free evenings except for Tuesday, so I couldn't even get it done in my spare time. Not that I want to, anyway.'

'You're getting very uncompromising, did you know?'

'Yes, I know. I'm thinking of leaving.'

'I always feel like that before a press conference,' Alan agrees.

'No, seriously. I've started applying for jobs.'

'You won't earn more than you're getting here,' he says flatly. 'Not at your age. And you mightn't even get such a free hand. Big H. may have his faults but at least he's lazy. You could end up with a diligent boss who won't delegate. Your only alternative is to work for some crappy little one-horse organization where the PR department is just you. Then you'll have ten different bosses, from the MD to the sales and marketing directors, plus the personnel manager and God knows who else thrown in, all telling you what to do and giving you all the shitty jobs they don't want to do themselves.'

'Have you finished putting me off?' I inquire. 'There is one other alternative, which is to get a job that isn't in public relations.'

He gazes at me. 'Not PR?'

'Don't sound so surprised! I've said often enough what I think of it. You have too, come to that.'

'But you can't just opt out,' he says. 'You'd have to start at the bottom in something else.'

'So?'

'So you'd lose a thousand a year in salary, for a start, plus having to take a job with less status than you've got now, plus wasting all that experience.'

'Surely it's worth it, to get a job you like better? It's only two years' experience, after all. I'm twenty-five. You're not suggesting I stay in this job till I retire, just for the sake of status and salary now? And what kind of status does writing about cosmetics give you, anyhow? Come on, Alan, you've been rude enough about it before!'

He shrugs. 'You'll find out the hard way.'

'Well, what's the alternative – tell me? You're always saying that PR's a waste of your talents. What are you planning to do yourself?'

'I shan't be here for ever,' he says crossly. 'I'll move around – move up. I'm taking that course to improve my qualifications.'

'But what do you see yourself ending up as?'

'I don't know, do I? It's too far ahead. I could go in for general management or I could stay in PR.'

'End up in Big Harry's shoes, you mean? The head of a PR department?'

'I could do worse,' he says belligerently. 'You've got to be realistic.'

'I suppose so. Probably no-one will employ me, anyway. I'll end up destitute. When you're Big Harry I'll sit on the steps of Bantam House and wait for you to throw me a crust. You could get into practice now and make me a cup of coffee.'

If I take a lunch-break today I'll have a look through the Sits Vac ads in the daily papers which are piling up, unopened and unscanned for mentions of Bantam products, on the secretary's desk. But before I do anything else I will go and see Hortense.

Hortense is in a meeting but her secretary's there.

'A temp for today?' she says. 'Well, I'll try ringing round the agencies but you may have to wait till Monday.'

'Could you call my extension and let me know?'

'Sure.'

She calls me ten minutes later. 'I've just remembered,' she says. 'Accounts had a good temp for three days this week but they didn't need her today. I've just phoned the agency to see if she's still free and they're trying to contact her at home. I'll call you back when I hear.'

If we don't get someone today I decide it would be quicker to write the news releases to go in the press kits directly on the typewriter. Trouble is, my typing isn't too good and I keep changing what I'm going to say. I have just thrown away the third draft when Hortense comes in.

'Fall at my feet and give thanks,' she commands. 'A temp is arriving in half an hour.'

'That's amazing! How did you manage it?'

'Jenny managed it,' she admits.

'She's fantastic then.' I ring her and tell her so.

'I know,' she says blithely. 'And modest with it.'

'You wouldn't like a permanent job, would you?' I offer. 'Steady hours except before press conferences; charming, easy-going people to work with . . .'

'Hey!' protests Hortense. 'Is this the thanks I get? I get you the perfect temp and you try to steal my perfect secretary.'

Beryl Evans is indeed the perfect temp. 'I'm not very good,' she says nervously, arriving exactly half an hour later. 'I've only just come back to work, you see, since my kids started middle school. My typing's not too bad but my shorthand is slow.'

'You do shorthand as well! That's fantastic. How slow is "slow"?'

'About seventy words a minute.'

'I couldn't talk that fast if I tried! But listen, are you happy to use it? Because it could save an awful lot of time. I've got this press conference on Wednesday, you see, and the last secretary couldn't type, so nothing's been done . . .'

Beryl is happy to use her shorthand. She is happy to take down my faltering dictation, complete with frequent reprises of 'Oh no, could we change that last bit . . . ?' She is happy to type news releases, with hardly an error, to answer the phone in a pleasant voice, to lend Alan an

172

aspirin for headache, to tolerate Big Harry when he bursts into her office and rifles through the filing cabinet, leaving the papers all over the floor when he's finished . . .

Arrangements for the press conference start to go wrong, as arrangements always do. The designer has changed the design for the posters, because he is young and enthusiastic and thinks he is paid to be artistic and not to convert Big Harry's ideas into paint.

And Nick, the Creative Director at the agency (who is paid to tell the designer not to be creative but to do what the client wants), has failed to spot the difference until too late. So the sample boxes – which have been photographed for printing in magazines as the Actual Product – are of one design and the posters are of another.

So Nick is afraid Big Harry will fire him from the Bantam account and then the agency will fire him from his well-paid expense account/company car job, and before he leaves he will fire the poor young designer . . . It takes six phone calls back and forth to calm him down, to persuade him not to murder the designer and to convince him that Big Harry will never notice the difference between the designs in any case.

After the fourth phone call, Beryl comes in with a cup of coffee. 'I wasn't sure how long you'd be on the phone, so I thought you might like this to keep you going. Would you like one of my sandwiches? They're ham.'

I am just refusing the offer when the phone rings again. 'Cathy Childs.'

'It's Julie, from Samson Photography. Barty asked me to ring to say the Cloud Ten photos are ready and he'll drop them in some time this afternoon.'

'Oh, while you're on – could you tell me how long it would take to do another studio session? We're going to have to change the logo on the boxes . . .'

'I'll get you that sandwich,' Beryl says.

At six o'clock we are still in the office. Nick has phoned again: he will have the sample box changed to the new design and pay for it to be re-photographed in the evening – at double rates – out of his own pocket. It must be nice in a way, to have a job you care so much about losing.

His anxiety has taken up a lot of time.

'I can stay another hour if you want,' Beryl says, 'but I'll have to ring my husband to let him know.'

'No, don't stay. We'll start again tomorrow – that's if you can come in tomorrow?'

'Oh yes. Have you any idea how long they'll be needing me here?'

'For as long as you want to stay, I should imagine. They've been advertising for a permanent secretary for ages. Every time Personnel find somebody suitable Mr Diggins vetoes them because they're not blonde, or for some other reason best known to him.'

'Would that be why I was turned down, do you think?'

'What?'

She smiles, embarrassed. 'I applied for this job,' she says. 'It's funny being sent here as a temp, isn't it?'

'You applied for this job and you were turned down?'

'I passed the first interview, with some man in Personnel, and the typing test and everything. He said it was fine by him but the appointment would depend on the second interview with the Public Relations Director, and he'd let me know the date and the time. Then I didn't hear anything so I phoned up and was told the job had gone.'

'When was that?'

'About three weeks ago.'

The job was still unfilled three weeks ago, except for Sharon, the temp who didn't like working for women.

'That's amazing! Big Harry promised Alan and me that we could sit in on the second interview! Then whenever we

174

asked he said there'd been no applicants recommended by Personnel!'

She shrugs. 'That's life, I suppose. It's a pity because the job seems interesting from what I've seen so far. Well, I'd better be off.'

'Yes. See you tomorrow. And thanks for putting up with my dictation.'

'Ask him,' says Wayne.

'Oh, I don't know. If I'm leaving . . . The next person mightn't like her.'

'But if she's better than anyone you've had so far . . . And you say she wants the job.'

'She did. She may not when she gets to know Big Harry. Or when she gets to know Alan and me for that matter!'

'What does Alan think of her?'

'I haven't had a chance to ask him. He's been at the factory most of the day and in a non-speaking mood for the rest of it. I'll talk to him tomorrow and see if he's willing to brave Big H. again. He's afraid of falling from favour.'

'Have you given in your notice yet?'

'No. No way, till I find another job! I've only applied for two so far. Wayne, have you seen the right-hand column of this menu?'

'You're not meant to look at the prices. It's on me. And don't pick grapefruit followed by a green salad; have what you want.'

'Fine. I'll have caviar and grouse.'

'Okay.'

'I didn't mean it! I haven't decided yet. What are you going to have?'

It seems funny to be taken out to dinner. Since February I've only been in restaurants for business lunches, or else to local wine bars with Vicky or Marcie or Elsa. Not tête-à-tête dinners in chic places like this with crisp linen and soft candlelight which casts gentle shadows over people's faces. Last time was with Barry at Marcello's. There was candlelight there too, fresh flowers and smiling waiters and beautiful food, but Barry and I were oblivious to all of it, unspeaking, each of us locked into our own private terror . . .

'Don't look so worried,' Wayne teases. 'If I can't pay the bill I'll let you wash up.'

'Yes.' I don't really hear him.

'You're not worried, are you? I know you said the other time that you didn't want to go out to dinner. Does it bring back memories?'

'No, not at all. It's lovely to go out. Have you chosen yet?'

'You don't talk about him much, do you?' he says gently.

'About Barry? No, well it was a long time ago now. I've got over it.'

'Eight months isn't very long to get over it.'

'Everyone else thinks it is,' I say bitterly. I didn't mean to say that. He is being sympathetic for the sake of politeness, because he's a nice guy. I am not going to start moaning to someone I have known for one week and will not see again after tonight. 'I think,' I say quickly, 'I'll have mushrooms *à la grecque* and then Dover sole. How about you?'

Over dinner he talks about his new job.

'Are you nervous about it?'

'Not really. Not about the job. I've met most of the people and the work's just a continuation of what I've been doing here. I'm more apprehensive about moving to a new place, finding somewhere to live and so on.'

'You could just find something temporary at first,' I suggest, 'to give yourself a base while you look around. You can always move again if you don't like it.'

'If I don't like it, I'll come back,' he says. 'My present

boss has said they'll find me a job if I don't want to stay on after the month's trial.'

'You must be good, then.'

He grins. 'Oh, I'm brilliant. Do you want a pudding? Oh no, you can't. Cheese and biscuits?'

'I'll have a pudding, if you're having one. Just this once.'

'No you won't. It's not worth making yourself ill for.' He's serious, what's worse.

'You're a terrible nag, has anyone ever told you?'

'Bloody cheek. After I let you have a whole glass of wine, as well. Waiter . . . .could we have two cheese and biscuits?'

Cheese is boring on its own, especially when there's a trolley full of apple shortcake and Black Forest gateau staring at you, so Wayne relents far enough to order a bottle of St Emilion to go with it. In tastebud terms, it's a million miles away from my customary supermarket plonk. It has the texture of velvet and the taste of nectar. It warms the soul and loosens the tongue. I tell Wayne the story of my childhood, about my brother Bill who used to steal Crunchies and now is a respectable lawyer; about my sister Lizzie who went on a school trip to France and came back engaged to an Australian ten years her senior; about my mother, who thought you could never trust men unless they were where you could see them, safely ensconced in an armchair, to be scolded and dusted round; about my father who thought women were wonderful, except for the one you happened to be married to, and who finally left home for one who would bring him breakfast in bed and clean up the tide-marks left round the bath without admonishing him for the trouble he caused.

And Wayne in return, his tongue equally loosened by the wine, tells me about his father who refused promotion all his life because he felt that work should not claim all your time and energy, and about his mother who had once taken Wayne and a schoolfriend fishing and nurtured a secret passion for it ever since. 'She gets up at dawn on cloudy Saturdays and sneaks off in the car with my cast-off waders and fishing tackle. She wouldn't confess at first where she was going; we thought she must have a secret lover.' And he talks about his sister, who spent a year in a commune and now appears to be founding her own, by having a baby every year.

The wine makes Wayne mellow. He orders some more. The second bottle makes me maudlin. 'I feel,' I say sadly, 'as though I've come adrift in life. I have to tread water all the time to stay afloat, but waves keep breaking over my head.'

Wayne looks worried. 'What do you mean?'

'If I knew that,' I tell him, 'I'd know the answer as well. Ignore me, it's the wine talking.'

'Will the jobs you apply for all have to be in London?'

'Not necessarily. That's what I mean really – I think. I could do anything, go anywhere; I've no ties. I even thought of selling the flat and going to Australia to see my sister but since I'm advertising for a flat-sharer I suppose I must have decided against that one.'

'How about going to Sheffield instead?'

'Sheffield?'

He laughs. 'It doesn't sound much of an alternative to Australia, does it? But if you heard of a job there – or perhaps if I did – would you leave London?'

'I don't know,' I say slowly.

'Think about it,' he suggests, 'while I go to the Gents'.'

Leave London. I don't know. Leave all my friends, and my flat – Barry's and my flat. And for what? For a city I've never been to and a guy I met in a supermarket a week ago. Put that way, it would be ridiculous. Put another way, if Barry had asked me to go to Sheffield, or Hong Kong, or the moon, after I'd known him for one day, I'd have gone. I don't feel that way about Wayne, but then many people

178

never feel that way about anyone, and don't expect to. Barry was an exception. How many exceptions can you have in one lifetime? Sometimes, as Marcie says, you just have to take second best.

I am staring pensively at the guy at the next table when I become aware that his girlfriend is staring resentfully back at me, so I shift my gaze to the flowers on the table, which are beginning to wilt by now. The candle has burned itself to a stub, its flame flickering feebly. Like a short-lived friendship, with nothing to sustain it. Tonight is his last chance to seduce me, if he wants to. This wine is making me muddled. He can hardly suggest going back for coffee, anyway. We've drunk about a gallon of it here.

The guy and his girlfriend stand up to go. Wayne, on his way back from the Gents', asks the waiter for the bill. I'm glad he pays by credit card; I'd hate to see all those notes on the plate and think that we'd eaten and drunk them all.

'Want to come back for coffee?' suggests Wayne.

'Okay.' Maybe I should take Marcie and Jim's advice. You can't be a hermit for ever. It's just that it seems so . . . Oh, never mind. 'Or you could come back to the flat,' I invite. 'It's nearer.' And it'll save me the indignity of an early-morning walk home tomorrow for a clean dress and teeth before I go to work.

'Fine.'

It's bitterly cold outside. By the time we get home we'll probably both be frozen solid. ('Before we get into bed, there's one thing I should tell you. I've got frostbite in my knees.' That would solve an awful lot of problems; we'd both be immobilized, one on either side of the bed, two little stick-figures with icicle limbs. 'I'm terribly sorry, but I can't seem to move my legs.' 'Me neither.' 'Oh dear, what a pity. Better forget it, then. Some other time, perhaps – when spring comes and the thaw sets in.')

'Are you cold?' he asks.

'Frozen frigid,' I say truthfully.

He looks at me quickly and grins. Oh yeah. He's not as goody-two-shoes as he looks.

'I'll make the coffee,' I say, as I open the front door. If he wants coffee he shall damn well have it. 'Black or white?'

'White.'

He'd better drink it, that's all. He'd better not leave it cooling on the floor till tomorrow morning.

'Shall I put a tape on?' he says.

'Yes, do.' How corny. He'll put on some snoozy music and turn the lights down. In my flat, too.

He puts on some heavy rock music and the lights stay on. He drinks the coffee. He makes himself at home, stretching out in the armchair, but doesn't take his shoes off. Actually, this is quite cosy. It's nice to sit here with someone, companionably not talking. If he's going to pounce he'd better get on with it before I fall asleep.

He comes and sits next to me on the floor.

'It was a nice meal,' I say. 'Thanks.'

He puts his coffee mug down on the floor. 'I wish I wasn't leaving London now,' he says. 'If I'd known I was going to meet you I wouldn't have applied for that job.'

If he's going to be nice I shall cry. Why can't he just get on with it, and discover I'm frigid, and walk out the door saying, 'Yeah, well, I'll ring you some time . . .' and get it all over with? And what if I'm not, after all? He puts his arm round me and settles himself more comfortably. I don't know how long it is since anyone cuddled me. I think it must be a long time.

'Is that someone at your door?'

'It can't be. What's the time?'

'Half-past one.'

'It can't be!'

'Maybe it's your neighbours or something.'

'I'd better go and see.'

It's Adrian. 'Are you difficult to get hold of!' he exclaims. 'How do people contact you, with no phone?'

'They ring me at work. Do you want to come in?' He does.

'I've just had my first night,' he explains.

'Your what?'

'First night. *War Game*. It went really well; the audience were great.'

'That's good.'

'I was going to invite you along but I couldn't get in touch with you. So when I was passing and saw your light still on . . .'

'Oh. I see.'

He is in the sitting room. 'Hi,' he says to Wayne.

'Wayne, Adrian.'

'Hi.'

'Adrian's an actor. He just had a first night.'

'Did it go well?'

'Great. The audience were great. It's called *War Game*; it's all about this guy who . . .'

'Coffee?'

'Yeah, that'd be great. Not interrupting anything, am I?'

'No, no,' say Wayne and I simultaneously.

'Great. It's about this guy, see, who . . .'

We all sit around – on chairs, decorously – sipping yet more coffee and talking about Adrian's play, Wayne's new job, my prospective flat-sharer. The tape runs out and I put another one on. The wine is making me feel sleepy and the coffee is making me sick. Or the other way around. Perhaps I should eat something. But I can't eat biscuits and I can hardly hand round apples. Or a third of an apple, seeing there's only one left.

'I must go,' Adrian says. 'Listen, do you want to come and see the play, Cathy? I can get you a ticket any night. That's if I'm not poaching on anybody's territory?' He looks at Wayne.

181

'No,' says Wayne, 'of course not.'

'Come too if you like,' Adrian offers.

'Thanks, but I won't be here.'

'Oh yes, the new job. Well – what night then, Cathy? How about Saturday, or will you have to be around for flat-hunters?'

'Next week would be better probably.' I wish he would fix something quickly and go home. Not that I don't want to go to the play but it seems unkind, in front of Wayne, to make arrangements for when he's gone.

We finally agree on Tuesday. It's the night before the press conference, but never mind.

When Adrian leaves, I move to go back to the sitting room, but Wayne says, 'I'd better go too.'

'Had you?' Perhaps it's just as well. Frigid or unfrigid, I'll find out sooner or later. You can't make use of people like that, use them as a kind of thermometer. Anyway, I doubt you can tell for certain in just one night. Maybe it's for the best.

Wayne doesn't look as though he thinks so. The relaxed mood is broken, the cosiness gone and a hangover looming. He looks hurt. He has no right to be hurt if someone else asks me out after he's gone. He knows that. But still he is hurt. He isn't looking at me. I pat his arm, in a sisterly sort of way, and say, 'It's been a nice week.'

He looks at me then, and hesitates. 'About tomorrow night,' he says. 'You've no idea what time you'll be finished?'

'Not really. But you've got your leaving party anyway, haven't you?'

'It's only a few drinks after work. Most of the guys have trains to catch. How about if you called round on your way home or something?'

'It could be quite late,' I warn.

He smiles. 'I don't go to bed all that early. Okay?'

'Okay.'

'See you tomorrow then.'

'Yes. Unless it's incredibly late. Just in case it is, good luck with the job.'

Mrs Pratt will be complaining about all the footsteps going up and down the stairs late at night. I must remember to tell the Pratts about getting a flat-sharer. Or maybe I'll leave it till I've actually got someone, so it's too late for them to object.

8

Carla phones me at work first thing in the morning, while I'm sipping my first cup of tea and talking to Beryl, to say that they're going to have the baby christened.

'Why the sudden decision?'

'Well . . . I don't know. It's hard to explain. When you have a child you feel you want to give it all the chances, you know? Even if you're not really sure if there's anything in it. Anyway, what I want to ask you is will you be Louise's godmother?'

'Carla, I'd love to. Um – does Jim agree? I mean, do you both . . .?'

'It was his idea to ask you,' Carla tells me.

'That's great. I'd love to, then.' Perhaps it's some kind of gesture; his way of making up. 'Tell me what I have to do.'

'I'm not sure; I hoped you'd know more about it than we do.'

'And don't you have to be confirmed or something? I'm not a paid-up member of any religion, you know that? I'm not sure I was even christened myself.'

'Well, it doesn't matter to Jim or me and I don't know who else is going to check up. We've got to go and talk to the vicar yet anyway, so we can ask him about the qualifications then, but in the meantime couldn't you have a word with that priest? The one you said came to see you the other day.'

'Father Delaney? He's the wrong denomination.'

'Does it make much difference nowadays? A godmother is a godmother, I would have thought. Anyway, don't worry about it because I'm sure you'll be quite acceptable.

As long as we all keep quiet about your lurid past.'

'When I was a concubine to the sheikh, you mean, or when I tried to poison my mother-in-law? The vicar isn't going to object to little details like that – be reasonable, Carla.' Beryl is listening open-mouthed; I think she believes me.

'Oh, of course not. No problem. The Church of England is very broadminded these days. Look, I must go; your future godchild is making a most unholy row.'

'I can hear her. Have a lovely peaceful day. And Carla – thanks a lot for asking me. I'm flattered, really.'

'So,' Beryl says as I put the phone down, 'you're going to be a godmother? Would that be your sister's child?'

I'm glad to know that someone else is as nosy as I am. I can't stand people who pretend to be – or perhaps they really are – uninterested in other people's affairs. The kind of upright citizens who put the phone down the instant they realize they've cut in on a crossed line and who studiously ignore any letters left hanging around. The type who consider it dishonourable even to read the entries on someone's kitchen calendar (which tell you fascinating things like who came to dinner with the calendar-owner last week, how much she owes the milkman, how many days her period's overdue and when the dog is going to the vet). I have no scruples about my interest in such things, regarding it not as snoopiness, which is vulgar, but as an indispensable means of gathering information about the richly varied facets of human life. Or at least that's the best excuse I've come up with so far.

I reckon Beryl, as a fellow life-inquirer, deserves a full and informative reply but our conversation is interrupted by Alan, arriving only fifteen minutes late.

'Hi, Alan. You're early. Late, but early-late. Is it some special occasion?'

He turns his back and starts unpacking his briefcase to

indicate that such jibes are beneath his contempt.

'I'll go and see if the mail's come,' Beryl decides, sliding hastily off the corner of my desk. She raises her eyebrows at me as she goes out.

I've given up asking Alan what's wrong when he's in a mood. He either won't answer or else he goes into long explanations about the injustice of landlords, employers, friends, lovers, relations or life in general, which tell you nothing except that he's in a mood. So I let him go on ignoring me and slamming books about, and concentrate instead on drafting some notes on Cloud Ten to give to Diane Crosswell when I see her this evening.

I'm not good at notes. They start off as briefly-jotted ideas and turn into fully-grown sentences halfway down the page, so I have to go back and turn the jottings into sentences too.

'Beryl, could you type this by the end of this afternoon? It's for a beauty editor I'm seeing tonight. How are you getting on?'

She is getting on fine. She has sorted out all the work into order of priority and is making her way through the list methodically.

'On Monday and Tuesday,' I say, 'we'll have to do the ring-round. That's phoning all the journalists we've invited, to remind them and to see if they're planning to come. Then we can do the name-badges: I've got some cloud-shaped ones arriving on Monday.'

'Is there any chance I could come along on Wednesday?' Beryl says. 'I'd like to see what goes on.'

'It would be nice if you could, but it really depends on Alan. I've been giving you all my work so far because of the press conference, so Alan's will be piling up. What we normally do is get a couple of girls from a promotions agency to hand out drinks and so on, but if you'd like to do the reception duties I could ask Alan if he'd mind.'

'Yes, have a try. If he says no, never mind.'

'Are you still keen on this job, Beryl? Permanently, I mean?'

'I would be, if it was going. I wish I knew what that Mr Diggins had against me, before he even met me.'

'I'll try to find out. Like some coffee?'

'Please.'

'Alan. Coffee?'

'Yuh,' he says, without looking up.

I think the atmosphere will have to thaw a bit before I start asking him favours about sparing Beryl on Wednesday.

'Carla just phoned,' I say chattily, 'to ask me to be godmother to Louise.'

'Who's Louise when she's at home?'

'The baby,' I say patiently. 'Have you any idea what a godmother's supposed to do?'

'Is it likely,' he says, 'that I would have?'

Either I have offended him in some way or else Jerry's 'rapturous reunion' was one-sided.

'By the way,' I say, 'did Jerry tell you I saw him the other night?'

He put his pen down. 'How you can have the bloody nerve to ask,' he says slowly and with venom, 'I really don't know.'

I stare at him. 'What do you mean?'

'I mean,' he says, 'that your interference in my personal life is just about unforgivable.'

'Alan, he picked me up at the gates and said he wanted to talk to me . . . I didn't . . .' I am stammering stupidly. I have never heard Alan talk like this. He is really angry. He stares at me as if he hates me.

'You told him about me,' he says. 'You talked to him about me and gave him advice. You had no fucking right to interfere!'

187

Put like that, it sounds terrible. I sit down the other side of his desk. 'Yes,' I say slowly. 'You're right. I shouldn't have done. I'm really sorry.'

'It's a bit bloody late.'

'Why – what happened?'

'It doesn't matter what happened!' Alan yells, his voice rising to a scream. 'It's the fucking principle of the thing. Why don't you keep your bloody nose out of other people's business?'

'Alan, I didn't mean . . . I'm really sorry. He seemed so upset; I didn't know what to say to him. And I was sick. Otherwise I might have thought a bit more . . .'

'Spare me the excuses.'

'Okay. I'm sorry. What else can I say? If I've done any harm I really am very sorry.'

'It's not a question of harm, I've already said. I just didn't want him turning up when I didn't expect him.'

'I didn't tell him to go round to your flat! He just shot off.' Without even giving me a lift home, I'm about to add when a thought strikes me. 'Oh my God – you didn't have someone else there?'

'No I didn't! It's just that the place was a mess, and I was a mess, in scruffy old clothes and I hadn't washed my hair . . .'

I don't believe this! 'Oh, Alan, Jerry's known you for years! He wouldn't worry about things like that . . .'

'That's not the fucking question!' he bawls. 'It doesn't change the fact that you went butting in where you'd no business to!'

'No, it doesn't. And I've said I'm sorry and I really am. If there's anything I can do to make things better . . .'

'Just stay out of my life!'

'All right.' As I make the coffee my hands are shaking. Alan and I have had our differences in the past, but nothing like this. Why didn't I think before I talked to Jerry? Why did I even get in the car, instead of insisting it was none of my business and he and Alan should sort out their problems for themselves? Just because I was too sick to argue and wanted to get it over with and get home. Not a very good reason for betraying a friend. And now it's too late and Alan will never regard me as a friend again. I put his coffee down in front of him.

'Alan, what can I say? Forgive me, will you?' I'm not good at apologizing. Barry and I used to skip it after a row. I'd make some silly joke and if he laughed I'd know I was forgiven, and the tension would break and we'd usually end up in bed. It's a method of apology that wouldn't be a wild success with Alan, so I have to swallow my pride and be humble instead.

'Forget it,' he says, without looking up. I am not forgiven.

To escape from the atmosphere I go to see Hortense about Beryl.

'Did you know that Beryl – who has turned out to be the perfect secretary – applied for the permanent job with Alan and me, and Big Harry wouldn't interview her?'

'Really? Wait a minute; I'll look it up. Are you feeling all right, Cathy?'

'Yes, why?'

'You look terrible. Your hands are shaking.'

'It's the drink. She came for the first interview about three weeks ago.'

Hortense finds the application form. 'Typing speed fifty, shorthand speed seventy; that's acceptable for the job, isn't it?'

'Perfectly.'

'Interview notes . . . mmm . . . mmm . . . sounds fine. Bob Griffiths interviewed her. Oh yes, I remember this one. He had quite an argument with your Mr Diggins. You'd better not let this go any further, Cathy, but Harry

Diggins turned her down on age. He said a married woman with school-age children would be unreliable.'

'Unreliable! For four months we've had nothing but temps who don't show up, can't type, or refuse to do half the work. At the rate Beryl works, she could take three days off a week and we'd still be gaining.'

'Well,' says Hortense, closing the file, 'I'm not the one you should be telling, am I?'

'Should I talk to Bob Griffiths?'

'If you want to. It won't do any good because he already agrees with you. It's Harry Diggins you'll have to speak to.'

'Again! I'm not his favourite person at the moment.'

'Take your courage in both hands, my dear,' says Hortense bracingly. 'You can't expect Personnel to fight your battles for you.'

Nor Alan. I have to ask him first, though, if he wants Beryl to stay. At least it may get him talking again.

'Big Harry said she'd be unreliable,' I tell him.

'All women are unreliable,' says Alan nastily.

I take a deep breath. 'But Beryl seems very good at the job. So if she still wants to stay, do you think I should speak to Big Harry and see if he'll change his mind?'

'If you believe in miracles.'

'But, what I'm getting at is – would you be happy for Beryl to have the job?' I don't believe in miracles. It would take more than that to make Alan happy.

He shrugs. 'I can't say, can I? She's hardly done any of my work so far.'

'Have you got anything urgent to be done?'

'That's not the point.'

'By the way, what would you think if she came along on Wednesday? Would you need her to be here that day?'

'It strikes me,' he says, 'that if she stayed she'd be more your secretary than mine.'

'No, not at all. It's only because there's a lot of paper-

190

work for the conference. Once that's over, she'll take the work on the normal basis.'

He shrugs again. 'You do what you like. I don't know why you're asking me. She seems to be your friend.'

I can either be sweetly patient or hit him over the head with the cut-glass ashtray. 'I'm asking you,' I say, not very sweetly at all, 'because she'll be working with you as well and because you're probably staying here longer than me.'

'I don't know why you're bothering, if you're leaving.'

'Because she'd like the job!'

'So?'

My hand hovers over the ashtray, longingly. I give up. When I'm halfway out of the office, he says, 'So what are you going to do?'

'I'll have a word with Big Harry. He can only say no.'

'He will.'

'Probably, yes.' I open the door again.

'So you're still going on with this stupid idea of leaving?' he says truculently.

I look him in the eye. 'You want me to stay?'

'Please yourself,' he says. 'I don't care.' And he picks up the telephone.

Big Harry's giving dictation to Hazel.

'Sorry, I'll come back later.'

'No, stay,' says Big Harry. 'I want a word with you. You can get on with that lot, Hazel. I'll call you in when I'm ready to do the rest.'

He swivels his chair in my direction and Hazel obediently gets up to leave. Hazel does what Big Harry tells her to do. Always. Big Harry is obviously waiting till she has left the room before he starts talking to me, so I get in first. Otherwise he says his piece and then dismisses you; by the time you remember what you came in to say you are firmly outside the door.

'I wanted to ask you about Beryl Evans,' I say.

191

'Who is Beryl Evans?'

'The temp. She's very good. Good typing and shorthand and pleasant on the phone and interested in the work.'

'And?'

'Couldn't we offer her the permanent secretary job?'

'Hmm. Don't see why not. Would she take it?'

Amazing. He doesn't remember turning her down. Should I tell him after all? It would be so much easier not to, and Beryl wouldn't tell. But there'd be a hell of a row if he ever found out. Better not.

'She applied for it before.'

He looks startled. 'And?'

'She got past the first interview.'

'Why didn't Personnel send her to me?' he says angrily.

'Perhaps she didn't sound suitable to you,' I say carefully.

'Rubbish!' he declares. 'I've never heard of the woman before.'

I decide not to pursue this point. 'What do you think then? I think she would be satisfactory.'

'All right,' he says. 'Good thing to have the vacancy filled. Send her in to see me, will you?'

'Okay.' I can't believe it was so easy. I stand up to go.

'Sit down a minute.' He actually says this, not barks it. He must be in a good mood today. I'm glad that somebody is.

He clears his throat importantly. Obviously some great announcement is pending.

'Err . . . how are the preparations for the press conference going?'

'Not bad. The badges and the posters will be ready by Monday or Tuesday at the latest. I'm going to meet the agency girls on Tuesday and I'll go in early Wednesday morning to set up the room at the hotel.'

'Good. Good.' He is not really listening. 'Tell me . . . er

192

'... Cathy. Tell me – how long have you been with us now?'

'Two years.'

'Mmm. Two years. Yes.' Long silence.

'Why?' I dare ask. Is this a way of breaking it to me that I've been pushing my luck with him for two years two long?

'I was thinking . . . perhaps a company car might be in order.'

'A company car?' I must go for a hearing test soon.

'Hm. Yes. Hm. Go with the job, you know. Press Officer for the cosmetics and toiletries division. It seems quite in order.'

'You mean – a company car for me?' I have to get this quite straight.

'Right,' he affirms.

'But I don't drive.'

This floors him. 'You don't . . . er . . . don't . . . er . . .'

'Drive,' I supply. 'No, I never got round to learning. Alan drives,' I add.

'What?'

'Alan. If you think press officers qualify for a company car I expect Alan might like one.'

'Hah.' He doesn't appear enchanted by the idea.

I wonder what this is leading up to. He must want something. It can hardly be a prelude to seduction; he tried that one two years ago, without that kind of subtlety. He can't want me to buy his wife's birthday present for him, because Hazel does that. Likewise go shopping for his new baggy suits. Likewise accompany him on business trips to the States, and sundry more informal duties that don't appear on the job specification form. So what does he want from me? Unless giving company cars to juniors is some kind of tax fiddle for him, but if so it's one I haven't heard of before.

'Still,' he says, 'these perks are worth having, you know. I'd give the matter careful consideration if I were you.'

'Okay.' It seems a waste of time to reiterate the pointless-
ness of having a car if you don't drive. It requires more than
mere logic to induce Big Harry to give up an idea once he
has got hold of it. Perhaps, though, I am being unfair in
attributing to him an ulterior motive. Perhaps he is being
genuinely nice, looking after my interests, getting me perks
to show he appreciates my work. You never know. I should
be more grateful.

'Right,' he says. 'Right.' He dismisses me by picking up
the phone, and I fade obligingly into long-shot.

'Big Harry wants to see you,' I tell Beryl.

'What about?'

'He doesn't take me into his confidence but I'd guess that
he's going to offer you the job.'

'You asked him!'

'Me?'

'I know you did. Thanks very much, Cathy. I really
appreciate it.'

'Sure you want it?' I tease her.

'Yes, I do. Even if one of the bosses has got a sore head
this morning.' She nods towards the inner office. 'What was
Alan shouting at you about?'

'Oh, it was my fault this time; I asked for it. By the way,
Big Harry knows you applied before but he doesn't
remember it. It's up to you whether you remind him or not
but I'd advise not, knowing him.'

'No I won't. Wish me luck, then.'

'Good luck. If I hear screams, I'll come and save you.'

'Is that meant to give me confidence?' She flicks at her
hair, straightens her skirts and goes out.

'Alan, I think I ought to warn you that Big Harry is having some kind of brainstorm.'

'Oh, what?' he says, quite normally, then dips his head
over the desk again, remembering that he is meant to be
not speaking to me.

194

'He's just offered me a company car. I think he must want something but I can't work out what.'

Alan flushes easily. He is a light shade of crimson now.

'Do you know something about it?' I ask, surprised.

'How the fucking hell should I?' he says vehemently. 'If anyone phones for me I'll be in Charles Fisher's office,' he adds, making for the door.

I let him go. Mysteries at Bantam, like dead fish in stagnant water, rise to the surface quickly. I have long ceased trying to fathom the murky shallows of company politics, and everything at Bantam is political.

Eight phone calls while Beryl and Alan are out of the office. I dash from one extension to the other like a demented hen. Also, my hangover, which has been hovering discreetly, descends now with massive tactlessness. It serves me right after last night. I try to remember that it was worth it at the time, but the very memory of the taste of wine makes my head ache.

Finally, I ring the switchboard and ask them to put all Alan's and Beryl's calls through to my extension. As soon as I've done this Alan returns, closely followed by Beryl. She doesn't look happy; in fact she is almost in tears.

'What happened?'

'He offered me the job,' she says, 'at a thousand a year less than advertised.'

'He can't do that!'

Alan bursts out laughing. 'What a bloody nerve!' he says admiringly. By tacit consent, Beryl and I turn our backs on him. Perhaps he was right to fear we'd gang up on him.

'Why, Beryl? What reason did he give?' Even Big Harry wouldn't be blatant enough to say it was because she was not young and blonde, and he'd be had up for discrimination if he said it was due to the fact she has school-age kids.

'Because I'm being taken on from being a temp,' she says

195

angrily, 'rather than "going through the official channels" as he put it.'

'But you went through the official channels – you applied for the job three weeks ago! I told him that!'

'I know, I told him too. He said that was just the point. In the normal way he said I wouldn't have been considered for the job, but since I was here as a temp I had proved to satisfy the basic standards. That's what he said – "proved to satisfy the basic standards".' She is crying properly now.

'Oh, listen, I'll go and see him . . .'

'No, don't,' she says. 'It won't do anything except get you in trouble. And I wouldn't take the job now, not if he offered me five thousand more. I'm sorry, Cathy, because I liked working with you, but as he said you'll be leaving anyway . . .'

'He said I'd be leaving?'

'That's what he told me. I said that you seemed to think that I was above the "basic standard" and he said it was an individual opinion and that you were thinking of leaving soon anyway.'

'But how did he . . .?' Instinctively I turn towards Alan, who has coloured up again like a traffic light. 'Oh, Alan, you didn't tell him?'

'How was I to know you hadn't already told him?' he says, looking out of the window.

'You know. You know I hadn't. I wasn't going to hand in my notice till I'd found another job.' I am almost joining Beryl in crying too; the office will be awash if we aren't careful. Big Harry would love that. There you are, he would say triumphantly, I always said women were too emotional to be in business. But Beryl reduces the flood risk by going back to her own office.

'I'll finish that typing for you,' she says, 'before I go.'

'It's not my fault,' Alan tells me angrily. 'Anyway, he can't make you hand in your notice till you want to.'

'I'll hand it in now, after what he's done,' I say 'How can I have worked for two years for a man who offers a person a job and then docks the salary?'

'Don't get hysterical,' says Alan uncomfortably. 'It isn't your battle, is it?'

'Injustice is injustice. I shall tell him . . .'

'No you won't. Calm down, for God's sake. He's always been like that. Don't blame him for your pre-menstrual tension or low blood sugar or whatever's bugging you today.'

'I haven't got . . .' But I have, actually – both of them. Plus an almighty hangover. 'All right. I'll leave it till tomorrow and think about it.' I'll talk it over with Wayne tonight, if I manage to see him after Diane Crosswell and if I live that long after he tried to poison me last night with all that alcohol.

I go back to my desk and start some work when another thought hits me. 'Oh God. The company car. So that was it. He wouldn't come right out and say why did I want to leave; he had to pretend he didn't know and then try to bribe me . . .'

'For God's sake, Cathy, give the man a break. What do you expect business people to be – saints or something? If he offers you a company car then grab it with both hands and don't start questioning the motives. This is industry, not a vicarage. What are you doing?'

'I'm going to give him my notice.'

'Fine,' says Alan. 'Good. Go hang yourself and see if anyone cares.'

On the way through Beryl's office I see her packing up to leave. 'I've left that news release in the tray,' she says. 'I'm sorry about your press conference and everything but you do understand, Cathy, don't you?'

I do. But I wish that someone would understand about my press conference.

I deposit my written notice on Big Harry's desk. He picks it up and reads it.

'Wait a minute.' We are back to barking again. 'Has this got anything to do with . . .'

'Yes. And ten thousand other things.'

'Okay,' he says. 'Okay. You've made your point. Tell Mrs Evans she can stay. For the full salary.'

'Mrs Evans is just leaving,' I inform him.

'Well, stop her,' he says, 'and tell her she can have the extra money.'

'She won't take it,' I tell him.

'My God!' he thunders. 'What do you women want if it isn't money?'

'To be treated like human beings,' I say, with the bluntness which only a hangover can bestow. 'It's not much to ask and it's cheaper than salary rises and company cars.'

'When,' he demands, 'have I ever failed to treat anyone like a human being?'

This question is so unanswerable that I make for the door before my hangover says something really rude.

'Look, Cathy,' he says, man-to-woman, 'why don't we just forget the whole incident? You put this piece of paper in the wastepaper basket where it belongs and I'll organize a replacement secretary.'

'One who can type?' I challenge. 'And one who can start five minutes ago and work fifteen hours a day until Wednesday?'

'I'll try.' Sarcasm is wasted on him. Beryl was wasted on him. My hangover is wasted on him. He holds out my notice. 'Chuck this thing away,' he says, 'there's a good girl.'

'No, keep it,' I say soberly. 'I mean it.'

'Cathy, don't cut off your nose to spite your face. You won't find another job like this one, you know.'

'No,' I agree. 'I don't think I will.'

* * *

Lunch with soggy chips. Phone calls, including one from Nick at the advertising agency, afraid that I will have betrayed his Fatal Error to Big Harry. I reassure him that I have not, that the new poster is truly lovely, that the redone photos can be captioned at the last minute on Tuesday evening, that the world will not end, that my head will not explode even though it feels as though it will . . .

Do hangovers just feel the same as low blood sugar by coincidence, or are all hangover victims in fact suffering from low blood sugar, and if they're the same thing is there a way of preventing the nasty symptoms without going to the extreme of laying off the alcohol? And is the fact that I seem to spend most of my time these days feeling lousy due to the fact that I'm developing rampant hypochondria, or is it due to the fact that my life is generally lousy and so feeling physically lousy is the inevitable result? Or should I stop agonizing about the state of my head, my stomach, my love life and the chips and concentrate on the basic essentials of life, like writing a really stunning news release on the subject of Toenail Picture-Transfers for the Older Woman?

Big Harry, not surprisingly, fails to find a temp who will work for three hours this afternoon. Hortense, not surprisingly, refuses to give his urgent request for a competent temp by nine A.M. Monday morning high priority, since Beryl has called in to Personnel and explained to Hortense why she is leaving. I pass the Personnel office just as Hortense is telling Big Harry in her forthright and heavily accented voice: 'There must be some reason why you cannot keep your staff.'

She must also have learned from him that he cannot keep his Press Officer (Cosmetics and Toiletries), for she comes into my office during the afternoon to try to persuade me to reconsider.

'Hortense, you've just said he's a bastard, so isn't it logical that I want to leave?'

'He was a bastard two years ago. Why didn't you leave then?'

'That's what I've been asking myself for two years. I've finally come to my senses.'

'You know, Cathy, take it from me – jobs like the one you have will not fall at your feet.'

'I don't want another job like this one. I've wasted two years of my life on writing about toenail transfers and I've decided that's enough.'

'Don't say that,' says Hortense, 'or you'll make me think about all the years I've spent selecting people to sell the toenail transfers.'

We have a laugh and a cup of tea and both go back to our socially useful jobs.

Four o'clock, and Alan leaves early to meet Jerry up in town.

'Alan,' I say, as he's putting his coat on.

'I know,' he says quickly. 'I'm sorry too.'

'Have a good weekend.'

'Yuh. See you.'

Five o'clock, and Diane Crosswell phones to ask if we can make it seven thirty at Escargot and Friends, instead of seven o'clock. That means we'll finish half an hour later and I may not get to see Wayne. I have given up kidding myself that it doesn't matter to me, that I'm simply afraid of disappointing him. I am simply afraid that if I have to survive the rest of today and all the days beyond it without just one more dose of his friendly attention and affectionate arm-round-the-shoulders, I shall quite definitely disintegrate. Which is disturbing because it makes me realize I've come to depend on him, in just one week, and that in the circumstances he is the last person I should have become dependent on, and that anyway I should be dependent on myself and not expect other people to salvage me from the wreckage of my screwed-up emotions.

So. Seven thirty it is. I get there early and ask the waiter if he knows of a fool-proof hangover cure. He consults the wine waiter, who argues with the chef. They can't agree on whether the Angostura bitters should be used as well as the Worcester sauce or instead. I decide the whole idea was a mistake and settle instead for a slimline tonic with lemon, which is equally nasty for about a third of the price.

Diane is late and apologetic. 'Have you been waiting for ages? You must think I'm a real pain – all this rushing about being harassed and busy. I hate people like that myself.'

'Not at all. I envy you. I gave in my notice at work today so I'll soon be very un-busy. Shall we get the business bit over first and then we can talk about sensible things while we eat?'

She orders a vodka and lemonade, while I stick to tonic, and she reads through my hungover script on toenail transfers.

'That's great; I can use that word for word. You're too good for public relations, Cathy. You'd be amazed at the garbage we get in from some of the other manufacturers.'

Over lasagne (and several more vodkas for Diane and no more slimline tonic for me – a little goes a long way and then starts coming up again), Diane tells me about her new business.

'A friend and I are setting up a little publishing house, packaging health and beauty books – that's preparing the text and artwork for publication for the bigger firms. We started off with three trial projects, expecting to have no offers at all for years, and got them all accepted by two quite well-known publishers. So we'll have plenty of work to launch us; it's All Systems Go from this week onwards.'

'It sounds great. It must be really good to be your own boss.'

'You should try it yourself,' she advocates, with the zeal of the newly-converted.

'I would, only I have two handicaps. No skills and no money.'

'You can write and deal with people and you've got business experience. And you don't need money, just a friendly bank manager.'

'And a lot of nerve.'

'That's true,' she concedes. 'And the arrogance to believe that somebody somewhere can't live without your professional services.'

Her enthusiasm carries her through the evening. The restaurant fills and empties again as she expounds her theories on businessmen and recounts anecdotes of life on a women's magazine. She is witty, funny and good company. Wayne will be in bed by now, getting some necessary sleep before his early start tomorrow. I will have missed him. I'll probably never see him again; perhaps on a flying visit from Sheffield to see all his friends in one weekend.

'Shall we have some more coffee?' suggests Diane.

'Yes, why not?'

'You're not in any hurry to get home are you, Cathy?'

'No, none at all.'

'That's good. It's nice to have a leisurely evening. I've been living on bought cheese sandwiches eaten at sprinting speed. It buggers your sanity as well as your digestion.'

My watch has stopped. By the time we emerge from the restaurant, though, all the pubs are closed, without any stragglers hovering outside, the cinema is open only for all-night porno, and the streets are devoid of buses.

'Can I give you a lift?' Diane offers.

'Thanks. Just to the top of the road will be fine.'

I'll call in at Wayne's, just tiptoe up the stairs so's not to wake everyone, and leave him a Good Luck note so he'll know that I made the effort to come, even though it was too late.

It's bound to be too late. He'll be asleep by now, for

202

sure. In the light of the hallway I scribble a hasty note. There is still a rim of light around his door. I'll just knock very softly. The door opens almost immediately.

'I thought I'd be too late.'

'I thought you weren't coming,' he says simultaneously, and then he is kissing me – my mouth, then my neck, eyes, face, then my mouth again.

This is the guy I'd marked down as 'warm, friendly and not very exciting'. I must have been mad. I must have been thinking of someone else. My mind is trying to be sensible, or at least to keep track of what his hands are doing. My body is unfurling to his touch, warming itself after its cold winter hibernation, expanding under the gentle, insistent pressure of his body. I switch my mind to 'off' and my body to 'automatic pilot'. Make love, not decisions. I couldn't stop now anyway, and Wayne is not likely to either.

Wayne stops.

'Cathy,' he says, his eyes and his voice blurry, 'I just have to be sure – is this what you really want?'

Being a rational, sensible creature I respond to this rational, considerate question by turning away from him and bursting into tears. But I stop almost at once. I don't cry now.

He comes over, and stands behind me with his arms around me. 'I'm sorry,' he says. 'But tell me what I'm sorry for. Is it for starting, or for stopping?'

I have to laugh at that, which is a mistake because my nose, clogged with tears, joins in with yucky snuffly noises. 'I wasn't exactly fighting you off,' I point out.

'So . . .'

'So I wish you hadn't asked me that question,' I admit.

'What's the answer?'

'I don't know.' All the elation has died out of me. We are two very ordinary people in a down-at-heel bedsit on a cold, dark November night, drawn together by age-old needs for warmth and sex and comfort and excitement, and perhaps by not much more. 'I'm sorry,' I say dully. 'I don't know what I really want. See, you shouldn't have asked. Why did you?'

'Because,' he says, 'you're the best thing that's happened to me in a long time and because I'm going to be away tomorrow. It isn't much to offer – the odd weekend visit, and phone calls at work. I don't want to love you and leave you in an emotional heap.'

'I'm already on the emotional scrap-heap,' I assure him. 'I abolished emotions months ago. I'd been meaning to break it to you gently that I was frigid, did you know?'

'And now you've broken it gently to yourself that you're not.'

'I suppose so. Except that I don't think I'm fully thawed.'

'Even a frozen chicken takes ten hours at room temperature,' Wayne points out. 'If you rush it you only end up with food poisoning. Take your time.'

'I'll go home then and let you get some sleep.' He has finished his packing; the room is stripped of everything that made it his for the time that he lived here. He has removed his personality, folded it neatly and stowed it in the suit-cases that stand in a corner of the room. It's as though he has already gone. Why prolong the leave-taking?

'Stay and have some coffee?'

'No, I'd better go.'

He doesn't try to dissuade me. He's probably keen to get it over with, too. 'I'll walk back with you,' he says.

Outside it is dark and drizzly, with no moon and no stars.

'There's no need to walk all the way with me. You'll get soaked.'

'It's okay.'

Poor guy. Frustrated and forlorn, rejected and rained on, his collar turned up against the cold. He takes hold of my hand, but my fingers are frozen.

'You ought to get some gloves.'

'I've got some, somewhere.'

Outside the house-door I hesitate. It would be silly to ask him in, since I refused to stay at his place, but it seems churlish not to. Wayne saves me the decision.

'Well then,' he says. 'I'll say goodbye.'

'Yes. Good luck and everything.'

'Thanks. Good luck with the press conference.'

He's like that; he remembers things, even in the midst of a change of lifestyle.

'Thanks.'

This is silly. There should be some easy formula for saying goodbye to people.

'I'll phone you,' he says.

That's it. The formula. The trusty old cliché which has liberated so many people from awkward partings. ('Don't call us; we'll call you.' 'I'll phone you.')

'Fine. Well, goodbye then.'

''Bye.'

He kisses me on the tip of my nose and then, gently, on the mouth. Then again on the mouth. Okay, I've changed my mind. He can stay. He can stay all night and complete the thaw. We can lie together mouth to mouth, body to body, skin against skin, with the duvet forming a roof above our heads. The duvet. The one I shared with Barry. No. No, I can't, not yet.

''Bye.'

'Goodbye.'

From the upstairs window I watch him walk down the street. He looks back once and I wave, but the window is darkened and he can't see me. When he turns the corner I'm suddenly aware of the darkness behind me, and grope for the light switch by the door.

What a day of disasters. Upsetting everyone I've come in contact with, almost. Alan, Beryl, Nick, Big Harry and now Wayne.

I get ready for bed, on my own. What a paragon of virtue

I am. Father Delaney would be proud of me. Big deal.

Thinking of Father Delaney – what did I do with that leaflet on meditation? Except that I can't go on Monday, I just remember, because I've arranged to go out with Elsa. Still, there's no reason why you can't do it at home. I had a quick try the other day, but I haven't looked at the pamphlet yet. Perhaps I didn't do it properly. It's so hard to concentrate. I find the pamphlet on top of the bread-bin. Wayne must have left it there while making the coffee the other night.

I'm not going to think of Wayne right now. Nor later either. What's the point of keeping on thinking about people who are gone? Though as Barry's mother said, when he died, 'I'll never believe that he's gone. He'll always be alive, to me.' I knew what she meant but somehow, coming from her, it sounded possessive and grim.

I'm not going to think of Barry either, or of death. It's the wine that has this effect on me, and late nights. Depression is a physical thing, an imbalance of chemicals. My chemicals are disturbed. Like those evil-smelling substances that Barry used to decant into test-tubes and shake and peer at intently.

Not Barry. Not Wayne, not goodbyes and partings and being left alone in an empty flat with no love and no plans and no future.

So. Meditation. The mantra phrase is meant to clear your mind, so the pamphlet says, of all its everyday clutter of thoughts. No more clattering, churning, unwelcome thoughts – faces and voices and phrases and endless, circling words. Peace. A time to listen, to be receptive, to let the presence of God be felt.

Sounds ideal. Just what I need: Father D. was right. Cross-legged on the floor, back straight, eyes closed, silently reciting the magic, meaningless phrase to empty my mind.

In time with my breathing. Rise and fall. The presence of God. I don't know. I thought I'd felt it, or something like it, a couple of times in the past. In church, with Barry beside me. Once or twice, just a hint of a presence there – not an alien being enthroned on a cloud, but something as much a part of me as myself. Only once or twice, a brief glimpse, a hint. The rest of the time, just nothing. Repeating meaningless words, listening to stories written centuries ago by uneducated fishermen. Not much relevance to daily life. 'Consider the lilies of the field', when the world is all motorways and airports now, with jet-propelled people hogging the fast lane.

'I'm not the religious type,' I told Barry. 'In all the times I've been going to Mass with you I must have clocked up about ten seconds of real prayer.'

'That's great,' Barry said. 'Ten seconds of realization of a whole dimension of life that some people close their eyes to for ever.'

Barry was like that: he always took the optimistic view. Even at the end . . . I'm meant to be emptying my mind, not letting it fill like a tank with a steady flow of long-dormant memories.

So, try again. A blackness and a blankness, a detachment from the ceaseless, directionless motion of body and mind and external things. A silence as deep as death. Could it have been like that for Barry? A gentle darkness in which to float free, released from time and space, from hurry and anxiety, from doubt and mistrust and fear? Or did he detach himself from life with difficulty, hanging on to the fraying threads of it until they faded out of meaning and left him, unanchored, drifting in the void?

Right, that's it. I'm not going on with this meditation thing. What's the point of clearing your mind of its workaday anxieties about friends and jobs and how to pay the bills, only to find that they've made room for the major, suppressed anxieties about life and death and suffering and peace?

Back to reality quickly: making coffee and pouring a drink while the kettle boils, and opening a packet of cigarettes. I don't care if it is escapism and all of it's bad for the health. Whose business is it if I need to escape, and kill myself in the process? If there are things you just can't face then it's better to do anything rather than think about them – isn't it?

Marcie's right. It's out to catch you, this religion lark. All it does is make you feel uncomfortable and make your life more difficult. You have to be brought up to it, to thrive on a masochistic lust for truthfulness, brushing aside the comfortable deceptions and carefully-built defences and facing life raw and naked, without weapons and without shields.

I've got so far towards it several times but I lose my nerve when it comes to shedding all those defences. How can you finally make that act of trust, cast yourself on the mercy of a God you can't even see, confident that he will reward you with sanity and not leave you bruised and broken and mad? I can't bring myself to that point. Perhaps I'm spiritually frigid as well.

'And nobody can be good all the time anyway, so it's just hypocrisy.' I remember arguing with Barry.

'Not hypocrisy,' Barry objected. 'Just plain human failure. As you say, it's a difficult way to live. You're aiming for perfection.'

'So why even try? Why not just sit back and enjoy being a sinful slob?'

'Because,' he said, putting his head on one side to consider his reply, 'people don't enjoy sinking to the bottom. Deep down, you know, you're worth more than that. If you're not reaching upwards you're not really living.'

We had quite a few discussions like that. We kept our own views, on the whole, but we both unbent a little, influenced each other a little over the years as married people do, blurring their outlines where they touch.

Cigarettes give you a nasty taste in the mouth at this time of night, and an even worse one to wake up to in the morning. I finish the coffee and the gin I'm not meant to have, and in token deference to my diet munch a single Ryvita before I go to bed.

Under the duvet I could have shared with Wayne. Alone on the single pillow, winter-cold to the ears. Oh Barry, if I could have you back for just one night . . .

You know, I can't remember the last time I slept with him – the last time we had sex. It must have been fairly ordinary, I suppose. The very last time was a non-starter and so doesn't count. Barry was either too ill or too anxious or too guilty, or all three. Impotence was the final indignity.

It had happened once before, I remember, but that was different. Returning late from a party, I was drunk and sleepy and he was stoned and overconfident. In his mind he was Super-Lover, but his body refused to cooperate, and he drooped like a joint that's been smoked by too many lips. Too passively pissed to help out, I lay and giggled feebly at his wasted energy till he rolled over on to his back and peering accusingly under the bedclothes yelled, 'Up, damn you!' and I laughed so much I had to get up and go to the loo. Later, I read an article that said wives should be warmly supportive and sympathetic through episodes of impotence, and I felt suitably guilty.

The last time was different; there was no laughter then, only silence and secret anxieties – me wondering about Janice, and Barry thinking about . . . I still don't know.

This is useless; I'm never going to sleep. I get up and light another cigarette and put on a record and the late-night TV horror film without the sound. When it ends, I watch the dot in the centre of the screen till it bleeps at me and it sounds like my thoughts, a single high-pitched wail.

9

I finally get to sleep, but am awakened half an hour later by someone hammering on the door. I run to open it thinking the house must be on fire, and this stocky, red-haired bloke walks in.

'I've come about the room you advertised,' he announces.

I am outraged. 'Do you realize what time it is?'

'Five to nine,' he says. 'Why?'

'Oh, is it?' I say lamely. 'It feels a lot earlier.' I fold my dressing gown more securely over my chest. 'Would you like a cup of coffee?'

'No thanks,' he says briskly. 'I've got a list of places to see if this one's no good.'

I decide I don't like him. He walks past me and pushes open my bedroom door.

'That's my room,' I tell him. 'The one that I'm letting is down here.'

'I'll need to see the whole flat,' he says. 'The kitchen and bathroom are shared, right?'

'That's right.' The kitchen and bathroom are not shared; they are mine. I am not having this guy in my bath. Or keeping his cheese next to mine in the fridge. And I know who'd end up cleaning the loo.

He flings open cupboards in the kitchen. 'Not much space.'

'I'd clear a cupboard,' I tell him, 'and half the fridge.'

'What about washing?'

'It's compulsory.'

'No,' he says patiently. 'Is there a washing machine?'

'No, there isn't. There's a launderette down the road.'

I'm not having his socks dripping over the bath either. Come to think of it, I'm getting less keen by the minute on having any part of him in any part of the flat. It's not often you taken an instant dislike to someone but this guy I feel I have known five minutes too long.

'The room's a reasonable size,' he says. 'The rent's a bit high. Would you take a pound a week less?'

'Sorry.' Good. He won't take it.

'Worth a try,' he says philosophically. 'Okay, I'll take it. I'll move in tomorrow; one week's rent in advance.'

Over my dead body. 'Actually,' I say, 'I've got other people coming to see the place yet.'

He looks annoyed. 'First come first served,' he claims.

'Not the way I do it. I'm going to see everybody and then decide.'

'You can't do that,' he says. 'It's discrimination.'

'I have to live with the person,' I point out. 'I'm entitled to be discriminating.' I didn't mean to be so blunt, but at least it will get rid of him quickly and let me open a window. His best friend hasn't told him about deodorants and I don't want the next person (if anyone comes) to think it's me.

'You mean you don't like me,' he says accusingly.

'I think perhaps,' I say carefully, 'we might not get on.'

'I can get on with most people,' he says. Then, belligerently, 'Why not?'

'You're the wrong star-sign,' I say at random. 'I can only live with Leos.'

'I am a Leo.'

Shit. He would be.

'You've got red hair,' I say desperately, resenting him for making me sink to kindergarten level. Why can't he take a hint and get out?

'So have you!'

211

'That's what I mean. It wouldn't work. Two fiery tempers in one flat.'

'I'm very even-tempered,' he says crossly.

I have run out of arguments, short of telling him that he smells and I can't stand the sight of him. And I have the feeling he wouldn't regard those as reasons for not wanting him.

'Leave me your phone number,' I suggest, 'and I'll let you know.'

'When?'

'Monday.'

'I might have found somewhere else by then.'

We stare at each other with hostility.

'That's the risk we'll both have to take.'

He leaves, slamming the door, and without giving me his phone number.

I am left feeling slightly shaken. I had no idea I could be such a cow. So much for my theory of taking the first person who comes along. 'You can live with anyone really,' I had told Carla airily. Except if they smell and are totally obnoxious. It's not that I'm at all intolerant, but people like him should be strangled at birth.

I'd better get some clothes on before anyone else turns up. I am struggling into my jeans (I haven't got fatter; denim shrinks in the wash) when I hear someone calling through the letter box. It's a young couple with matching sweatshirts and hairstyles.

'I don't think your doorbell works,' says the guy.

'No, it doesn't. I'd forgotten. Come on in.' I hadn't expected a couple. 'Is it both of you . . .?'

'Yes.'

'Oh. The room isn't all that big.'

They inspect it unenthusiastically, holding hands.

'Would we have to share the sitting room?' the girl asks.

'Yes.' I can see this wouldn't be a success; I'd feel I

was playing gooseberry in my own flat.

'We could put the stereo on the chest of drawers,' the girl says to the guy.

He shakes his head. 'What about the telly?'

'We could always take some of the furniture out,' she says. 'We've got our own bed,' she tells me. 'We wouldn't need this one.'

'Ah.'

'And the wardrobe; if we moved the wardrobe out, there might be room . . .'

Someone else is knocking at the door. 'Excuse me,' I say. They carry on replanning the room together.

'The doorbell doesn't work,' says a plain, dumpy girl clad in home-knitted woollies.

'I know. I'm sorry. Come in.'

The young couple drift out, hand in hand. 'We'll let you know,' they murmur.

The new girl surveys the room. 'It looks all right,' she decides.

'Would you like to see the sitting room?'

'Not necessarily. I'd sit in my own room. I believe in people having their own space. I need peace in the evenings to get my head together.'

'Oh, do you?' I think of the evenings with Carla and Jim or Vicky and Keith, when we play each other's new records full blast and have Cointreau and sardines on toast.

'And I'd go home every weekend,' she continues.

'Oh, would you?' What's the point of having a flat-mate you never see? I thought I just wanted someone to share the bills, but I'm beginning to see that that isn't enough; I want someone to be company as well. Preferably good company – someone amusing and articulate, with the same sense of humour as me. And someone who doesn't smell and won't take over the place and make me feel pushed out. Oh dear. It seems a tall order, suddenly.

'And I don't smoke,' she says virtuously.

'I don't mind people smoking. I smoke.'

'Do you?' She looks scandalized. 'Oh, I don't think I could live with that.'

When she leaves, I stick a notice on the door: THE DOORBELL DOESN'T WORK. This obviously puts people off because there is a lull of five minutes, time to let me put the kettle on and make some tea, but not time to drink it.

The next person is a six-foot-two African guy.

'My name is John Mwedzi,' he says. 'I have come in answer to your advertisment.'

The old-fashioned phrase conjures up another; 'in answer to prayer'. Which he probably isn't: he'd fill the whole flat. Already the hall looks smaller than it is.

'Come in and I'll show you the room.' It might be worth taking him just to see my mother's face when I told her my new flat-mate was not only male but black.

He gives the room a cursory glance. 'It is very nice,' he says.

'This is the sitting room. Kitchen. Bathroom.'

'Yes,' he says. 'Very nice.' He is very solemn. Worried. As though looking over a flat is a matter of life and death. He keeps looking at me expectantly, waiting for me to say something.

'I'm seeing everyone who answers the ad,' I explain, 'and then letting them know.'

'Yes, of course.' He lets out his breath.

'That's if you're interested,' I add. He hasn't said he is yet.

He looks surprised. 'Oh yes, very much,' he says. 'It is dependent on you.'

I wonder if he is used to being turned down because he is black. That would account for the expectancy and the sigh

214

when I give myself a let-out. 'Have you looked at a lot of places?' I ask.

'Very many,' he says feelingly. 'You see . . . there is also my wife.'

'Oh I see.' Another couple. 'The room is a bit small, actually . . .'

'Of course.' He accepts this with resignation, looking defeated. It's obviously a gambit he's heard before.

'I mean from your point of view,' I say hastily. 'You might find it very cramped. I really only expected single people to want the room.'

'Yes,' he says. Then, 'From the point of view of my wife and I, it would be all right. We have been living in separate bedsits, you see, two miles apart. We have not been able to find a house where both of us can live.'

I can't quite work this one out. 'Why not?'

He smiles ruefully, which makes his face look nice. 'Landlords will sometimes take one black person, but two is too much for them.'

'So you've had to live apart, even though you're married?'

'Yes. For eight months.'

'Eight months! That's terrible.'

He looks down at his feet. 'Yes,' he says. 'Yes.'

Eight months. I have been without Barry for eight months and he has been without his wife. I don't want a couple here, especially not a couple who will virtually be on honeymoon.

'You couldn't decide on the room without your wife seeing it,' I say helplessly.

A ray of hope creeps into his eyes. 'I could bring her,' he says. 'She is downstairs in the street.'

'It's pouring with rain!' What kind of man leaves his wife in the street?

He hesitates. 'We have been to a lot of places,' he explains. 'Now I go ahead to see first. Then if the person doesn't shut the door straight away she can come.'

'Yes, I see.' So he isn't a monster; he is protecting his wife from repeated humiliations of landlords fumbling for plausible excuses. It is becoming more difficult by the minute to turn him away. It's just that I don't want a couple. If I explained . . . 'The idea,' I say carefully, 'was to have a flat-mate to share the place. For company. My husband died eight months ago, from cancer.'

I don't know why I am telling him this – to show him that other people have problems too and that I can understand his, or to break it to him gently that he and his wife don't fit the requirements.

'I am very sorry,' he says gravely. 'So you have been on your own for eight months too.'

There. The coincidence has struck him too. Perhaps, as Barry's Aunty Ida used to say, this is Meant to Be. But two lodgers, when I wanted one . . .? Still, as long as we got on well, two nice lodgers would be better than one awful one, and he seems nice. Certainly better than the others, anyway.

'Look,' I say. 'Why don't you ask your wife to come up and we can talk about it?' The issue seems to be deciding itself, without any conscious participation by me. I would need a very strong reason for refusing them now.

He hesitates. 'There is one other thing,' he says.

'What's that?'

'My wife,' he says. 'She is pregnant.'

Oh great. There's the strong reason. *Three* lodgers. And Carla thought she was joking when she said don't share the flat with a baby.

That would also explain why his wife is standing outside in the rain rather than toiling up flights of stairs to be met with outright horror by countless landlords.

I can see that the situation is really tragic – he looks really tragic – but something in it suddenly makes me laugh. He looks at me in perplexity.

'I'm sorry,' I apologize. 'But you aren't exactly topping the popularity polls as tenants, are you?'

A reluctant smile spreads across his face. 'Not exactly,' he agrees. 'Young, black and pregnant. It isn't everyone's favourite combination.'

If he has a sense of humour, despite their present circumstances, then I think this could work out. And with four people in a smallish flat, a sense of humour is going to be essential.

Another couple appears in the hallway.

'I'm sorry,' I say. 'I think the room is taken.'

'I will fetch my wife,' says John.

While he is gone I go and look at the room again. It is really not very big. Not for two people and a cot. I go and look at my own room, which is not much bigger. I go back to the spare room and look at that again.

John appears. 'This is Naomi,' he says.

Naomi is tall and striking-looking, with a high cheek-boned face marred only by dark rings of tiredness under the eyes. She would be thin except for the fact that she is enormously pregnant.

'Hello,' she says, with no enthusiasm.

'Hi. Listen,' I say, full of my new idea. 'I've been having second thoughts about this room; it really is much too small for three people and . . .'

Naomi promptly bursts into tears.

'No, no!' I say, appalled. 'I didn't mean that I didn't want you here; it's just that the room . . .'

But she is sobbing heartbrokenly, tears pouring through her fingers as she cups her hands over her face. John puts his arm around her and tries to calm her, but she sobs and sobs.

217

I can't stand it; I shall join in if she doesn't stop.

'Go through there,' I tell John, 'and sit down, and I'll make us all some tea.'

While the kettle is boiling I go and remove the sign that says THE DOORBELL DOESN'T WORK and scrawl on the back of it, SORRY, THE ROOM IS TAKEN. Then I go back to the kitchen and make the tea and a whole pile of toast as well.

'I don't know if you've had breakfast, but I haven't and I'm starving. Do you think you might feel better if you had something to eat?'

Naomi is still half-sobbing into a handkerchief. 'My wife is very tired,' John explains. 'We have been to so many places and the baby is nearly due. She thought that we had found somewhere at last.' He looks at me reproachfully.

'Yes, I see. But I didn't mean that you couldn't have the room. I'm sorry; I should have put it better . . .'

Naomi looks at me. 'We can live here?' she says. Her eyes, which were haggard, suddenly lighten and look beautiful.

'Yes, of course; we agreed. As long as you like it.'

'It will be wonderful,' she says. 'I can't believe it.' She starts to cry again and John clears his throat.

'But you were going to say . . .?' he says.

'I was just wondering if we could change the rooms around. That room is quite small and so's mine, but this one is a lot bigger. If we made my bedroom the sitting room . . . The only problem is the fitted wardrobes.'

He is immediately interested. 'Let me take a look.'

Naomi stays sitting on the sofa, leaning back.

'Have some toast?'

'I am not hungry. A cup of tea . . .'

'Sugar?'

'One spoon please.'

She has not even glanced at her surroundings, but has sunk into the sofa in a haze of exhaustion.

'When is the baby due?'

'Soon now. Three or four weeks.'

'What are you hoping for, a girl or a boy?'

'I don't mind. As long as the baby is all right and as long as we have a home . . .'

I am afraid she is going to cry again, but John returns.

'It would not be too difficult,' he says, 'to take down the wardrobes and put them up in here. The alcoves look the same size.'

'That's good. I could get a carpenter to come and look at them.'

'I am a joiner,' says John. 'I can do it myself.'

'You are?' I am amazed at this good luck. 'That's wonderful. And do you think the sofa and everything would fit in there?'

He goes back again to look. Naomi stares through me at the opposite wall.

'The sofa would fit,' he says, 'and the table and chairs but I think not both armchairs. Only one.'

'That would be all right. We could leave one in here, couldn't we? It might come in handy for sitting in to feed the baby or something. Have you got any furniture of your own?'

'No,' he says, 'only the cot for the baby. And the sheets for the cot. We must buy some sheets and blankets for the bed.'

'I've got lots of sheets if you don't want to get your own. No blankets, but there's a spare duvet if you want. It hasn't even been opened; it was a wedding present but we already had one.'

Naomi removes her gaze from the wall. 'You are married, then?' she says. John frowns fearsomely at her but she doesn't see.

'My husband died.'

'Oh no!' she says. 'So young? Oh no!' Her eyes fill with tears again. I am touched. 'Why did he die?' she asks. Again, John nudges her and frowns.

'Naomi.'

'I don't mind,' I say. 'He had cancer. It all happened very quickly. He didn't suffer long. In that way you could say he was one of the lucky ones.'

'But such a shock for you. So terrible.' Naomi's apathy is forgotten; she sits forward, holding her tea-mug on her knees.

'Yes,' I say. 'Yes.' It is a relief to talk about it. Except that people don't ask, don't want you to pour out your woes. And except that whenever I think about it, even now, the tears which I've held back so long start to pound against the flood gates in my mind. 'But I'm over it now,' I say quickly, 'and I've got lots of friends who've been really kind, so everything's fine. I hope you won't mind people calling in quite a lot.'

'Of course not. It's your flat,' John says.

'Have you got friends around here? Or family?'

'Our friends mostly live a few miles away, near where Naomi lives now. Our families are in Ghana.'

'Is that where you come from originally?'

'Yes. I have been here five years, and Naomi four.'

'Have you been back to Ghana since?'

'Once,' Naomi says. 'After we got married we thought of going back there to live but we wouldn't now. Not with a child. Sometimes the people are queuing for hours for food and sometimes the shops have just run out of things, and the children don't have enough. Here we can give our child so much more.'

In one room of a London flat. Shared with a total stranger. After eight months of living apart in a city that doesn't want to know. It doesn't sound like 'so much more' to me.

'Would you like to have a look round now?' I ask Naomi. 'See the kitchen and everything?'

'Yes, all right.'

She looks at everything silently, nodding approval. 'We will be quiet,' she says suddenly. 'We will keep the baby quiet. If it cries I will take it for a walk. At night too.'

'I hope you won't – it'll get pneumonia! I don't mind a bit of noise. This place has been quiet for too long. It'll be nice to have a baby in the house.'

For the first time she smiles. 'I feel hungry now,' she says. 'Can I change my mind about the toast?'

'I'll put the kettle on,' I say, 'and make some more tea.' But John forestalls me.

'I'll do it. You both sit down.'

'I could get used to this,' I say appreciatively.

In the open doorway, two girls appear. 'Is the room really taken?' one says.

'Yes, I'm afraid it is.'

'Oh. Did you know your doorbell isn't working?'

'I know. Actually, I think it's just as well, because pretty soon there'll be no room for visitors.'

And then suddenly all three of us are laughing and the two girls look at us as if we are mad and go away shaking their heads at one another.

'I can mend the doorbell as well,' says John. 'I will come this week and do it.'

'He's good at things like that,' Naomi says. 'He can do carpentry, electrical, plumbing things – anything you need.' She gazes at him with pride and he looks embarrassed.

'You can't fix immersion heaters, I suppose?' I say hopefully. 'It keeps making funny noises and switching off.'

'I think I know what that might be,' he says. 'I'll take a look.'

'You know,' I say complacently, 'I think this is going to be a great success.'

221

For no reason, except perhaps general relief, we all start laughing again and through the window I see that the rain has stopped at last and the sun is trying to shine.

In spite of the notice, people continue to bang on the door to ask if the room is really taken. In the end I go out, leaving a notice on the front door as well, and a note which I put in the Pratts' letter box, telling them the cowardly way that from next Sunday the house will be slightly more occupied. I hope they won't complain, but I wouldn't put any money on it.

In the meantime I go round to Vicky's, but she is out and Keith is too stoned to remember where she is, so I go to the phone box instead to ring up Carla and Marcie and my mother to tell them about the new lodgers.

The conversation is handicapped at the start by the fact that each of them in turn thinks I am joking.

'No, seriously Cathy, have you found someone?' Carla keeps saying.

'I've told you, Carla (Marcie/Mother) – a black family. A young couple with a baby on the way.'

Jim takes over the receiver from Carla. 'Come off it, Cathy. What is this, the Black Nativity? Christmas looming, an unborn infant and no room at the inn?'

Eventually they believe me, which is worse because they all promptly tell me, in no uncertain terms, that I am mad, a fool, unrealistic, idealistic, and blind to the many obvious snags.

'Give it a week and you'll be at each other's throats, and then how the hell will you ever get them out?' Jim demands.

I go home thoroughly depressed. What on earth have I done? Why didn't I listen to my own sense of reason? How could I have taken on a whole family instead of a single person? By the time I get home, I feel almost affectionate towards the little red-haired guy I disliked so much this morning. One thick-skinned person who didn't pay much attention to personal hygiene would surely be easier to live with than a whole black family, with a baby who will cry half the night. A married couple who will probably have rows and throw things. Or else they'll stop speaking to each other and address their remarks to me, and I will be pig-in-the-middle.

Or else, even worse, they'll be amorous, kissing erotically in the kitchen and pulling apart and giggling when I tiptoe humbly in, apologizing for my presence, to make a cup of tea. Another couple in the flat which was Barry's and mine. A couple who would undoubtedly prefer, as Barry and I preferred, to be on their own in the nice little flat with no guests and no intruders – such as me. They will make love noisily and I will lie awake trying to blot out the sound from my ears and from my mind.

The sink will be full of other people's washing-up; the bath will be strewn with other people's little hairs; the flat will not smell of me but of strangers. Why the hell did I do it, just for the sake of not worrying about the bills? And for the sake of some company to drown out the sound of my own thoughts, so loud sometimes that they echo around the empty rooms. That won't happen now, whatever else. I certainly won't be able to hear myself think. Or will I? You can be as lonely in a crowded flat as in an empty one. And at least, till now, the flat has been a refuge from the outside world. And what if, when I leave my job, I can't find another one and have to hang around at home all day, with the flat full of nappies and motherhood?

I thought of us, you know, having a baby, when we first moved in. Not that either Barry or I wanted children for quite a long time, but still I looked speculatively at the spare room when we viewed the flat and thought – just speculatively – that if and when a baby should arrive the place would do quite nicely. Well, now there will be a baby there, though not in that room, which will be my solitary bedroom. And not my baby and Barry's but a strange couple's whom I hardly know.

Pull yourself together, Cathy. All this negative thinking. You've been ringing the wrong people, that's all – people you knew would disapprove. So now phone someone who won't criticize, who will tell you you're right to act on your intuitions and that something which decided itself so neatly has to be Meant.

But Aunty Ida is on her annual holiday to Majorca and my sister Lizzie, who never criticizes anybody, is in Australia and Wayne, who made me feel that I was all right, not so odd and neurotic after all, is in Sheffield. And there would be no use phoning him, even if I had a number, because I effectively told him he wasn't wanted. Not just in bed but in the rest of my life. When I let him know I wasn't ready to sleep with him he was neither resentful nor persistent. He made it clear there would be no pressure; he asked me to stay for coffee and chat instead. And I refused.

He was kind, he was friendly: he would have settled, at least for a time, for an easy relationship without commitments – emotional or physical. A bit of company, a bit of interest in each other, a bit of affection, a bit of warmth in a cold November – I could have given all that and received it too if I hadn't wasted our time in games of will-he-won't-he/can-I-or-can't-I? If I wouldn't admit him to the holy of holies at least I could have let him wait in the hall instead of opening the door on a chain, like a suspicious Mrs Pratt, and then slamming it in his face at the first sign of closeness. If I hadn't done that, I'd be plus one friend now, to ring up for long-distance chats. Oh well, too late now. I'll know next time.

Moving to Sheffield wouldn't have worked; you can't cast your fate on one person you've known for a week, throwing off all your friends and familiar places, like a drowning man throwing off lifebelts and clinging to a leaf. Not that I'm drowning; I only think I am. I Will Survive: the trick is not to think too much.

In the end, I phone Elsa and she and one of her flat-mates come round and we go to the cinema, which is filled with under-age children on a Saturday afternoon, and see a re-run film on street crime and teenage sex. It's awful, but it's loud and action-packed and could have been specifically designed for people who don't want to hear themselves think.

Outside, it has started to rain again.

On Monday morning it is still raining. Continuing cold and showery, the weather forecast said, with occasional sunny intervals. So where are the sunny intervals, I'd like to know?

A postcard arrives from Aunty Ida in Palma, with a picture of hotels and restaurants with signs that say 'Real Fish and Chips' and 'Tea Just Like Mum Makes' and 'English Spoken Here'. On the back, Aunty Ida's eccentrically punctuated scrawl shouts WISH YOU WERE HERE DARLING. WEATHER MILD. BUT NEED A CARDI SWEET BOY CALLED CARLOS BRINGS ME BREAKFAST. IN BED. ALL MY LOVE DARLING AUNTY IDA.

Carlos, I am assuming, is one of the waiters, though knowing Aunty Ida I can't be sure. Aunty Ida, now in her seventies, attracts 'sweet boys' and 'sweet girls' too, of all ages, by the sheer exuberance of her personality.

When Barry and I were first together, Aunty Ida was in raptures. 'Such a sweet girl,' she enthused. Which certainly made a refreshing change from the reception I got from Barry's mother – who would never dream of sending a postcard and in fact wouldn't speak to me at all now if it wasn't for me ringing her faithfully every other Sunday to hear all the latest about her constipation.

I prop Aunty Ida's postcard on the edge of the bookshelf in the sitting room (I wonder if John can move the bookshelves too?) and think of her with affection. I will write to her later and to Lizzie too. I won't be going to Austrailia, not this winter anyway. If I'm going to crack up I'll do it in the safety of my own half of the world. Not that I have any reason for cracking up. Looking at life dispassionately, mine has a lot going for it. It's only from the inside that it doesn't feel so good.

The new temp, Penny, is nineteen, willing and terrified. She types the envelopes upside down, blobs the copy with undiluted correction fluid and answers the phone with a frightened 'Yes?'

To start her off on the ring-round I phone the first journalist myself to show her how it's done. 'Hello, is that Kay Thomas? Cathy Childs, from Bantam Cosmetics. Did you receive our invitation to the launch of the new range on Wednesday? That's right, the Baritz Hotel, eleven thirty for twelve. You'll try to come? That's great. Or you'll send . . . how do you spell that? Selim K-A-R-I. Okay. We'll look forward to seeing one of you then.'

Penny is listening attentively.

'Here's the list of names,' I tell her. 'Just put a tick or a cross or a "don't know" and write in the names of anyone who's coming instead of the person invited. It takes a long time, I'm afraid, by the time you've left messages for people who aren't there and then they don't ring back so you have to phone them again . . . it'll probably take you most of today and tomorrow. Okay? Would you like to try the next name on the list now?'

She phones through, gets the right person, says, 'Hello, this is . . .' then hisses at me, 'Do I say your name or my own?'

'Yours.'

'This is Penny Sands.' Pause, then she loses her nerve and blurts out: 'Are you coming on Wednesday, or what?'

After that I write her out a script: 'Good morning, this is Penny Sands from Bantam Cosmetics . . .' At two thirty Alan passes through her office and tells me she is still saying 'Good morning' so I go in and change the script to 'Good afternoon'.

Big Harry has put the Cloud Ten poster up in his office and sharp-eyed Hazel has noticed it's not the same as the original. He comes into my office, annoyed. 'Why didn't you tell me you'd changed the design?'

'I'm sorry, I must have forgotten.'

'You shouldn't have agreed the change of design without consulting me.'

'No, I'm sorry.'

'All right.' He eyes me apprehensively. He's been all kid-glove with me since I said I was leaving. I should have tried it years ago. 'All right. You thought this design better?'

'I think so. What do you think?' Actually I don't like it. The colours were better on the last one.

'Mm. All right. Go ahead. By the way, make a note to draft a speech to the Retail Association by Friday, will you? Hazel will give you the details.'

'Who's giving the speech?'

'The MD. About ten minutes' worth; mention the research behind the new ranges but don't make it technical.'

'Do I give the draft to the MD or you?'

'To me. Say mid-afternoon on Friday.'

The MD thinks Big Harry writes his speeches; he sends them back marked in red ink with suggested amendments and Big H. agrees to them like a lamb, without consulting the author. Perhaps in turn I should delegate the writing to someone else, without letting Big Harry know. I'm sure the audience would listen to it with equal indifference.

They would thank the MD for his edifying speech and he would accept their praise with becoming modesty, in placid ignorance of the fact that his weighty words were scripted by the janitor.

Alan is communicating again, but depressed. 'Jerry and I are thinking of splitting up. We seem to be getting nowhere. What do you think?'

I am tempted to remind him that he told me not to interfere in his personal life. 'I don't know. Where aren't you getting that you want to go?'

'You know what I mean. We don't get through, don't communicate at a meaningful level.'

'Perhaps you need marriage guidance or something.'

'Are you being funny?'

'No. They deal with any kind of relationship.'

'Jerry wouldn't go. He'd feel silly. I would too.'

'Well, maybe not then.'

'I suppose I could suggest it. What d'you think?'

'You could.'

'Or I could go on my own first of all. Huh?'

'Yes.'

'Yes, which?'

'Yes, either. Whichever you think.'

'You're very negative, Cathy.'

'I know. It's the weather.'

'It's always either the weather or the time of day or the time of the month or something. You women have moods like barometers.'

'Yeah, right. Can you pass the phone book, Alan? A to D?'

'The problem with Jerry is, he lives for his work. Outside the theatre he ceases to function.'

'Yes. Have you got the number of A. S. Dickens & Son in your address book, Alan?'

'Here you are, have a look. See, his personal life is just

a distraction for him, a mindless relaxation after work. He's not prepared to put any effort into it.'

'He was upset last time you split up. Why have you cross-ed out Josie Phillips' name here? Has she left?'

'Where? No, that's an underline from the line above. You see, Jerry had a very weird upbringing really: his mother . . .'

'Just a minute, Alan. I promised to phone Dickens before half-past three. Can you tell me after?'

At five o'clock there is so much work still to do that I phone Elsa to ask if we can make the wine bar another night. At eight P.M. I finally leave the office and get home at a quarter to nine to find I have no food, so I have to go out again in the rain to the late-night delicatessen. I watch the end of the news and fall asleep on the floor in front of the gas fire.

Mrs Pratt wakes me at ten o'clock by knocking on the door to say what do I mean by getting a lodger without first asking them? I tell her it's two, nearly three lodgers and that they are black and very nice and she is dumbfounded, so I smile and excuse myself for not asking her in as I'm just on my way to bed, and shut the door before she recovers her power of speech. At twenty past ten I hear her shouting instructions to Mr Pratt from the hall, and he shuffles up the stairs and knocks on the door, but I don't answer it and he calls down irritably, 'I told you she'd be asleep.'

Then, as a judgement on me, I can't sleep at all but keep making mental lists of things still to be done before Wednesday. Ridiculous, all this preparation. Just to launch a new make-up range that people will buy and use and get used to and forget, and then the whizz-kids at Bantam will have to concoct a new product, a bit different and a bit the same, and the Creative Team will agonize over its name and image and packaging, and Nick from the ad agency will start sending slogans and sketches and colour charts and the whole thing will start again. Without me. I wonder who they'll get. And I wonder who'll get me. I forgot to look in the paper today for jobs.

By Tuesday, Alan has decided he's leaving Jerry because Jerry has done something unspeakable. Only before I can hear what it was Vicky rings to say she's leaving Keith and can she move into my flat? She gets upset when I say I've got someone now .

'Can't you tell them no?'

'It's too late, I'm afraid. I've already told them yes.'

'But if you explain that a friend wants to come in now? They'll understand that. They can find somewhere else.'

'They've been looking for eight months, Vicky; I can't do that.'

'Well, what am I meant to do? I can't live with that creep a second longer, I tell you.'

'You're welcome to stay till Sunday if that's any help, till the new people come.'

'No thanks, that wouldn't make much difference. Marcie said you were going to have a party?'

'Did she? Oh yes, I said I thought I ought to soon.'

'A housewarming for your new flat-mates?' she says jealously.

'I hadn't thought of it like that. In fact I don't think Naomi would appreciate parties just now; the baby's due in a few weeks and she's really quite tired.'

'Baby? Cathy, are you sure you know what you're . . .'

'Listen, Vicky, can I call you back? I have to go out now.'

Out, to the ad agency to pick up the posters and name-badges, to the hotel to give a final check to all the arrangements, to the promotions agency to meet the two girls who will help dispense booze, badges and a benign atmosphere. Then back to the office to help Penny type badges and collate news releases.

Penny stays late but even so we don't have time to make

up the press kits. I can't stay any longer or I'll be late for Adrian's play, so I take all the press-kit folders and news releases and photos home with me. I'll have to make up the kits when I get back tonight. Or, if Adrian has other things in mind, very early tomorrow morning.

Not that I'm planning anything; that would be clinical, wouldn't it? But seeing that I've now discovered I'm not frigid, or at least on the thaw, celibacy is beginning to seem an overrated vocation. It's all Wayne's fault. I could forget sex, or treat the occasional urges as a temporary aberration, while it remained a distant memory. Sex in theory is easily resisted; it's the warm, human-to-human contact that transforms it from past recollection to present immediate necessity. And Adrian is neither the platonic nor the patient type, unlikely to consider the evening complete if it ends at the front door.

So you see, there would be no reason not to. No strings, no complications, no hesitations, no yes-I-will-no-I-won't, as with Wayne. No virtuous and-what-about-your-wife, as with Jim. Just a simple calculation of one and one makes two makes one. Third time lucky. Marcie is right: it doesn't have to mean anything. And if I have any qualms afterwards, at least I'll have something specific to agonize about instead of, as now, agonizing about everything and nothing.

'*War Game*?' Alan said when I mentioned it. 'I haven't seen the play but Jerry says it's weak and badly directed.' I refrain from saying that Jerry thinks any play he hasn't directed himself is badly directed.

In fact the play is great, if a bit disconcerting because the actors mingle with the audience at certain points which breaks your concentration a bit because you stop thinking about the play and start worrying in case you're expected to do something. The play is about this soldier who joined the army because his best mate joined, but who buys himself

231

out when he finds he's expected to be aggressive and learn how to kill people. Then in civvy street he finds that he's still expected to be aggressive and violence is all around him – at least in the army it was controlled and limited.

Adrian plays the best friend who enthuses about new weapons and improved ammo but is sickened by the sight of street violence against an immigrant lad. He's quite good actually; I forget that he's Adrian, someone I know, and believe that he's Gareth, who's never understood that war means killing real live human beings.

During the interval I go out on the balcony to get some air but it's freezing cold and raining yet again so I go back to the auditorium, unwilling to mingle with the happy couples and groups in the bar. When the play ends and they stream out into the streets, talking and laughing and huddling under umbrellas, I go backstage to meet Adrian.

A handful of the cast are sitting round, in various stages of undress, discussing the play.

'Cathy! Over here.' Clad in underpants, sweater and one sock, he introduces me to the rest of the cast. It's funny, having seen them so recently in their stage roles, to see them now half-dressed and half made-up and unfamiliar in their own selves. The sensitive hero is loudly articulating his view that the lighting in the second act was off-cue.

'Come on,' says Adrian, pulling on jeans and gymshoes. 'We'll go on over to the pub. The others'll join us when they've finished arguing.'

The pub is full of people from the audience, who look at Adrian with recognition. I feel good, in reflected limelight.

'Nice to be famous, isn't it?'

'I'm not famous yet,' he says seriously. 'But I will be. What did you think of my performance?'

'Very good. I forgot it was you.'

'Did you?' He is pleased. 'That's how it should be. What are you drinking?'

In a corner of the bar Adrian discovers Terry, the lighting engineer. 'Nick's out for your blood,' he warns. 'He says you buggered the lighting in the second scene.'

'Why d'you think I'm in here?' says Terry imperturbably. 'Are you going to introduce me to your girlfriend?'

'Cathy. Terry. The ultimate lazy slob.'

'What an insult,' Terry protests. 'I'm sure she's nothing of the kind. What are you having, Cathy?'

'I've ordered them already,' Adrian tells him.

While he fetches the drinks, I sit down beside Terry.

'I have to confess there's a grain of truth in Adrian's description,' Terry says disarmingly. 'I've been in here all evening, left my assistant doing the lights, but don't give me away.'

'But now you'll get blamed for his mistakes.'

He shrugs unconcernedly. 'Some you win, some you lose. I've got paid for spending an evening in the pub. That can't be bad, can it?'

'Don't believe anything he tells you,' Adrian says, coming back with the drinks. 'He's a bullshitter.'

'Now that's not fair. I'm as forthright and sincere as they come. I'm happily married with two lovely kids, Cathy. There, isn't that honest? Now I can be lecherous with a clear conscience.'

'Adrian,' booms a stocky guy who was the sergeant major in the play, 'you really fucked up my cues in the target-practice scene. What the fucking hell were you playing at?'

'Improvisation,' says Adrian uncontritely.

'You mean you forgot your fucking lines.'

'I didn't.'

'What other fucking reason could there be . . .'

''Scuse me a minute, Cathy,' Adrian says. 'I'll just buy this idiot a drink.' He starts to elbow his way to the bar, followed by the sergeant major.

'Desertion,' says Terry mournfully. 'If you were my girlfriend I wouldn't desert you.'

'I'm not his girlfriend.'

'So why isn't he doing his level best to persuade you to be? I would myself if I didn't have a wife with a shotgun. Would you have me, Cathy, if I didn't have a trigger-happy wife? You've finished your drink. I'd buy you another but it would mean deserting you altogether. Tell me honestly, which would you prefer – my company or another drink?'

'I'd prefer both,' I tell him, 'but if it's a choice I'll settle for the company.'

He laughs. 'Here, we'll compromise – have half my beer.'

'Thanks.' What I'd really like is something to eat. I should have brought my usual snack with me but I came out in such a hurry I forgot. Maybe when Adrian comes back I could persuade him to go for a hamburger or something.

'Let me tell you my life story,' says Terry. 'It takes a long time, although I'm so young, because I leave in all the boring details. It means that I have a captive audience; you can listen to me and I can look at you. What could be nicer?'

'Who for?'

'For me, of course. Only would you mind sliding along the bench a bit? Because I have this arthritic left side and it has to be kept warm.'

I have to laugh; he is so blatant and takes himself so unseriously. At the bar, the actors are arguing over which of them blew his lines. Adrian waves at me above the heads and calls something but I can't catch it. I shrug and shake my head to show him I can't hear.

Terry has moved up and put his arm around me.

'Ah,' he says, 'that's good for my arthritis!'

'Did you know that the worst thing for arthritis is beer?' I tease him.

'That's why I need the heat treatment,' he says earnestly.

234

'To counteract the bad effects. Snuggle up a bit closer, will you?'

Adrian fights his way back through the crowd.

'I couldn't hear what you were saying,' I apologize.

'I was just saying "Come over here" but I've come to you instead. Lay off will you, Terry, you lecherous bastard?'

'She's enjoying it,' Terry protests, 'aren't you, Cathy?'

'I've come to rescue you,' Adrian says. 'If we stay here I won't get a minute's peace from this rabble. And neither will you, by the look of it.'

'Last orders, please!' the barman calls.

'Rabble,' repeats Terry. 'Rabble indeed. Ah well, if you're really off there's nothing for it but to go home to the bosom of my family. Unless you'd like to change your mind, Cathy, and come with me instead?'

'With a gun-toting wife? No thanks.'

Adrian glances at me. 'You seem to be getting on well with him,' he says, as Terry disappears through the crowd.

'He's funny.'

'He's a lazy bugger. Come on, let's go down the flea-pit and see a blue movie.'

'Can we get something to eat?'

'Good idea. I'm hungry.'

Out in the street it is raining still, and cold.

'Christ,' says Adrian. 'Will it ever stop raining? This is meant to be "occasional cold showers". So what did you think of the play?'

'I thought it was good. Who wrote it?'

'Oh, some guy. No-one famous.'

'When was it written? Is it contemporary or is he dead?'

'Probably dead. Most of them are. Did you like that bit at the start of the second act where I lit a fag and then stubbed it out without thinking because I was nervous of the careers guy?'

'Yes, that was good.'

'I mean, you noticed it? You realized why it was done like that?'

'Yes, it was quite effective. There's a hamburger stand over there, Adrian.'

'We don't want hamburgers. I know this little pasta house down the road.'

The pasta house down the road is full and there is no point in waiting; the chef has taken last orders for the night. I feel unreasonably annoyed, though it's nobody's fault.

'We could just go back to that hamburger stand,' I suggest.

'We'd get soaked,' he says. 'They'll probably do hot dogs or something in the cinema.'

'What film is on, do you know?'

'Blue movies. It's the all-night porno pit.'

It is too. 'I thought you were joking,' I say.

'Why? Don't you like blue movies?'

'Well . . .'

'You'll like them,' he promises. 'They're good for a laugh if nothing else.'

The porno pit does not do hot dogs. I suppose people have other things to think about.

'I'll get some chocolate,' Adrian offers.

'I can't eat sweets, actually.'

'Crisps? Peanuts? Ice cream?'

'No, not those either.'

'I'll just get some chocolate,' he says. 'Don't worry, we won't stay too long, then we'll go and find you some food.'

We find our way to the seats, past lots of single men in raincoats, and Adrian eats his chocolate. I give up being strong-minded about my diet and have a piece, which is a mistake because it makes me hungrier, and thirsty as well.

On the screen, lots of naked people are screaming at each other and slamming bedroom doors and running up and down stairs, wobbling uncomfortably. Adrian slides down in his seat and watches attentively.

After twenty minutes, I am getting slightly bored. I don't reckon sex as a spectator sport. You either do it or you don't. Watching other people do it is like watching other people eat: tantalizing when you're hungry and off-putting when you're not.

'Enjoying it?' Adrian says, removing his gaze from the screen.

'I'm really hungry,' I say apologetically.

'It's sublimation, all this eating,' Adrian tells me. 'It's a sign of frustration. Concentrate on the film and you'll see you'll forget what a hamburger is. Fucking hell – look at that!'

The girl who has just been writhing so energetically with the blond guy gets up and goes out (presumably to go to the loo), leaving him exhausted, and meets the black guy, who has just been leaping around on the other girl, and has come out for a breath of air. Undeterred by their recent expenditure of energy, they fall into a heap on the landing and have an action replay, rolling precariously close to the stairs.

'Look at that!' says Adrian admiringly, as the couple achieve athletic contortions.

'She must have remarkable bladder control.'

'Eh?'

'She went out to go to the loo and never made it.'

'She's making it now all right. Aren't you enjoying this?'

'Mm, well . . .'

'Just forget that you're hungry,' he says, 'for a few minutes. Don't you find this erotic?'

I watch the film and try to find it erotic; I look at the close-ups of the couple's anatomy and start to fantasize about food: poached eggs and sausages. With chips would be nice. And a fried tomato and mushrooms. I think

Adrian's got it wrong. Wanting food is not a sublimation of the sex drive; in my case I think sex is a sublimation of the eating drive. If someone offered me steak and chips right now on condition I gave up sex for life, I would take the steak without a second's regret.

Adrian shifts in his seat; the film is obviously getting to him. He puts his hand on my knee and wanders upwards. I don't think he's fantasizing about steak and chips.

Behind me, I catch the unmistakable smell of chips and swivel round to see where it's coming from. Adrian takes this cooperative movement as encouragement. 'Let's go back to your place,' he whispers seductively.

'Okay.' If he only gives me time to scramble the eggs I've got in the fridge I'll do whatever he likes.

Adrian's car is parked in the car park behind the theatre. He drives like a maniac, ignoring all traffic signals.

'The lights are red,' I say weakly, as he drives through them.

He grins. 'I'm in a hurry.'

'I have to eat,' I say firmly, when we get to the flat.

'You're a real passion killer, aren't you?'

'On an empty stomach, yes. Want some scrambled eggs?'

'Can't you have something quicker?' he complains.

'Okay.' I settle for cheese and biscuits and eat them hastily, shedding crumbs, under his impatient gaze. I'm still hungry really and I'd rather wait, anyway, for the food to take effect on my blood-sugar level; I feel weak and slightly peevish. If I waited for that to wear off it would be better, but then Adrian would be peevish and if not weak, decidedly uncomfortable, so I give in gracefully.

Adrian has played this scene before, I can see. Moreover, he has rehearsed it thoroughly, cutting down all the preliminaries to a matter of minutes. I feel like a passenger who's accustomed to catching the local shopping train and finds himself on the inter-city express.

But what I did expect? This is a one-off, not a marriage. Just because I got used to married sex . . . What was it Barry said about the difference between roast dinners and a bag of crisps . . .?

Barry. I have the sudden conviction that if I have sex with Adrian I will banish Barry for ever, never be able to think of him again. I thought that was what I wanted, but I don't. If I lose him, wipe out the memory, I shall lose a part of myself. Adrian leans away from me to unzip his jeans.

Indignation is like indigestion; once it attacks you it won't stay down. Who the hell does this guy think he is, grabbing the goodies for the price of one drink and a ticket to a pathetic film? Treating me like a vending machine – put in the statutory sum of money and the snack of your choice is instantly available. And isn't it slightly sick to woo-and-screw the wife of his dead friend? Not that there has been much wooing: no cuddling, no kissing, no laughter, no love to be wasted. Sex without loving. It makes as much sense to me now as sex without touching.

'No,' I say. 'No.'

He pauses momentarily, then decides I can't mean it.

'No,' I say, sitting up.

'What?'

'No.'

'What the f. . . What do you mean, no?'

'I'm sorry.'

'You're sorry! *You're* sorry!'

'Yes.'

'What's the matter? You want me to slow down or something?'

'I want you to stop.'

'You . . . listen, are you serious?'

'Yes. I'm sorry.' I keep apologizing these days. I seem to have a lot to apologize for.

'Are you frigid?' he demands.

'No.'

'I think you are,' he says furiously.

'I thought I was,' I agree, 'but now I don't think I am.'

'So what's the problem? Wrong time of the month? Not taken your pill? Religious objections – what?'

'No.'

'What then?' he almost shouts.

'I'm sorry,' I say again. 'I don't want to.'

He looks at me, astounded. 'You don't want to?'

'No.'

'Well,' he says. I get the impression that this possibility is one which hadn't entered his mind. He stands up and makes for the door, tugging at his zip. 'There is a word for women who do what you've just done.'

'There are several. The best is probably "cruel".'

'Not the one I had in mind.'

'No, but it's true as well. And unfair, and unkind,' I say penitently.

He shakes his head. 'I don't understand you, I really don't.'

'No.'

'You didn't appear to have any objections before.'

'I didn't think I had.'

'Shit,' he says. 'Shit.' He goes out, closing the door behind him – closing, not slamming it. It is quite a lot more than I probably deserve.

I sit on the edge of the sofa and examine my feelings with clinical detachment, but I have no feelings at all apart from a vague sense of pity. No thoughts, no feelings, a total absence of intellect, emotions and soul. Just a body that won't obey its cues. That's the trouble with vending machines: so easy when they function, but they're always breaking down.

Mechanically, I set out the piles of press kits and start to fill the folders for tomorrow.

10

Tell me honestly: do you think I'm heading for a nervous breakdown? Don't be polite about it; I really want to know, because if I am I'll go to a psychiatrist or something, though he'll probably only offer Valium and I-told-you-so.

It's ridiculous, isn't it? To start feeling like this after eight months, just when according to public opinion I should be 'getting over it'. So why does it seem to be getting worse?

I took it well at first: I did, really. Okay, I had moments of rebelling against my fate, as everyone does. Why me? we all scream. Why me, out of all those millions of others? – conveniently ignoring the fact that those millions of others are dying of hunger, or grieving over lost children, or wasting their lives in loneliness because they don't want the pain of loving but only want to be loved.

I don't feel like that any more. Occasionally I feel bitter. Well, how many girls get widowed at twenty-five? But I don't really expect any longer that life will be rosy for me just because it's mine. I've changed in quite a few ways, in the past eight months.

For instance, I could never stand being on my own. It may even have been one reason I couldn't stick doing a Ph.D: all that studying in late-night libraries and lonely rooms. I saw solitude as a last resort, like a schoolboy poring over a skinny-mag, making do with paper ladies for want of any real ones. Now I actually need to be alone – not all the time, just a breath of solitude in a crowded day.

Or perhaps it's just age that makes me hanker after peace. But no, it can't be that because Marcie, who's older than me, can't bear to be alone. She surrounds herself with people and with activity; she's busy, successful and popular precisely for that reason – because she's afraid of not being busy, successful and popular.

I know it's fear because I've felt that way too. You can only make the fear go away if you have the nerve to stare it in the face. Not to push the unwelcome thoughts away as they tumble into your mind until, like falling snow, they pile up into a drift that can't be shifted even with a snowplough. A drift that threatens to topple over and suffocate the thinker.

Is this a nervous breakdown then? Or am I just going mad?

The press conference and my period arrive on the same day. Perfect timing. It always makes me feel drowsy, as though I could sleep for a week. Menstruation that is, not press conferences, though come to think of it they have much the same effect.

Perhaps some day someone will invent an antidote: after all, it's quite a severe problem; journalists suffer from it not once a month but several times a week. And we haven't had a really good medical discovery for some time: nothing more exciting than the endless stream of 'cancer is caused by cyclamates/hair dye/cutting your toenails' theories.

The only interesting bit of the press conference is usually the lunch when, after the presentations, speeches, audio-visuals and monologues, we can get down to real conversation on topics which have nothing to do with eyelash condition or multi-vitamin nail varnish. Then the mood relaxes, nursed along by a few generous martinis, and lingers on to the end of the conference, unmarred by a discreetly swift distribution of press kits and sample boxes.

Unless Big Harry has a hand in the proceedings. As he has today – delivering his 'spontaneous' spiel, trapping the youngest and prettiest of the beauty writers with ponderous anecdotes on chemical processes; pressing drinks and ignoring refusals, topping up glasses and breathing down necks. Why are the men at the top in public relations so bad at relating to the public? Perhaps it's because they see it as Public Relations instead of having a chat with a few individuals.

There's not a bad turnout today, which should please Big Harry anyway. And me. There's always an awful half hour before a press conference is due to start when you wonder if anybody will come. It's worse than having a party – at least then you know there are bound to be a few who'll come along for the free booze; you can't bank on that with a press conference because chances are your event will be rivalled by several others, all gushing with quadruple whiskies and Harvey Wallbangers with ice.

So, if they come, they come for the story alone. And they have come, most of them, which means I succeeded in persuading them that Cloud Ten will be a good story. Which means that I've done a good job, because that's what I'm paid for; to make people want to write about toenail transfers and glitter dust. What a way to earn a living.

'Not a bad turnout,' says Big Harry, pawing goodbye to the last remaining beauty writer. 'Only a few defectors, hmm? Better get on to those straight away, Cathy. As soon as you get back to the office.'

'I'll line them up and shoot them.'

'What?'

'I'll send them a press kit.'

'That's right. With a covering letter.'

'Sure.'

'Saying – ah, saying that you're sorry . . . uh . . .'

'Sorry they couldn't make it?'

'Sorry . . . uh . . . mm. Sorry they – ah – couldn't . . . er . . . couldn't make it. You know the kind of thing.'

'Yes.'

243

'And perhaps a short résumé of my speech – just briefly you know.'

Great. More work. I could have run off copies of his speech last week and included them in the press kit, but he refused to let me, because that would imply that the speech was planned and not spontaneous.

'Would you like another drink before you go, Mr Diggins?'

'Huh? Oh – is that the time? I'd better be getting back. I can leave you to clear up, can't I? And get back as quickly as you can, will you: I'd like those letters sent out today.'

'I'll take a minicab then.'

'A minicab?'

'It'll take me quite some time to get back to the office by tube and then bus,' I point out. 'And there is a lot of stuff to carry.'

'Yes, I suppose so. How much is a minicab likely to cost for that distance?'

'I don't know. If you'd rather wait twenty minutes and give me a lift . . .'

'No, no. Can't spare the time. Yes, the best thing is for you to . . . uh . . . take a . . . um . . . a . . .'

'Minicab?'

'To take . . . ah . . . take a, yes, a minicab.'

'Fine. I'll see you later then.'

He gets as far as the door, with one of the remaining Cloud Ten sample boxes tucked under his jacket for his wife; and turns back as a thought lumbers up to him.

'Ah, Cathy.'

'Yes?'

'You . . . ah . . . did a good job this morning. Yes,' he repeats, pleased with the phrase, 'a good job.'

'Thanks.'

'The quality of your work,' he goes on, ponderously, but quite fluently for him, 'would justify a rise, in my opinion.

Perhaps quite a substantial one.'

'But there's only a month to go before I leave. Surely it wouldn't be worth . . .'

'It would of course be dependent on your staying on.'

'Ah. What about Alan?'

'What do you mean?'

'We're on the same salary. Would he get a pay rise too?'

Anarchy! Big Harry freezes visibly. 'Matters of salary depend on the Personnel Department,' he says coldly. 'I can only make recommendations.' Which hedges the issue of whether he would recommend Alan.

'Alan does the same job,' I point out, 'and he works just as hard. And he's prepared to stay on, whereas I'm planning to leave.'

'Think it over,' Big Harry says brusquely, pushing his way through both swing doors at once, so they crash behind him, saloon-bar style.

Poor Big Harry. I'm upsetting his digestion, not playing the game. Now that I've committed myself to leaving, I can't resist breaking all the rules I've been chafing against ever since starting in business. I've nothing to lose. Except glowing references. And my head.

By the time I've phoned for a minicab and got back to the office it's half-past three. Penny is typing laboriously. 'Any messages?'

'Only a few.'

'Could you type some letters if I dictate them?'

She looks horrified.

'Or shall I write them out for you to copy type?'

'Yes please.'

By half-past five I feel so tired I decide to go home. Now the press conference is finally over I feel flat. I'll go home and have a bath and watch television.

When I get home, though, John is there with an outraged Mrs Pratt.

'I've come to mend the doorbell,' John says. 'If that's all right with you?'

'It's very all right with me. Are you sure you don't mind? Mrs Pratt, you've met John, have you?'

'He tells me, he's moving in,' she says ominously.

'That's right. On Sunday. With Naomi, his wife,' I add. Otherwise she'll be spreading tales around the neighbourhood about That Girl Upstairs and her So-Called Lodger.

Mrs Pratt sniffs and seals herself off behind her front door.

'Come upstairs, John; I'll make some tea.'

He produces a bunch of flowers from his work-bag. 'From Naomi.'

'That's very kind. Will you thank her from me?'

'I can have a look at the immersion heater as well. If I wouldn't be in your way.'

'I'd probably be in yours. Or can I help?'

'No, not really. It's probably easier on my own.'

'I'll stay out of the way then; I'll go out. And while I remember, here's the spare key.' Barry's key.

It's only when I am out on the street that I wonder where I am going. So much for my lazy evening on my own. Not that I want to be on my own. And not that I want to be unoccupied. What the hell is the matter with me these days? Maybe it's just physical: my period, tiredness, not having eaten much today. I suppose I should have eaten before I came out. Somehow I can't really see the point, eating every two hours just to keep going. Keep going for what?

I know: I'll go and call on Father Delaney, ask him, as Carla suggested, about being a godmother. It's a bus ride away but I might as well walk to kill time. On the way there it starts to rain again, steadily and persistently. I have never known so much rain.

When I die it will be by drowning, and my epitaph will be:

She Couldn't Stand All the Rain.

By the time I arrive I am soaked through. I think about going straight home again. If I turn up in this state he'll thing there's something wrong; he won't believe I've come all this way in the rain just to ask what a godmother does. Still, it's equally silly to come all this way in the rain for nothing.

Teresa, the housekeeper, opens the door. 'Father Delaney's saying evening Mass. Then he's seeing a young couple about a baptism.'

'Oh I see. Never mind; it wasn't important.'

'Will you come in and wait?'

'No. No, I won't wait. Thanks all the same.'

'You're wet through,' she exclaims. 'Won't you come in and wait in his study? The fire is just lit. And I'll make you a cup of tea,' she adds persuasively.

'All right. Thanks.' I might as well. I'm too tired to argue, too tired to walk home in the rain again.

Teresa shows me into the study, brings me a cup of tea. 'Sit yourself down.' She goes out, closing the door as the phone in the hall begins to ring.

There's an old black and white television in the corner of the room and I switch it on. A report on a famine, result of war, somewhere in the East. Starving children with swollen bellies and faces like skulls: hardly human, let alone childlike. Limbs like a bird's. Eyes in a five-year-old child that are old with the knowledge of what the world can do.

I switch it off. I can't take other people's sufferings. I can't take my own. I offer advice to all and sundry without getting hurt by their hurt: Vicky and Carla and Alan and Jerry and all the world. Married and single, hetero- and homosexual alike. Like some kind of guru. Good old Aunty Cath, the problem-solver. Silly bitch thinks she knows all the answers to all the questions. Pity she's got such a mental block about her own. Coped okay with her husband's death – quite well really – then just as she should have been getting back to normal the woman went crazy, completely neurotic. Started trying homeopathic medicine and meditation and all those weirdo things. Found she was getting obsessed with death. I mean – really weird.

The fire is lit but not giving out warmth yet; the logs are just beginning to catch. Over the mantelpiece is a large crucifix – an agonized Jesus nailed to a wooden cross. Not a comfortable reminder to have in your living room. On the opposite wall, a clock ticks out the minutes, the hours, to eternity. There are papers on the desk – a diary with committee meetings, hospital visits, youth club meetings, church services.

What makes an intelligent man like Father Delaney spend his life in the service of dying old ladies, the local yobbos from the high-rise flats, and the Catholic Women's League? Running meditation groups and jumble sales? What an incongruous mixture. Contemplation of the eternal and redemption of the parish debt. Other people's problems, other people's lives. Sharing in all the sorrows and probably very few of the joys. Hearing in the confessional all the sins, the sordidness, the selfishness and the failures. A seedy sort of job in a seedy sort of place, with a meagre wage and a dingy little nouse as recompense. And a dying man over the mantelpiece to remind him, as if he could ever forget, that closeness to God demands a willingness to suffer.

So how come suffering alone doesn't bring that closeness? Why can't I instantly meditate successfully: doesn't my status as tragic young widow automatically elevate me to the heavenly heights? Why can't I get that sense of peace that others seem to get from it: don't I qualify?

But I know why it is. Here, in this acquiescent room with its silent suffering and its ticking clock, I know that the problem is fear. It was not so far from the truth to call it spiritual frigidity. It's not fear of turning into a 'Christian', of wearing the shapeless uniform and the relentless smile, but fear of suffering. Fear of losing my defences, of facing up to the raw facts of life, of living every ticking minute in the service of God, twenty-four hours a day, with no oases of selfishness. No 'Haven't I done enough?' or 'Just this once I can't be expected to . . .'

Don't I deserve a bit of peace, though? Haven't I suffered enough? Looking at the bleeding image of that beaten, unbeaten man, the answer comes: 'You haven't started yet.' But it's hard. It's so hard. Why do they say religion's a soft option? No defences, no excuses, no let-outs, no limitations. 'Be perfect, as your heavenly Father is perfect.' It's impossible. Even to attempt it is impossible. Well, not impossible. But so hard. Again, that dying figure passively accepting its fate, to save a world that doesn't want to know: 'You're telling *me* it's hard?!'

But you have to have defences, escapism, else you'd go mad, wouldn't you? If you didn't protect yourself. If you let yourself think. If you let yourself stop thinking, stop filling your head with thoughts that rest on a painful subject and whirl away before it can grip your mind. If you stopped filling your waking moments with activity – work, people, exercise – anything not to face that terrible silence where images rise unbidden: images of a dying man on a cross, a starving child in a dusty street, a wasted life, a wasted grey-faced young man in a hospital bed . . .

Barry. Not the living, laughing Barry but the Barry I have banished all these months, pushed from my mind for fear he took over my heart and my reason. Barry, in the lonely hours of the night. 'Cathy, hold me. I've got such pain.' 'Shall I call the doctor?' 'No. Not yet. Don't leave me.' But I had left him. Left him all alone in that high, cold, anonymous hospital bed with the curtains drawn round. Alone behind the shuttered eyelids, lost beyond my reach and cold beyond my warmth. 'Come away now, Mrs Childs; your friends have come to take you home.'

Don't cry. Father Delaney will be back soon, or Teresa to take the teacup away. Don't cry. Don't think. Don't suffer. Bleeding man on a wooden cross. You're not joking, it's hard. Not joking. Not pretending any more. Oh my God, Barry, why did you have to leave me?

Holding the mantelpiece, head against the wood, bleeding with tears that start in the heart and force their way up with a retching relentlessness.

Sit down. Calm down. What will Father Delaney say? What will everybody say? You ought to be over it now. Ought to find yourself a new man. A new job, a new life, a new heart to replace the old broken one.

Head on the arm of the chair, fingers clutching the tassels; body twisted one way then the other; racking sobs that fight for breath; pain that scalds the mind.

The door opens. Teresa, hesitating, 'Don't upset yourself now. Anything I can do? Father Delaney will be back soon.' She's seen it all before. Crazed and frightened people mourning the loss of their fantasies. No illusions, no escape. Alone in the presence of a suffering God. Help me; I can't bear it. Be still and know that I am thy God. All you who labour and are heavy-burdened. Blessed are those who mourn, for they shall be comforted. Comfort me then; I am mourning. Ask and you shall receive; knock and the door shall be opened. Help me. Barry. Help me. Be still.

The logs shift in the grate and the clock ticks and the housekeeper answers the phone in the hall, and the suffering Christ looks down on the sobbing maniac tearing out her heart along with the shabby tassels on the chair. And I only came to ask what a godmother was.

'You never spoke about it to anyone then?' says Father Delaney.

I must have been crying for about an hour by the time he returns. My voice comes out slurred and thick, like an old movie soundtrack.

'No. You did ask me to tell you, didn't you? Several times. But I couldn't then. I couldn't even think about it to myself. And then later on it was too late. People didn't want to know; they were embarrassed. Oh, I told them bits, things they asked: how long he was in hospital, what the tests showed, things like that.'

'But nothing about how you felt?'

'I didn't know how I felt at first. I didn't feel anything.'

'You didn't stay with him after he died.' It is a statement, not a question.

'I wanted to. I felt he hadn't . . . hadn't quite gone yet. That he still needed me. I wanted to stay there beside him all night, just in case. I felt it would be the last thing I could do for him.'

'But the hospital staff wouldn't let you.'

'They said it would be better to go home. They persuaded me. I wasn't in a state to argue. They phoned Carla and Jim and they came and took me away. Carla was pregnant. I couldn't remember anyone else's phone number, so I gave the doctor theirs. Jim was afraid she'd lose the baby; she cried all night. I didn't cry.'

He sighs, heavily. 'I wish I could have been there.'

'I wanted to call you, before, but Barry wouldn't let me. You were just getting over pneumonia. You'd gone to that place to convalesce.'

'I know. The priest here should have called me. I cursed the poor man for a fool when I returned.'

'It wasn't his fault; he offered but I refused. I didn't want to see you, to be honest. I thought you'd make me cry.'

'I would have.'

'I know. I wish you had. Your dinner's burning; I can smell it. You go ahead and eat.'

'Are you hungry?'

'No. No thanks.'

'Nor me. We'll both eat later on. I'll just go and turn the oven off.'

'Are you sure . . . ?'

'Certain sure. It doesn't smell very appetizing, you have to admit?'

I sniff the air critically. 'Overcooked greens. And liver?'

'Stuffed heart,' he says ruefully. 'Cheap but not very cheerful.'

Returning, he puts a log on the fire. 'Can I tempt you to some Bulgarian sherry?'

'I never knew there was such a thing.'

'Well, it says on the label it's Bulgarian. I'm not at all sure that it's sherry. But if you care to risk it . . .'

'I'm meant to be off alcohol,' I remember.

'Why's that?'

'Low blood sugar. I'm supposed to eat every two hours too, but I keep forgetting.'

'How long is it now since you ate?'

I make a mental count. 'Five hours. It doesn't matter.'

'It certainly does. What can you eat?'

'No, really . . .'

'Bread and cheese?'

'I can't eat white bread.' What a pain I am. Poor man.

'I think it's brown; I'll have a look. Tea or coffee?'

'Tea please. I'll come and give you a hand.'

'You'll stay where you are, by the fire. It's like the Arctic in that kitchen. I won't be long.'

Peace in the silent, suffering room. After the anguish, a curious stillness. You fear the worst when you hide from it. Meeting fear head-on brings the revelation that there's nothing left to be afraid of. Peace. Be still and know that I am thy God. Traffic outside the window; inside, the ticking clock and the sound of Father Delaney rattling plates in the kitchen. 'Donald!' he calls. 'Would you take the phone for me when it rings? I have someone here.'

'One of my youth leaders,' he explains, coming in with a laden tray. 'He's living here till he finds himself a flat. Now, tell me. But eat at the same time.'

'Tell you what?' Now that the food is here I do feel hungry. It makes you light-headed, all this grief.

'Tell me what, she says, after eight months of silence! Tell me everything,' he says firmly, 'from the beginning.'

'The very beginning,' I say slowly, 'is long before Barry got ill. The beginning was really Janice.'

'Then begin with Janice,' he says imperturbably. He helps himself to a goodly hunk of cheese, butters two slices of wholemeal bread and settles himself on the opposite chair. He reminds me of the radio programme I used to listen to as a child. *Listen with Mother*. ('Are you sitting comfortably? Then I'll begin.')

'Janice was a girl who came to work in Barry's lab. She was very young, very shy, and she did everything wrong. I met her when she hadn't been there long. They were all working late one night on some project and I called in after work with fish and chips and everyone sat down to eat except Janice, who was washing some test-tubes. Barry told her to leave them, but one of the others had already asked her if they were ready yet, so she was hurrying to do them, obviously flustered, and as she finished she pulled out the plug in the sink and sent the whole lot flying with her elbow.'

I glance at Father Delaney, but he is listening attentively. 'I know it doesn't seem relevant,' I say.

'Go on.'

'So everybody groaned. It had happened before, or several things like it; Barry had told me. He said the trouble was the poor girl was so nervous, being more or less straight from school and in her first job, that it made her clumsy.

Anyway, Barry got up – she was in tears – and put his arm round her and told her to come and eat. You could tell by the way she looked at him and the way she looked at the others that he was the only one there who was kind to her.'

'Ah.'

'Yes, ah. The next time I saw her, wherever Barry went in the lab she seemed to be half a step behind him. It became a joke; the others teased him about it. In the end he told them to drop it because Janice could see they were laughing at her. She tried: I could see she tried to be sensible, but she adored him. She used to get me to talk to her about him; she would seize on little scraps of information and hoard them away like a hamster. She talked about him as though he was a god.'

'Were you jealous?'

I shrug. 'She loved him. She couldn't help that. I could hardly blame her; I loved him myself. Yes, of course I was jealous.'

Father Delaney leans forward and takes another piece of bread. 'Another cup of tea?'

'Yes please.' I hadn't noticed I'd drunk the first one.

'And what about Barry?' Father Delaney says. 'What did he feel?'

'Embarrassed at first, I think. He used to joke about it to me, once he knew that I'd noticed. It had to get fairly obvious before he noticed it himself; he wasn't vain. I used to call her his shadow. "And how was your shadow today?" That kind of thing. I went on about it a bit. I suppose I thought that as long as he could laugh at her he was quite safe. Or I was quite safe. But then he stopped laughing.' I stop, in memory.

'What happened?'

'Nothing, really. He just changed in the way he spoke about her. If I made a remark about her dropping things, he'd defend her. It made me . . . not very nice. I stressed

254

her shortcomings, and said things like, "I thought you said she was useless?" But he just said, "Not now; she's changed." And she had, too. She seemed calmer; she still gazed at him adoringly, but there was a kind of serenity about her.'

'And him?'

'I don't know. He seemed to treat her normally. He was gentler with her than the others, but then he always had been. They had jokes together. She was more relaxed, more confident. They didn't exclude me, when I was there, but I felt excluded anyway. And at home he was very quiet. You know what he was like normally: full of enthusiasm, talking all the time. Well, he seemed to change. Several times I'd come in and he'd be sitting in a chair just gazing into space. He wasn't unloving or anything, just – distant. Absent-minded.'

'When was this, Cathy?'

'It was when we still thought we were going to France. At first I thought he didn't want to go, that he'd changed his mind. I tried to talk to him about it, but he said no, that everything was fine. So I said, just casually once, that I was having a few second thoughts myself and he said quite violently, "We've *got* to go or it'll be too late." It shook me up a bit. I asked him what he meant but he seemed puzzled himself; he genuinely didn't seem to know.'

'Did he know then, about the illness?'

'No. No, as far as we knew then there was nothing wrong. Then I thought I was pregnant; it was probably wishful thinking. When I discovered it was a false alarm I felt as though I'd lost my last chance of keeping him. It was soon after that we heard that his job in France was postponed. the guy who was leaving had trouble selling his house and the move was delayed for several months. I thought the world would end. I was sure then that Barry was in love with Janice and that he was counting on the move to get him away before his feelings caught up with him.'

'How did he react to the news of the delay?'

'Disappointed, initially, and then he seemed relieved. He didn't talk much about it. He started to look a bit pale, and he was even quieter. He was staying at work very late every night. He actually was working. I checked up on him once. I shouldn't have done but I did. Janice was there too sometimes, I think; I don't know for sure. I told him he was working too hard, getting too tired and depressed. And he said, "I want to get this project finished." I thought he meant before he left for France, but afterwards I wondered if he knew in some way . . . I know it sounds silly . . .'

Father Delaney nods slowly. 'I've wondered the same thing myself,' he says.

'You have?'

'You remember that night I came round?' he says. 'Soon after you'd heard that the move had been postponed?'

'Yes, I remember.'

'You went out to the kitchen at one stage to make some coffee or something, and Barry and I were talking – about nothing especially serious. Suddenly he said, à propos of nothing, "Do you think people know when they're going to die?"'

'Are you sure?' I ask. 'I mean, sure it was then, so early on? He hadn't had any tests or anything, then.'

'I know. Yes, it was definitely at that time. I remember you talking about some friends who were going to give a party for you – a kind of not-going-away-after-all party, you called it.'

That's right. And Barry said that? What did you answer?'

'I was a bit taken aback. I think I said something to the effect that people often did know. I was going to ask him why he had asked but you came back into the room just then and he changed the subject to something else.'

256

'So he did know,' I say slowly. 'I thought, at the end, that he knew but I wondered how long . . . I got the RC chaplain, you know, at the hospital, to come and see him the morning before he died. He did that service – the one where they anoint the hands and feet: what do they call it?'

'The sacrament of the sick.'

'That's it. It was obviously intended for dying people and I wondered if I'd done the right thing, whether it wouldn't upset Barry, the implication that he hadn't got long to go. But he seemed relieved in a way, more relaxed.'

'Did you know then? Had the doctor told you?'

'The doctor wouldn't commit himself; none of them would. But it was obvious in the end. He got so weak so quickly; he seemed to be dying before my eyes. And when the chaplain said to me, "Do you think he is going to die?" I said that I knew he was. I think the chaplain assumed the doctor must have told me because I heard him ticking the registrar off and saying he should have been called before. Anyway, he said that I must talk to Barry, because Barry knew too. I said, "Are you sure about that?" and he said yes, he'd seen it before and I must be the one to bring up the subject because Barry might be afraid of upsetting me.'

'So did you?'

'Well, not then. I thought I wouldn't at all, in fact, because when I went back to him he was in such pain. And then his mother came, and kept rabbiting on about all the things he was going to do when he got better. I followed her out of the ward when she left and said, "Look, do you want to stay, because he hasn't got very much longer?" I didn't want her there and I don't think Barry did either but I didn't want her saying that I'd kept her from her own son. But she stared at me as though she hated me and said, "What the hell do you mean? He can't be that bad. He's sitting up." She almost shouted it. And I said, "They've propped him up so he can breathe. He's really ill. You can see that." '

'That must have been hard for you, to have to tell her.'

'It was her reaction that was hard. She grabbed me by the shoulders and shook me till my teeth felt loose. She said, "Don't you ever talk like that again!" and then she walked out. Then the first thing she said when I phoned her after Barry died was, "Why didn't you call me? I should have been told." '

'Some people can't accept the idea,' Father Delaney says. 'You can tell them over and over again but if they don't want to hear they just won't. So, did you talk to Barry eventually about the fact that he was dying?'

'In a way. It was late that same night. They'd given him something for the pain and he slept a bit, then he woke up with it and it really was bad. I went to find the sister and she said he couldn't have another injection yet and I got really angry and said, "What harm is it going to do now, for God's sake?" so she gave him one. But it took a while to work. He was very weak, but he suddenly started struggling to get his arm out from under the covers and he caught hold of my hand, and his eyes were really . . . desperate.

'So I sat on the bed beside him and put my arms round him and said, "It's nearly over now, darling. Don't fight it, just let yourself go. Close your eyes and I'll hold you." He didn't close his eyes; he kept on looking at me, but he did relax. Then after a while his breathing got very shallow and then I couldn't feel it at all, and his eyes kind of glazed over but they still weren't closed. The nurse had to close them for him. Oh God . . .'

I didn't think I could cry any more. I don't know where all these tears are coming from. Eight months of 'being a brave girl', of 'keeping a stiff upper lip', like you're taught as a child. I must have been storing up grief in the hollowness of my heart till it burst through the walls like a geyser through solid rock, showering the frozen waste with its scorching tide.

'I must go home,' I say finally. 'It's terribly late. I'm sorry. I'll go home.'

'You'll do no such thing. I'll make up the spare bed and you'll stay here the night.'

He shows me the way to a sparsely furnished room, freezing cold, and unearths an ancient hot-water bottle and an even more ancient dressing gown. 'Though I'd advise you to sleep in your clothes if you're not accustomed to frostbite. Anything else you need, now? Sleep well, then. And no more thinking till morning.'

Morning is heralded by a tousle-haired youth – presumably Donald – who brings me a cup of tea and three pieces of toast.

'What's the time? Oh hell, I'll be late for work!'

'You're not to go in. Father Delaney's orders.'

'Oh yes? Is that what they mean by the authoritarian church?'

'You've got it,' Donald says cheerfully. 'Father Delaney is worse than the Pope when he puts his mind to it.'

Worse than Wayne, with his orders to take care of myself. Except that I can't complain about Wayne, since he's gone. I'm not complaining about Father Delaney either; it's a relief to sink back into sleep, unbothered by toast crumbs and the cold hot-water bottle in the bed.

When I next awake, it's lunchtime. The unlovely smell of Teresa's cooking floats up the stairs and attacks my defenceless nostrils, bringing back memories of school dinners from the dim and undeserving past.

Stewed stringy chicken in watery gravy polluted by overcooked carrots. 'Are priests allowed to go out to restaurants? If so, I'll take you to Marcello's one time. They do beautiful chicken in this amazing herb-flavoured sauce, with onion and green and red peppers and . . .'

'You're making my mouth water. But you save your money: those places aren't cheap!'

'And then afterwards,' I say tantalizingly, 'there's this wonderful gateau with cream and fresh peaches and brandy . . .'

Teresa brings in the rice pudding, brown and solid, without any jam. 'Will I leave you the cheese and biscuits for tonight, Father? I'm off to see my sister in Watford now.'

'That'll do fine Teresa, thank you. Give your sister my kind regards.'

'I'll see you tomorrow then.'

'I could book a table for tonight,' I say persuasively. 'And what about the guy who's living here – Donald? We could all go. My treat.'

'I won't hear of it! It would cost a fortune, and you don't want to go to a place like that with a tattered old priest in a shiny suit.'

'Please come,' I say seriously. 'If you'd like to. You've been so kind to me – and to Barry. Regard it as a thank-you from both of us.'

He bows from the waist. 'In that case I'll be honoured to accept the invitation. Considering which, I can safely leave the rest of this pudding without any fear of starvation!'

After lunch he says, 'Now you'll tell me the rest, including the parts you missed out last night.' But I chicken out again. Yes, I know I said I wouldn't. But after the storm last night, and the steady showers of the past eight months, I need to dry out before I stand out in the rain again. So, 'I have to go to work,' I insist, not meeting his eyes. 'But I will talk later, I promise – later on.' So he lets me go, and on the way to work I decide to have a party after all. I never thanked people properly for their help when Barry died; I can't return all the dinners and drinks and things, let alone all the kindnesses. So the party will be an acknowledgement of their friendship and a kind of fresh start. You can face the future if you can face the past. And it will give me a deadline to work towards. Before the party I will bring myself to admit to myself what I couldn't admit before. And then I will celebrate my release and I'll start getting positive and getting a job and getting healthy too, because I won't need the fags and the booze and the layers of protectiveness with which I destroy myself. And maybe I'll even phone Wayne and ask how he's getting on and show that I like him after all, without expecting anything in return. He's done all the giving so far; he ran all the risks of rejection, while I played safe and played cool, so now if he doesn't want to know then that's only fair, isn't it? It's my turn to be the one to get hurt. In the meantime there are people to phone and invite to the party, using Bantam's phone bill and time as a kind of leaving present. Alan is here, so I can invite him straight away.

'Friday night. Yes, tomorrow. I thought of Saturday, but the Mwedzis arrive on Sunday. Friday will give me time to clean up. Ask Jerry too.'

'I might,' he says, 'or I might not.'

Hortense can be invited directly too, and Suky and Steve and Davy and Patsy and Hazel. Then, on the phone, Carla and Jim and my brother Bill and Vicky and Keith (if he's still around by tomorrow) and Marcie and Desmond (is his name Desmond? I can't keep track) and Elsa and her flat-mates and John and Naomi and a host of other people. I'm not counting numbers. If you work a party out like that you lose your nerve and start wondering how they'll ever fit in the flat; if you don't keep count they invariably fit in somehow. I'll buy bread and cheese and wine and beer, and warn the Pratts tonight, while they're still in a state of shock about the lodgers and can't protest too much.

I invite Penny too, and she says she'll come. 'Can I bring my boyfriend? And is it bring-a-bottle?'

'Yes it is. And do. By the way, Penny, you said there were some phone calls yesterday but I can't find the messages file. It isn't on my desk.'

261

'No, it's in the filing cabinet.'

'In the . . . How long has it been there?'

'Since I came,' she says proudly. 'I filed it away.'

Since Monday. Good God, it's Thursday now. I find the file, and it's stacked with message slips: some for Alan and some for me. I turn the pile upside down and start from the Monday ones. Calls from journalists to say they could or couldn't come to the press conference. A message from my mother – will I ring her some time, not urgent. Tuesday: more calls from journalists. One of the photographers called – I ordered some prints from a contact sheet without giving the sheet number. Several messages for Alan, one from Jerry – please call him back immediately. Diane Crosswell the beauty editor phoned: please would Cathy Childs call her back, at home?

On Tuesday too, a Mr Slindon called. Mr Wayne Slindon. He left no message, no number, and didn't ring again.

That's it. I'll do it now, not postpone it any longer. I call his old office and ask the secretary if she knows his new number. She sounds curious, asks for my name and says, 'It's business, is it?' I grit my teeth and reply, with my new resolve to be honest and do it the hard way, 'No, actually it's personal,' at which she says, 'What was your name again?'

Finally she relents and divulges the name of the Sheffield firm and, with my morale at rock bottom, I dial the number and ask for Wayne.

'Mr Slindon's secretary speaking.'

She sounds blonde. I bet he's taken her out already.

'Hello, could I speak to Mr Slindon please?'

'Could I have your name?'

'Cathy Childs.' She'll tell him and he'll say 'Who?' and have to think for a moment.

'From which company?'

'Bantam Cos . . . No, it's a personal call.'

'Oh, I see. Just a minute, please.'

There is a pause. ('Who is she, Wayne?' she'll be saying. 'You told me last night there wasn't anyone.' And he'll disclaim: 'Oh, just some bird I took out a few times in London. Won't leave me alone . . .') Interesting to know I can feel jealous again. A definite sign of thaw; the ice is being eroded by the floods. It was safer, being encased in ice, but it's better to be warm and human and risk getting hurt. At least I think it is. I seem to have lost a layer of skin as well: I'm sure I was much thicker-skinned before.

'Mr Slindon is in a meeting.'

'I see.' I've used that one myself; I know what it means. 'Well, thank you.'

'No – he said could you hold on just a minute; he'll try not to keep you long. He has the managing director with him.'

'Oh. Yes, I'll hang on.' Maybe . . . I'll have to wait and see. I've nothing to lose anyway. Honesty time. Yes, I have; I really like him.

'Cathy? Sorry to keep you waiting.'

'Hello Wayne. Have I called at a bad time?'

'No, not at all. How are you?'

'Fine. All right. How are you getting on?'

'Very well.' He sounds confident. Self-sufficient. 'I'm starting to find my feet. I'm in digs but looking for a flat, and the job seems okay. The people are very friendly.'

'Oh, that's good.' Why the hell did I ring? He's into a new life now, with people who are friendly – not cold and cagey like people in London whom he'd probably rather forget.

'How did your press conference go?' he continues, to fill the silence left by my drying up.

'Not too bad; a lot of people turned up. I gave in my notice at work this week.'

'Have you found a new job?'

'No, but I've started looking.' In case he thinks I'm dropping hints for him to renew his suggestion about a job in Sheffield, I hurry on. 'And I've got some new flat-mates moving in on Sunday – a couple from Ghana, expecting a baby.' I'll keep the conversation general and ring off. It's not that I'm a coward, but what's the point in going over old ground when he probably doesn't want to know?

'A what? I can't hear you very well,' he says. 'Hang on while I shut the door, can you?'

Another pause, and voices, 'I'll be with you in a minute,' he says to somebody.

'Listen, I'm interrupting your work,' I say, as he returns to the phone. 'I'll go now; I only rang to see how you're . . .'

'No,' he says. 'I wanted to talk to you. I rang you on Tuesday, did you know? I wanted to say . . . if I messed things up, on Friday night, I'm sorry.' He's braver than I am; I'd never have got round to saying it myself.

'No, you didn't,' I assure him. 'It was me, changing my mind all the time.'

'It's just that I didn't know where I stood and . . .'

'I know. It was my fault.'

'No, it was mine.' He starts to laugh. 'This is silly. What I wanted to say, except that I lost my nerve, was I don't know whether you want anyone around since your husband died but it doesn't have to be the torrid scene; I can just be a friend, or . . . well, whatever you want.'

'That's very nice of you,' I say. 'And actually I didn't ring just to see how you're getting on: I called to say if you want to come down any time I'd be really glad to see you.'

Alan walks into the office, shoots me a questioning glance, and sits down at his desk to listen.

'In fact,' I continue doggedly, 'I'm having a party on Friday night but I'm sure you'll be too busy . . . I mean, if you could manage to come you'd be very welcome.'

'I'd love to, but I don't know what time I could get away. There's quite a backlog of work here and as the new broom

I think I'm expected to make a clean sweep. By the time I got the train . . .'

'Yes, of course. Never mind.' My nerve fails again. He meant a casual, occasional friendship, not a demand for long-distance travel.

'If I turned up too late for the party, though,' he continues, 'I could borrow Stewart's flat for the night and see you on Saturday morning – would that be okay?'

'Yes.' There you are. It can work out. For no reason, I start to laugh.

'You sound better,' he says. 'Are you?'

'Yes, I am.'

'Is the diet helping?'

'Yes. No, to be honest. I haven't been really keeping to it, but I will. The reason I'm feeling better is because I broke down and cried last night, all over poor Father Delaney, and he made me talk about Barry, instead of pretending I'd got over it all.' Alan is agog by now; his ears are on stalks.

'You're not really over it, are you?' Wayne says.

'No, but I'm working on it now.'

'That's good. Look, I've got to go. I've left the director waiting; I said you were an urgent query from my old office but I'd better not push my luck!'

'You didn't! Yes, you'd better go then, hadn't you?'

'Cathy,' he says, as I'm about to put the phone down.

'Yes?'

'Did you say you had a family from Ghana moving into your flat?'

'Yes.'

'That's what I thought you'd said,' he says. 'I'll see you at the weekend.'

''Bye.'

'You're not going to tell me that was business,' says Alan dryly.

'No, I'm not going to tell you.' His face falls. I relent. 'Okay, what do you want to know?'

'I don't want to know anything,' he says with dignity. 'I wouldn't dream of interfering in anyone's personal life. Even if I was interested, which I'm not.'

'Coffee, Alan?'

'Thanks. And a biscuit if there's any left.'

When I phone Diane Crosswell, she answers the phone in a breathless, frantic voice.

'You sound busy already!'

'I'm desperate,' she says. 'I'm glad you phoned back. I've got something to ask you. You'll need to think about it, I expect; I'm not asking you to decide immediately but I need to have some idea because really I don't know what else . . .'

'What is it?'

She sounds really upset.

'Rosemary – my partner in this business we're setting up – her husband's in the army, right? And he's being posted to Germany, as usual at short notice, and she wants to go too.'

'Oh dear. So she can't . . .' A tiny flicker of hope begins to stir. No, it can't be.

'So I either have to find someone else or drop the whole scheme altogether. She's willing to go on working till the last minute if only I can find someone to take over when she goes. And I wondered, as you said you were leaving your job . . .'

'Yes.'

'So look, I know you'll have to think about it and you may feel it's not your line, but if you wanted to come and have à chat I could tell you whatever you wanted to know.'

'Yes, fine.'

'You mean you'll think about it?'

'No, I mean I'll do it.'

'Are you sure? That's marvellous! Are you sure?'

'I'm sure, but are you? I haven't any experience of the kind of work you're doing.'

'That doesn't matter – neither had Rosemary; she worked in advertising. But you've general experience of business and you can write about cosmetics and beauty and so on, which is an added bonus. As long as you don't mind learning you'll soon pick up the rest.'

'I don't mind learning. My brain will be glad of the exercise.'

She laughs. 'Is it that bad where you are? How did the press conference go?'

'It went. No, it was okay. I've given in my notice here already, by the way.'

'You have? That's amazing. I can't believe how this is working out. Listen, we haven't talked about your salary, or whether you want to put some money in and be a partner, but come along to my house and we'll talk it over. When are you free?'

'Monday evening? It'll have to be after work; I've had enough time off recently. But if you're free tomorrow I'm having a party, if you'd like to come.'

'Great! Yes, I'll come – give me the address. Is the party for your birthday or anything?'

'No, at least it wasn't meant to be. Thanks – you've just given me an excuse for celebrating!'

'We'll both celebrate,' she promises. 'I'll bring some vodka.'

Through the window I notice that the rain has stopped and there is a break in the clouds. Perhaps we're in for a few bright intervals after all.

11

Marcello's used to be one of Barry's favourite restaurants.
It's strange to go there again this evening. If I was going
with anyone else but an aging Catholic priest and a youth
club leader with a spotty face and trousers too short in the
leg, it would feel like betrayal. As it is, it feels like an
absolution.

It's a good evening, actually. We're a strange enough
trio; we attract a few curious glances as we go in. But
Donald's shyness rapidly evaporates once we get him on to
the subject of his youth club protégés, then he launches into
an unexpectedly funny recital of the holiday jobs he took as
a schoolboy. And Father Delaney was always good company after a couple of drinks. The food is as fantastic as I
remembered it and the waiters as deft at juggling plates;
the memories are all good ones. By the time we leave, I feel
that I've laid the ghosts of the past.

Even the memory of that very last time at Marcello's
wasn't really bad, once I brought myself to think about it
instead of skirting around it.

We hadn't intended to go out that night. Barry had promised to come home early from work. 'I won't be late,' he
said. 'I want to talk to you.'

For weeks I'd been wishing he would talk to me, but
when he said that I realized it was the last thing I wanted to
hear. Picture the scene – straight out of TV soap opera:
'Darling, there's something I have to tell you.' Close-up
shot of wronged wife's harrowed expression. 'Oh Barry
. . . Not . . . ?' 'I'm afraid so. We've had some good
times together, Cathy, but now it's over.' 'Oh my God,

Barry, how will I live without you?'

Well, it wasn't going to be like that. If he'd stopped loving me then I wasn't going to plead and I wasn't going to cry. I would pack my bags, and disappear into the night, leaving him to what happiness he could find with Janice.

Only he wouldn't be happy. I knew him well enough to realize that. Catholic consciences are uncomfortably insistent, honed to razor-sharpness by examinations of conscience and 'acts of contrition': 'Oh my God, because Thou art so good I am truly sorry I have offended Thee . . . ' every night since childhood. 'Bless me Father for I have sinned. I have been selfish and impatient and have said unkind things about people. Oh yeah, and I left my wife and I'm shacking up with this other bird . . .' How could he be happy again if he did that? Some people could, but not Barry. Not Barry who agonized after a party, quite genuinely, in case he'd hurt somebody's feelings by saying something thoughtless. 'D'you think he realized I didn't mean it that way, Cath? Perhaps I should ring him and say I'm sorry, I'd had a few drinks . . .'

I knew him well enough to be certain that if he lost touch with his God (whom I'd begrudged him at first, as an unwelcome third in our relationship) he'd cut himself off from all peace of mind and every chance of happiness. And, whatever he'd done, I couldn't wish that on him.

So I decided, at work, that I wouldn't let him tell me because once the words were out it would make it so hard for him to go back on them. Instead I'd have one last wordless try at making him see that I loved him, that he didn't have to make any hasty decisions, that I would go with him to France or to Timbuctoo or I'd wait at home – anything that he wanted till his love for Janice had healed and he could be with me without wishing he was with her.

I would leave work early and cook him his favourite meal: chilli con carne with slightly garlicky salad and fluffy rice.

And I'd put on some music and turn back the bed and show him, without any long explanations or heavy discussions, that perhaps, if he stayed, it might become bearable again. Anything to stop him saying he didn't want me around any more. If he said it after all, I would go without tears or recriminations or appeals to his compassion – but I would try this way first.

By seven o'clock the chilli was simmering nicely and the water was boiling for the rice. I have a way with rice. You add a few drops of lemon juice to the water and then the grains don't get sticky and it never lumps. I found myself thinking that Janice probably didn't know about that. How ridiculous can you get? As if Barry would suddenly fall out of love with her because she couldn't cook rice. 'I'm sorry Janice, this isn't going to work. I can't take living with your lumpy rice . . .'

At eight o'clock I'd taken the chilli off the gas ring and put it in the oven on a slow heat. The rice had gone dry so I added a bit more water and put that in the oven too. It wouldn't be so nice but it couldn't be helped.

By half-past eight it was all getting a bit dried up. He couldn't be much longer, surely. He said he wouldn't be late. Perhaps he'd had to stay on to finish something. Perhaps he hadn't realized the time. Perhaps he'd gone to the pub for a quick drink with one of the others and then felt he had to stay and buy a round. Perhaps he and Janice . . .

At ten past nine he came home. 'I'm sorry,' he said. 'I'm sorry.' He was grey in the face with exhaustion, taut lines of strain from the sides of his mouth disappearing into his beard, his shoulders slumping with defeat. 'I've got to talk to you, Cathy,' he said.

'Later,' I said. 'We'll eat first. You look shattered.'

The dinner was beyond retrieval. It looked like a packet dehydrated meal before you add the water, and it smelt worse.

'I'm not hungry,' he said. 'I'll just have a drink.'

'I tell you what: we'll go to Marcello's. They won't be fully booked on a Monday. You'd feel better after a meal, wouldn't you?'

'I don't feel too good at the moment,' he admitted. 'Okay then, we'll go.'

We walked to the station in silence, made small talk on the tube. Marcello's was fairly crowded, even on a Monday, but they found us a table for two. In the corner, in the dark. I was glad of that. I wasn't going to cry, I'd decided, but just in case I did . . .

We skipped the starters and ordered pasta for main course; we were both of us almost past eating. By the time the food arrived it was ten o'clock. We forked our way through the lasagne in silence. After half a plateful I stopped. Why keep up the farce? Let him tell me now and get it over with. How could I change his mind in one evening? He'd known me for two and a half years. If he didn't know by now that I loved him, that I wouldn't want him to leave me, then it was a lost cause anyway

'Have you finished?' he asked. 'Me too. I'll get the bill, shall I? We could go for a walk.'

So we left Marcello's with its laughing, chattering people and its warm lights and went out into the unwelcoming February night. Along the embankment the dossers were hunched under flattened cardboard boxes and dirty newspapers. 'How do they live,' I said, 'in this weather?'

'They don't,' Barry said. 'Not very long.' One of them asked Barry for a light and he gave him the lighter and all our cigarettes too. 'Poor sods,' he said bleakly. 'What a way to go.'

'Barry,' I said finally, when we had walked for a while without words and without direction. 'What did you want to talk to me about?'

He stopped immediately. 'Come here,' he said, 'and hold

me. We're both going to need it.'

His tone frightened me. 'Tell me quickly,' I said.

'I should have told you before,' he said, 'but I kept hoping that it would all come to nothing. I should have given you some warning, Cath, but I didn't want to worry you before I knew for sure.'

'Just tell me now.' For all my good resolutions, I was shaking.

'I've been passing blood,' he said. 'I've had a lot of pain.'

'What?' It was so far removed from what I'd expected to hear, I couldn't take it in.

'I've been passing blood,' he repeated. 'When I pee. Quite a lot.'

'But darling, you must go to the doctor at once! You shouldn't leave it . . .'

'I went,' he said.

'You went? When?'

'A few weeks ago.'

'A few *weeks*!' But Barry was always helpless when he was ill. If he had a slight cold he'd collapse, demanding remedies in a quavering voice. Now he had coped with this thing alone, without telling me.

'Yes. I went to the GP and he sent me to the hospital. I went back there today. I've got to go in for a biopsy.'

'When?'

'Tomorrow. First thing in the morning.'

'Tomorrow!' I seemed to be repeating everything he said.

'Yes. I wanted to ask you – will you come with me? I mean, you can't stay, but just to come in with me in the morning.'

'Of course I will.' At least he wanted me. But Jesus, I'd rather have had a dozen Janices than this. 'Barry, what do they think it is? Did they say?'

'They can't be sure till they do the biopsy. It could be lots

272

of things. It might not be cancer. Don't let's worry about it till we know.'

'No, we won't jump to conclusions.'

But why had they arranged for him to go in so soon, with waiting lists as long as they were?

We walked nearly the whole way home; it was miles. At every tube station we thought we'd just walk to the next one. Finally we got on a couple of stops from home, then we had to walk back to the flat. We were both exhausted, trembling from weariness and shock. I made some coffee and we took it to bed. Then we lay awake all night in each other's arms.

'Barry,' I said, as the first glimmerings of light seeped through the gap in the curtains.

'Yes?'

'What do you think, yourself?'

'I don't know.' A pause. 'I don't feel right.'

'In what way? Ill, you mean?'

'Not really ill. Just strange – not normal.'

'It could be the anxiety – do you think?'

'It could be. You'd better get some sleep, Cath.'

'I'm not sleepy.'

'Me neither. You wouldn't make some more coffee would you? And is there any of that grass left?'

'Should you smoke, if you're having an operation tomorrow?'

'Bring it anyway. I need something.'

'Okay.'

It was then that I suggested trying to contact Father Delaney who was away on convalescence, and Barry said no, let the poor guy recover in peace. But the suggestion must have triggered something in his mind because when I came in with the coffee he was praying, eyes closed and lips moving. I put his coffee on the floor by the bed and sat by the window, drawing the curtains back to give him enough light to roll a joint from the rest of the grass.

'Your coffee's getting cold,' I said finally

He drank the coffee but left the joint untouched. 'I'll have to start doing without that stuff,' he said soberly.

Donald collects his bike from outside my flat, excuses himself and goes home: he has to be up very early tomorrow morning. It already is very early tomorrow morning. Father Delaney delays his departure long enough to come in for a cup of coffee and the rest of the story on Barry.

'So your fears about him and this girl – Janice – were unjustified, then?' he says.

I look at him sitting opposite me in Barry's chair, a shabby, balding, middle-aged man with the innocent eyes of a child. 'Yes,' I say. 'I was wrong.'

He smiles, rewarding me. 'I thought there must have been some mistake,' he says. 'It's my belief he'd no sooner have hurt you than fly to the moon.'

He pats me on the shoulder as he leaves. 'Many thanks for the meal: a great treat.' And he gets on his creaky old bicycle and rides home to the comfortless presbytery and Teresa's stolid cooking.

He's a good man; it was worth the lie. While he's been in the business of priesthood long enough not to expect perfection from human beings, Father Delaney was fond of Barry; it would have distressed him to think Barry capable of what he saw, in uncompromising terms, as the adultery that Christ had ordained thou shalt not commit.

Not that I knew whether things had gone that far; to be honest, what Barry had or had not done worried me less than what he felt. I'm inclined to think if he'd slept with her, the guilt would have killed the whole relationship; without actual sex he would feel freer to love her and it was his love, rather than just his body, that I didn't want to share.

I never asked him and he never told me, though I think he tried to. Earlier that last afternoon, before his mother came, he was sick and I sat by him, holding the bowl. He lay back on the pillows, pale and sweating, and said, 'You're a great wife, did you know?'

'Thanks.'

'I mean it. Really. I do better out of this marriage than you do.'

'Don't be silly, Barry!'

'I'm not a very good person. I've done some things I really wish I hadn't.'

If he would only not die, I wouldn't care what he had done. 'It doesn't matter,' I told him. 'You're lovely. Whatever you've done – it's nothing.'

But there had been something. Sarah, one of the girls from the lab, called to see me after he died. She was nervous and ill at ease, as people often are in the presence of the bereaved. She had been deputed by Barry's colleagues to offer all their condolences – selected, probably, by virtue of her being one of the longer-standing employees and female – for women are better, according to men, at dealing with nasty emotional things.

So poor Sarah stammered her words of conventional sorrow and shifted her weight from one foot to the other and asked in a fearful half-whisper about flowers and funeral times. 'Some of us would like to come along,' she apologized, 'if that's all right with you?'

'Yes. Fine.'

She got to the door and, having half-exited and already bidden goodbye to the cluster of other people in the flat, suddenly blurted out, 'Janice wants to come too.'

'Okay,' I said.

She looked at me searchingly, compassion and curiosity mingling. 'I mean, I could tell her it's invitation only,' she stumbled. 'I mean, if you don't want her there . . .' She ground to a halt and a look of terror crossed her face: what had she said?

'No,' I said limply. 'Let her come.'

And so she had come and had broken down halfway through, her sobs fading to an echo as Sarah supported her out of the church. They were still outside on the steps when we all came out. Janice came up to me with tears streaming down her reddened face. She looked like a schoolgirl; she wasn't much older than that, after all. 'I'm sorry,' she sobbed. 'I'm so sorry.'

I didn't know if she was apologizing for breaking down in church or for breaking into the marriage, or just offering condolences for his death. But it was impossible to hate anyone in the face of such naked suffering, and at least she hadn't avoided me as a few others had, or made bright remarks about how I would soon be over it. So I put my hand on her arm for a second, before I was reclaimed by relatives.

And when she wrote to me later, an emotional letter about Barry, I sent her a picture of him that I'd taken at Christmas, in a paper hat with a sprig of holly in his beard.

I call on the Pratts, half an hour before the party's due to start, with a bottle of wine.

'I hope the party won't be too noisy tonight. Just bang on the door or something if it is.'

Mr Pratt asks me in. 'The wife's out, I'm afraid. Townswomen's Guild. No, I don't suppose it'll be too noisy. You don't have parties very often; glad to see you have a bit of fun,' he says unexpectedly.

'Thanks.'

'Will you have a glass of this wine if I open it? The wife doesn't drink much nowadays.'

'Okay, I will. I might as well get a head start on everyone else! I'm just wondering now if people will turn up. We've just had a press conference at work and that was the same – that half hour before it's meant to begin. I must be mad, doing it twice in one week!'

'Oh, they'll turn up, don't you worry. You've got a lot of friends. We see them popping in and out. You're not lonely, anyway.'

'No.'

'We thought you might be, when your husband died. We thought you might move away.'

'I thought about it. But I won't move now, not for the moment.'

I'll stay here now and grow back into shape, let the jagged edges heal, become a whole person again and not a torn-off half.

So, 'Yes,' I tell Mr Pratt, 'I'll be staying here a while. You know about my new flat-mates moving in on Sunday?'

'Yes, the wife told me.'

'I'm afraid she isn't very pleased.'

'She doesn't like the idea of living with black people. It's just that she's never known any. She'll come round. We had some where I used to work – West Indians. We got on all right.'

'The Mwedzis are from Ghana; they've been over here five years. I think you'll like them when you know them. Why don't you come up for a drink one evening next week?'

'We could do that. I'll ask the wife. There's someone at the front door – is that one of your guests?'

'It's Carla and Jim. I'll see you then, Mr Pratt.'

Everyone comes to the party. Except Wayne, that is, but I didn't expect him really. It doesn't matter, I'll see him tomorrow morning.

Alan arrives with Jerry after all; Elsa comes with her flat-mates, one of whom is wearing a cowboy outfit, complete with spiky metal spurs; Vicky and Keith arrive separately. Keith brings a can of beer, two friends and a tinfoil package of something. 'We've found a new pusher,' he tells me confidentially. 'This stuff's really ace. You'll have to try it.'

'I might later.' There are so many people I haven't seen for a while and there's news to catch up on, drinks to pour, later arrivals to welcome.

'Cathy, darling.' It's Marcie, with Desmond and some other guy as well. 'You look beautiful.'

'But of course; look who sold me the clothes!'

'It's the way you wear them, darling. That's your flair. Mine is persuading you to buy them. Now aren't you glad you did? Jim darling, don't you think Cathy looks stunning?'

'Amazing,' he says.

'Amazingly what?' she asks, smiling at him.

'Amazingly amazing. Come and dance with me, Marcie.'

Half an hour later they are still dancing. Someone turns the music up and the lights down.

Carla is in a corner getting pissed on Anjou Rosé and swapping childhood reminiscences with Steve from work. 'Oh, we used to play doctors and nurses too,' I hear her say delightedly.

Hortense is talking to Hazel about Big Harry. 'You'll have to do something with him,' she is saying. 'He can't keep his staff. They haven't all got your loyalty.'

Diane Crosswell is in deep conversation with Desmond. Suky is chatting to Naomi and John, who come for a brief drink and a few introductions and stay, in the end, for a couple of hours. Vicky is nowhere to be seen.

Alan and Elsa and I are in the throes of inventing a new form of dance which involves a lot of contortions and giggling, when Keith taps me on the shoulder. 'When do I get to talk to you?'

I leave Elsa with Alan and sit on the floor to talk to Keith.

'Vicky and I are splitting up,' he says. 'Did she tell you?'

'Yes, she did. I'm sorry to hear that.'

'We're not really compatible,' he says. 'She's too frenetic, doesn't know how to enjoy life. Have a drag; this stuff is really ace.'

I have a couple of drags, to be sociable, but he soon gets beyond the sociable stage and floats off on a cloud of fragrant smoke. I leave him smiling at his own fantasies and go and dance with Elsa's flat-mate Nick – the one without the spurs. It's a surprise when Carla and Jim come up to say they are leaving.

'The babysitter's only sixteen; we said we'd be back by one o'clock.'

'I'll get your coats.' The coats are in the bedroom, on the bed, but when I go in they have taken on a life of their own, moving in time to the couple underneath. 'Jim, I don't think I can get your coats just yet.'

'Why not?' He pushes the door open. 'Excuse me,' he says politely, and emerges with both coats over his arm.

'Who was it?' I say curiously.

'Vicky. With someone I didn't recognize, but it certainly wasn't Keith.'

Carla peers over his shoulder into the gloom. 'One of Elsa's flat-mates,' she pronounces. 'Ed, is he called?'

I feel illogically annoyed at the use being made of my bed. For the first time it occurs to me that it was a bit anti-social of Barry and me at that first party together to appropriate one of the bedrooms. Whoever owned the bed might not have wanted strangers copulating all over it. And it must have been a nuisance for them to have to break into the room in the morning. It never bothered me before.

I return to the party. Keith and his friends are lying on the floor and people are dancing round them. I dance with Jerry, then with someone else – one of Keith's friends, I think – then Nick again.

Someone changes the tape, then later puts another one on, all slow tracks.

'Lovely party, Cathy.' It's Elsa.

'Are you going already?'

'What d'you mean, already? It's half-past three.'

'Is it really? I thought it was about one.'

People are leaving now, giggling and stumbling down the stairs and going 'Sssh!' in stage whispers. Slamming car doors and driving off eccentrically, offering lifts and calling goodbyes. The flat seems suddenly empty. Glasses are everywhere, and overflowing ashtrays. Fag-ends and somebody's shoes. A couple of chairs, which were used in a one-hand weightlifting contest, are upside down and the sofa cushions are on the floor, one of them quietly absorbing a tipped-over bottle of wine.

I could start clearing up. On the other hand, I could go to bed. It'll still all be there in the morning, unfortunately.

I rescue the wine-bottle and half-heartedly pick up a couple of chairs.

'Too late for the party,' Wayne says. 'The story of my life. The door was open so I came in.' He's shaved off his beard, I notice.

'Hello! When did you . . . ?'

'I got a lift down with a guy from work who was going to Battersea – only the car broke down just past the end of the motorway and we spent hours trying to fix it. We didn't even manage it in the end; he got a tow home and I got a taxi here. How was the party?'

'Nice. You're shivering – you must be frozen! I'll see if there's any whisky left.'

There is not. 'Just flat beer and some wine, though most of that's on the sofa.'

'Don't worry. I'll have coffee.'

'Have you eaten?'

'A long time ago,' he admits.

'Would you like . . . let me see . . . bacon sandwiches?'

'Don't start cooking, this time of night. Yes, I would.'

His lips are blue and his teeth are chattering. The floor in front of the gas fire is unsittable-on, soaked with spilt booze and littered with broken crisps.

'Light the one in the bedroom,' I tell him, 'and thaw yourself out. Put the duvet round you or something.' The kitchen floor is sticky with beer. I wash out a couple of wine-filled mugs and empty the kettle, which has a fag-end floating in it.

Wayne goes into the bedroom but comes out again at once. 'There's somebody in there.'

Vicky emerges, followed by Ed, in his cowboy suit. They both look tousled and sheepish.

'We seem to have outstayed our welcome,' Vicky says.

'Not at all,' I assure her. 'Stay the night if you like.'

'I think we have,' she says. 'Is that breakfast you're making?'

'Bacon sandwiches. Want one?'

Vicky says yes and Ed says no simultaneously. She shrugs. 'No, then. We'll be going. Great party, Cathy.'

'Glad you enjoyed it.' We both start laughing and Wayne joins in.

Ed looks confused. 'Goodnight,' he mumbles.

''Night, Ed. See you Vicky.'

I have half closed the door when she whispers, 'Sorry about the duvet.'

'What?' But she has gone, running down the stairs after Ed. I return to the bacon sandwiches and Wayne goes to light the bedroom fire.

'Are you warmer now?'

'A bit. Look – was your duvet like this before?' he asks.

'What . . . oh no! What happened to it?' The duvet, which lasted Barry and me all our married life, is split in about six places; the filling sags out through the gashes like

281

the guts of some passive small animal crushed on the careless road.

'At a guess,' says Wayne, 'I'd say that the cowboy forgot to take his spurs off.' He starts to laugh.

'Oh no . . .'

Seeing my dismay, he stops laughing. 'It can probably be patched up,' he consoles.

'It doesn't matter,' I lie. 'It's probably time I got rid of it anyway.'

I fetch the spare duvet, the one I promised to Naomi and John. 'They won't mind if it's used for one night, if I put a clean cover on.'

'Tell me about them,' Wayne says.

'Tell me about your new job first. D'you think you'll stay?'

'I think so. I've found a job that might do for you as well, if you think you might fancy Sheffield.' He raises an eyebrow at me tentatively.

'Well . . . I've been offered one, actually, since I last spoke to you.'

'In London?'

'Yes, in London. To be honest with you,' I add, 'I think I've decided I don't want to leave here just yet. This place may not be perfect and the people may not be either, but I've been around them a long time and they feel like part of me.'

He looks at me. 'And you feel you've lost enough parts of you already?'

'Something like that.' I'm impressed by his perception. 'I don't mean I wouldn't go away to stay, but I don't want to move out permanently right now. I'm sorry.'

'Don't be. It's good that we both know what we want. I can come down for weekends or you can come up to Sheffield once I've found a flat. Or we could sometimes meet

282

halfway: my sister lives in the Midlands. Would you do that?'

'Yes, I could meet you halfway.'

He laughs. 'Sounds symbolic, doesn't it?'

'Profound and meaningful,' I agree. 'Do you want some more coffee?'

'I wouldn't mind.'

When I return with the coffee mugs he has fallen asleep, hunched in front of the fire. I spread the torn duvet on the floor and tip him gently towards it and he topples unresistingly. I tuck the new duvet on top of him and, after a moment's hesitation, kick off my shoes and join him between the layers.

He opens one eye and slides an arm round me. 'All right?'

'Mm.'

Wayne moves his head and his chin brushes my cheek.

'Why did you shave off your beard?' I ask idly.

'Uh?' He forces himself awake. 'I thought I needed a change . . . You want an honest answer?'

'Yes.'

'Carla told me your husband had a beard.'

'That was the reason you got rid of yours? But why?'

'I think it was the reason,' he says. 'I wasn't keen to look like him, I suppose, in case I did too badly out of the comparison. According to Carla, he was the perfect husband.'

'I'm not comparing,' I tell him. 'Honestly. I like you as you are. And Carla was very fond of Barry so her view of him is a bit biased.'

'Isn't yours?'

'It was,' I say. 'Of course. But I think I'm more realistic now. On the whole it was a very happy marriage but no, it wasn't perfect, any more than any relationship is.'

His arm round me tightens. 'Not being perfect myself,'

he says, 'I'm relieved to hear you say that.'

The wind is rattling the window and fresh showers drive gusts of rain against the pane. In the next room the debris of yesterday lies waiting to be cleared, but just now, poised in the no-man's-land between yesterday and today, it's enough to be warm and dry inside the sandwich made by the old duvet and the new. And, lulled by the rhythmic sputtering of the fire and the comforting breath of another human being, it's enough to know that tomorrow the rain may stop, even if just for an hour or two.

Outstanding fiction in paperback from Grafton Books

Barbara Pym

Quartet in Autumn	£1.95	☐
The Sweet Dove Died	£2.50	☐
Less Than Angels	£1.95	☐
Some Tame Gazelle	£1.95	☐
A Few Green Leaves	£1.95	☐
No Fond Return of Love	£1.95	☐
Jane and Prudence	£1.95	☐
An Unsuitable Attachment	£2.50	☐
Crampton Hodnet	£2.50	☐
A Very Private Eye (non-fiction)	£2.95	☐

Elizabeth Smart

By Grand Central Station I Sat Down and Wept	£2.50	☐

Maggie Gee

Dying, in Other Words	£1.50	☐

Ruth Prawer Jhabvala

A Stronger Climate	£2.50	☐
A New Dominion	£1.95	☐
Like Birds, Like Fishes	£2.50	☐

To order direct from the publisher just tick the titles you want and fill in the order form.

Outstanding fiction in paperback from Grafton Books

Muriel Spark

The Abbess of Crewe	£1.95	☐
The Only Problem	£2.50	☐
Territorial Rights	£1.95	☐
Not To Disturb	£1.25	☐
Loitering with Intent	£1.25	☐
Bang-Bang You're Dead	£1.25	☐
The Hothouse by the East River	£1.25	☐
Going up to Sotheby's	£1.25	☐
The Takeover	£1.95	☐

Toni Morrison

Song of Solomon	£2.50	☐
The Bluest Eye	£2.50	☐
Sula	£2.50	☐
Tar Baby	£1.95	☐

Erica Jong

Parachutes and Kisses	£2.50	☐
Fear of Flying	£2.95	☐
How to Save Your Own Life	£2.50	☐
Fanny	£2.95	☐
Selected Poems II	£1.25	☐
At the Edge of the Body	£1.25	☐

Anita Brookner

A Start in Life	£1.95	☐
Providence	£1.95	☐
Look at Me	£2.50	☐
Hotel du Lac	£2.50	☐

To order direct from the publisher just tick the titles you want
and fill in the order form.

All these books are available at your local bookshop or newsagent, or can be ordered direct from the publisher.

To order direct from the publishers just tick the titles you want and fill in the form below.

Name _____

Address _____

Cold Showers

Cathy Childs is frigid.

She is a widow at twenty-five, trapped in a frustrating PR job
and a fast metabolism that means she has to eat every
two hours.

You've got to laugh.

So she does – elbowing aside her grief and the teeming
irritations of office life with a shrug and a smile.

Her friends say she needs a man – the husband of one agrees
and tries the direct approach.

What a jerk.

Not that she doesn't want to bounce back. Hmm. Maybe
Wayne – the man she met by the frozen vegetables – can defros
her heart as well as the asparagus . . .

*'Lively, humorous and well observed . . . thoughtful and moving
Cathy's struggle not to romanticize her former life, and her
honesty about her own feelings, give it integrity and strength'*
BOOKS AND BOOKMEN

*'Clare Nonhebel's ability to make the ordinary absorbing is
very real'*
THE TIMES

Front cover illustration by
John Clementson

ISBN 0-586-06680-2

FICTION

UNITED KINGDOM £2.95
NEW ZEALAND $10.95 RRP INC. GST
AUSTRALIA $8.95 (recommended)

00295

9 780586 066805